Make Me A Liar

MELISSA LANDERS

HYPERION

Los Angeles   New York

First Edition, December 2023
10 9 8 7 6 5 4 3 2 1
FAC-004510-23285
Printed in the United States of America

This book is set in Adobe Caslon Pro/Monotype.
Designed by Phil Buchanan

Library of Congress Cataloging-in-Publication Control Number: 2022951838
ISBN 978-1-368-09838-0
Reinforced binding

Visit www.HyperionTeens.com

SUSTAINABLE FORESTRY INITIATIVE
Certified Sourcing
www.forests.org
SFI-01681

Logo Applies to Text Stock Only

To my husband, Kevin.
Thank you for taking care of your girl.

Chapter One

I LIKE TEENAGE BOYS, JUST NOT ENOUGH TO WEAR ONE.

Who could blame me? The high school years were brutal for guys. Everyone knew it. I'm pretty sure that if the average person could head-hop like me—if they could transfer their mind into someone else's body—no one would use their gift to walk around in a fog of testosterone and armpit stank with unpredictable dangly bits going bonkers in their pants.

Yeah, no, hard pass. (Pun intended.) I would rather live a year of consecutive Mondays than spend one hour inside a guy's meat suit. Which was why I didn't take male clients.

Until the day I met Josh Fenske.

He wore me down one Friday after school when I watched him drown in literal garbage. The bell had just rung, and I was sneaking off to the super-secret parking spot I had discovered behind the cafeteria. Ordinarily, I wouldn't have noticed Josh—or anyone else—in my rush to beat a hundred other cars out of the parking lot before it turned to gridlock. But focused as I was, not even I could miss the sight of a redheaded sophomore going ass over teakettle into the dumpster.

Nor could I miss the elephant-size boy who had launched him in there. The jerk's name was Mark Something-Or-Other, a senior who'd transferred in a few weeks ago after his last school expelled him for punching a bus driver in the boob. Or maybe it was giving a janitor a wedgie. That part didn't matter. The point was Mark had major damage. I could tell from the way he kept torturing his prey by shoving Josh's head into the garbage each time the poor kid tried to stand up.

It was the saddest game of Whac-A-Mole I had ever seen.

At that point, I could've stepped in. I'm not heartless, and I can handle myself. But that would have made matters worse. The thing about bullies is they're not feminists. Shocking, I know. A guy like Mark would lose even more respect for Josh if a girl rescued him. And if I beat Mark in a fight, which I absolutely would, he would roll twice as hard every day afterward to save face. Which would make Josh an even bigger target. The only way to break the cycle of abuse was for Josh to stand up for himself in a public display of fierce badassery.

That I could do.

So I stayed out of sight and waited until Mark left before offering Josh my services. In exchange for a modest fee, I would use Josh's body to fight Mark. And I would win, guaranteed, or his money back. Josh accepted, and just like that, I had broken my cardinal rule and booked my first male client.

I knew the job would be weird. I was prepared for some level of awkwardness, having to wear a boy's body and whatnot. What I didn't expect was for Josh to show up to his appointment an hour late, wearing nothing but a black eye and a pair of Star Wars boxer shorts.

"Hey, Tia" was all Josh said. No mention of the wardrobe malfunction.

"Hey, yourself." I leaned down to squint at a cartoon Yoda near his waistband. Time and detergent had faded the Jedi Master, giving him a horrified expression. *Seen things, I have*, he seemed to say. *Terrible things . . . on the Dark Side of the Shorts.*

"You're late," I added. "I was starting to think you changed your mind."

Josh blushed hard enough to set his face on fire. "No. I didn't change my mind."

I pushed open the door and ushered him inside the backyard shed that doubled as my office. My dad had given it to me for my seventeenth birthday, a peace offering of sorts. Dad had never approved of my side hustle, but he tried his best to support me, and the shed was his way of showing it. The place was nothing special, just a five-by-ten, furnished with a few folding chairs and a black futon. But it was clean and private, and most important of all, secured with a padlock to protect my body when I left it behind for a job.

"So, tell me what happened," I said.

Josh dropped his gaze. He crossed both arms over his chest and hugged himself, despite the heat wave that had turned the early May air into soup. I grabbed a blanket from the futon and handed it over. That seemed to help. Josh wrapped the fleece around himself and probed his swollen eye. "Mark jumped me."

"Where?" I asked.

"At the bus stop." Josh noticed a ladybug on the floor. He scooped it up and released it outside. "We live on the same street. That's how he knows me."

"Did anyone see?"

"You mean besides the twenty other kids at my stop?"

I groaned. It only took one person to start a rumor. Twenty witnesses could circulate the story in an hour. "Okay, that explains the black eye, but not the shorts."

"He, uh"—Josh scratched the back of his neck—"took my clothes, too."

"No."

"Yes."

"Please tell me you're joking."

Josh shot me a look. Not joking.

My chest burned with anger. Josh didn't deserve this. No one deserved having their dignity stripped away, but especially not a boy who caught and released bugs. I refocused my attention and considered what this meant for the job. Mark had upped the ante. Not only had he escalated his torture, but he'd also humiliated Josh in front of an audience. That told me Mark didn't care about getting caught. He had doubled down, so if I wanted to beat him at his own game, I would have to go all in.

"Don't worry," I told Josh. "I'm gonna shove my foot—well, your foot—so far up his ass, he'll be flossing with your shoelaces."

Josh cringed. "Maybe we should do something else. Something sneaky. Like get him expelled, but not let him find out it was me."

"No," I said. "Out of the question."

"Why?"

"Because your problem is bigger than one person," I explained. "Every school has an alpha dick. Right now, that's Mark. If we expel him, someone else will take his place, and then you're right back in the dumpster. We have to make sure no one screws with you ever again. I can do that."

Josh's facial expression told me he wasn't convinced.

"Think about it," I said. "Why are you here?"

"Because you can . . . you know"—he waved toward my face—"do mind control."

"Mind control is not a thing, Josh."

"You can take over bodies."

"Nope," I told him.

"You're a head-hopper, I mean."

Close enough. I preferred the term *immersionist*. *Head-hopper* was a label the media had invented two years ago when people like me started coming forward, and the term sort of stuck. No one knew how many of us existed or why we had all leveled up at the same time. Ever since the government passed a law forcing us to register like a bunch of pervy sex offenders, most immersionists kept their abilities a secret. Myself included. But according to the handful of interviews and studies I had read, it seemed we all shared three basic restrictions: our host had to be human, their body had to be alive, and they had to be willing to share their headspace. In other words, we couldn't hijack anyone's brain.

Try telling that to the public, though.

"Look," I said. "Simply put, you're paying me to change your reputation. Not by a lot. Just enough to make you a risk to guys like Mark." I held up an index finger. "Bullies are lazy. They want an easy target and a guaranteed win. So if they know you can throw down, they won't touch you. But they have to *know* it. And that means standing up for yourself in public. You don't have to flex every day. One time is all it takes . . . if you do it right."

"But I'm not giving you a lot to work with," Josh said, using one hand to indicate his skinny frame. "I can't beat Mark in a fair fight."

"You can't, but I can. And who says it has to be fair?"

Josh cast me a skeptical look.

"Your body is smaller than his," I told him. "But I'll be the one at the wheel. I won't lose, Josh. Trust me on this."

"But will it look legit?" he asked. "Real enough to convince everyone? I mean, you can't bust into the lunchroom and shout, 'Hey, Mark. I'm here to eat chicken nuggets and kick ass . . . and I'm all out of nuggets.' No one will buy it."

"You act like I've never done this before," I said, trying not to take offense at his complete lack of confidence in me. "This isn't my first rodeo."

Josh spread his blanketed arms wide. "Well, how do I know how many rodeos you've been to? It's not like you gave me a résumé."

I paused for a deep breath and reminded myself that I was a professional. Josh deserved my credentials. "Fine. I spent a year practicing immersion before I took my first client. That was three months ago, and since then I've done two breakups, two promposals, a few college interviews, and four coming-outs. I've never fought in a client's body, but my dad was a bouncer, and he taught me all his tricks."

"Whoa," Josh said, raising his brows. "Promposals, huh?"

"Really? That's what impressed you?"

"Just thinking about it makes my palms sweaty." He lifted a hand to show me. "How do you do it? How can you be so chill about stuff that terrifies everyone else? You make it sound easy."

It *was* easy. I didn't have to try to be brave for my clients. It came naturally, because someone else's heart was on the line instead of mine. In real life, aka my own life, I hated drama. My last breakup was so messy and embarrassing that I didn't even want to date anymore. But breaking up for a client? Effortless. I had zero reasons to feel anxious when I wasn't the one who would be crying into a pint of Ben & Jerry's afterward.

"It comes down to not being invested," I said. "When I go inside your head, I'll bring my own consciousness with me. I won't feel your emotions or have your memories. I won't know what you're afraid of, because I won't be you."

"You'll have no skin in the game," he added.

"Exactly. Which makes it easy for me to take risks that scare you."

"Huh," Josh said. "That's kind of deep."

"Speaking of risks . . ." I said with a pointed look. "There's no way for me to put a respectable hurt on Mark without getting you suspended. Three days, at least. The honor society might kick you out, too. Are you okay with that?"

"I guess so."

"You *guess* so?"

"I'm positive." Josh nodded. "No guts, no story. Right?"

"That's what I like to hear." I gave him a hearty pat on the shoulder. "Now, let's talk business. You remember my fee?"

"Yeah, about that," he said. "The money was in my pants, so . . ."

"Pay me later," I told him. "I know you're good for it. The most important part of our deal is keeping it a secret. You can't tell anyone about me. No one. Not your best friend, not your priest, not your mom. Not even yourself—so no journaling about it."

"But what if someone needs your help?" he asked.

"Then you come to me, and I'll decide if I want to offer them my services. But you don't mention me to that person." I pointed back and forth between us. "This only works if we stay quiet. If Mark ever found out that I did your dirty work for you . . ."

Josh swallowed hard. "I swear I won't tell a soul."

"All right. So now there's only one other matter to discuss."

"Which is?"

"Lunch."

Josh wrinkled his forehead.

"Before I exit your body," I explained, "I will take it to lunch. And I will stuff myself—technically *yourself*—full of the greasiest, cheesiest, sauciest, most nutritionally deficient garbage to ever see the inside of a fryer. And then I'll chase it down with a triple-fudge sundae and a shake."

His gaze lowered to my hips and thighs. "But why? You're not—"

"This isn't a weight thing," I interrupted. "It's an allergy thing." As evidence, I showed him the EpiPen I kept tucked in my pocket to save me from the perils of wheat, eggs, dairy, and a dozen other staples of human existence.

"What are you allergic to?" he asked.

"Everything that makes life worth living." I folded my arms. "I can't have good food unless I eat it in a different body. So I'm going to eat vicariously through you, Josh. This is nonnegotiable. Expect to wake up with level-five heartburn."

"Fine." He held up both palms. "Stuff me like a turkey."

"Oh, I will," I assured him with a smile. "Now that the details are out of the way, we can get to work." I sat on the futon and patted the spot beside me. "Come have a seat. You're going to give me a literal piece of your mind."

Chapter Two

"THE FIRST STEP IS TO RELAX," I TOLD JOSH, COVER-
ing his hand with mine. We sat side by side with our shoulders
touching. The contact allowed me to sense his tension and match the
rhythm of our breathing. "Close your eyes and concentrate on your
muscle groups, starting with your head and working your way down
to your toes. I want you to release all the tension in each group until
your body goes limp."

He nodded and inhaled. As he exhaled, his shoulder eased
down an inch, pressing closer against me. After the next breath, he
whispered, "By the way, how'd you learn to do this? Did someone
teach you?"

I stifled a laugh. I had never met another immersionist, let alone
had a guide. Only a few hundred of us had come forward to join the
registry, and the government kept those identities on lockdown, probably to stop us from networking. There were no schools for people
like me, no handbooks, no YouTube tutorials to explain the experience with step-by-step instructions, briefly interrupted by annoying

ads. No, I had to learn the old-fashioned way—by accident in a Chick-fil-A dining room.

"It's a long story," I whispered back. "I found some info on the dark web. After that, it was pretty much trial and error."

I didn't mention that my best friend, Valencia, had helped. I had committed a crime by failing to join the registry, and I didn't want Val charged with collusion for keeping my secret. But in all honesty, Val was the one who had made me realize I was an immersionist in the first place.

It all started with a craving for waffle fries. . . .

Val would constantly drag me into restaurants where I couldn't have anything on the menu except for a fruit cup. So there I was, sitting across the table from Val, drooling over her chicken sandwich and her waffle fries while I picked at a cup of mandarin oranges. I remember wishing I could trade places with her, and the next thing I knew, I tasted mayonnaise and saw Val's sandwich in my hands . . . except they were her hands.

She must have pushed me out of her mind right away because the whole thing lasted less than a second, just long enough for me to catch a glimpse of my body going limp on the other side of the table. I blinked and returned to my own head, and then promptly screamed and fell off my chair.

After picking me up off the floor, Val rushed me to my house to re-create what we had done. It took a few days of experimenting, but we figured out the basics. To transfer my mind into another person's body—and to stay there—required two main elements: cooperation and focus.

"No more talking," I told Josh. "I want you to imagine your mind as an empty room. There's no furniture inside. No windows, no decorations. Just four white walls and two doors—one door for the entrance and another one that leads to a walk-in closet."

"Are the doors open?"

"Not yet."

"What about the floor?" he asked. "Is it carpet?"

"Sure, if you want."

"What color?"

"Beige."

"Mm-kay," he said with a nod. "Got it."

"Now imagine yourself sitting cross-legged in the middle of the room, kind of like you're meditating. Your eyes are closed. You're warm and calm, focusing on each breath." I paused, waiting until he fully relaxed against me. "Now you hear a soft knock on the door, and you know it's me. You smile and open your eyes. You want to see me, so you push up from the carpet and walk to the door. Your body is loose and limber. You grasp the doorknob and turn it, and you let me in."

As I spoke, I tipped back my head and concentrated on Josh, imagining myself leaving my body and traveling to the door in his mind. My fingertips tingled, a sign of disconnect that told me the process was working. One by one, my limbs grew heavy as I floated out of my skin. A moment later, I stood facing an imaginary door that opened to reveal Josh, still clad in his Star Wars boxer shorts.

"Freaky." He grinned. "So does this mean we're both in my head?"

"For now." I leaned forward, struggling to cross the threshold. Some unknown force opposed me, like a strong wind pushing me backward. It happened during some transfers. I figured the resistance had to do with a struggle for control, because the force always disappeared as soon as my client left the room. I pointed at the closet. "I need you to go in there and wait until I call for you. Don't try to come out early. Just sit down in the closet and focus on your breathing, like you did before."

Josh chewed on his lower lip. "What's in there?"

Honestly, I didn't know. Every one of my clients had said they couldn't remember a single moment of their time outside the room. But I didn't want to scare Josh, so I told him, "The same thing that's in here—four walls and a carpet. Don't worry. You'll be fine. It'll all be over before you know it."

Josh hesitated for a beat, but he crossed the room and let himself into the closet. He closed the door behind him, and at once, the pressure against me dropped.

Now that I had control, I didn't need to stay in the imaginary room anymore. Turning my focus outward, I concentrated on my physical sensations—the pressure of my thighs against the futon cushion, the soft fleece blanketing my arms, the cool floor beneath my feet. Motion came next as I flexed my fingers and toes. And with my next breath, the transfer was complete. I lifted my head, stood up from the futon, and viewed the world (or the inside of my shed) as Josh Fenske.

I blinked a few times, taking in the changes. I wondered if Josh knew the throw rug he saw as gray was actually blue. I made a mental note to ask about his color blindness later. Right now, I had to deal with prepping my own body to leave it behind.

I hated this part.

Not only was it creepy seeing myself passed out with my head lolled to the side, but I felt a weird attraction between my mind and my flesh, a slight magnetism drawing me back to where I belonged. Maybe it was nature's way of making sure I could wander without losing my path home. That made sense, because even though the pull grew weaker with distance, I always felt it like a compass for my soul.

Which made me wonder what would happen if my body died while my mind was elsewhere. Would my soul find its home in a new body? Or would I always feel drawn toward my own remains?

I shivered. I didn't want to find out.

For that reason, I followed a list of safety protocols before I left for a job. First, I leaned down and readjusted my head so I wouldn't wake up with a stiff neck, which had happened more times than I cared to admit. Then I inspected each of my limbs, making sure nothing blocked my circulation. Satisfied with my body check, I scanned the shed for fire hazards—combustible liquids like nail polish and essential oils, or electronics that could short out and cause a spark. I didn't see anything at first, but then I remembered my cell phone and retrieved it from my back pocket. Faulty batteries could start fires. After one last look around, I left the shed and bolted the door with a two-inch steel padlock.

"Good luck getting through *that*," I dared no one in particular. The sound of Josh's deep voice shocked a laugh out of me. That would take some getting used to.

I set off across the lawn, the dewy grass tickling my bare feet as I walked toward the house in loping strides that covered the distance in half the time as usual. I had never piloted a body with legs as long as Josh's. I would have to get used to them—fast. Not to mention find him some clothes. I knew nothing in my closet would fit him, so I raided my dad's bedroom for a pair of Velcro sneakers, drawstring sweatpants, and a Grateful Dead T-shirt. Dad wouldn't mind sharing, as long as I washed and replaced his clothes before he noticed them missing.

Speaking of missing things, I should probably explain my absence to the attendance secretary, the ever-vigilant Mrs. Kazinski, before she called my dad at work. I logged on to my dad's School Link account and sent a quick message claiming I was sick with a fever. As for Josh, he would have to take an unexcused tardy. If I did my job right, it would be the least of his offenses today.

I checked the clock, noting I had thirty minutes until the next city bus. I had already bought a pass since Josh didn't drive. That left me with enough time to run a few drills in the basement gym. I jogged down the stairs and warmed up on the punching bag. I did the bare minimum—a few jabs and right hooks—to learn Josh's body. For an extra boost, I grabbed a Gatorade on my way out the door.

The walk to the bus stop gave me a chance to unwind, and I found myself daydreaming about what I would eat for lunch. I'd brought plenty of cash, and I had already decided on the restaurant. My favorite place was a family-owned diner called the Sparky Spoon. They made the best chili dogs in town, and their shakes weren't half bad either, depending on who was mixing them. Today that would be Nash. I knew his schedule because he was my ex . . . the same ex who had dumped me last fall to "focus on college," which apparently meant "bang sorority girls." But whatever. I didn't care about Nash. I wanted a chili dog, that was all.

I pushed him out of my mind when I boarded the bus. One hour and two transfers later, I stepped inside Harvey Davis High School and collected a tardy pass from Mrs. Kazinski, just as the fourth bell rang to signify senior lunch period—Mark's lunch period.

I couldn't have timed it better.

The only problem was Josh's boxer shorts. They provided no support for the beanbags that kept catching between my thighs. At first it hadn't bothered me, but the long walk to the bus stop had caused some serious chafing. Now I found myself ambling along the hallway with my knees spread and my hips pushed out like a bowlegged cowboy.

I couldn't take it anymore, so I snuck into the boys' locker room and borrowed a jockstrap from the supply closet. The strap looked ridiculous when I put it on over my boxers, but it bundled up everything nice and tight. For good measure, I tucked an athletic cup beneath the strap to protect me against a low blow. Not that I planned to fight fair, but I knew better than to count on a bully to hit above the belt.

When I finally reached the cafeteria, I paused outside the open doors and searched for Mark. I found him sitting alone at the end of a table near the emergency exit, farthest from the lunchroom monitor. A perfect spot to pick a fight, except the monitor on duty was Coach Bollard, otherwise known as the Boulder. I would have thirty seconds, at best, to take Mark down before the coach broke us up.

Staying out of sight, I studied Mark's body language and noticed a Coke in his right hand. He took a swig and set it down, and then used that same hand to pluck a french fry from his tray. He was a righty. The angle of his head toward a nearby group of girls told me he was right-eye dominant, too. I took in his posture, the way he curled around his food, his shoulders tense, and his butt poised on the edge of his seat. Those details might seem trivial, but they gave me a few key pieces of information. Mark would be quick to attack, he would lead with a lunge, and he would favor his right side.

The first lesson my dad had taught me was how to read someone's "tells." Even the tiniest actions could betray an opponent's next move and give away the advantage. My dad had been so adamant about paying attention that he had forced me to study hundreds of boxing matches until I could pause the fight and correctly predict what would happen next. Only then had he taught me how to throw a punch. Mark didn't know it yet, but he'd already lost.

Now to sell the performance.

Josh was right—everyone knew he was a quiet kid who didn't stand up for himself. He had proven it again that very morning by letting Mark take his clothes. But everyone also knew that quiet kids could snap, and in that rare occurrence, their explosions rang the loudest. Josh could push back, but to make people believe it, he needed to go nuclear.

I ruffled his hair and scrubbed his eyes until they felt puffy and red, and then I slapped both of his cheeks to create an angry flush. Satisfied with the transformation, I stalked into the cafeteria, breathing wildly through my nose.

No one noticed me at first, not even Mark. I made it all the way to his table without drawing a single glance. But all of that changed when I slapped the Coke out of his hand. At once, nearby chatter stopped. Mark froze. Hundreds of eyes widened and turned to me. A question hung in the air: *Did that really happen?* No one seemed to know what to think, least of all Mark, whose fingers were still curled around an invisible can.

"I'm done playing with you," I announced.

There was a collective intake of breath, and right on cue, a cell phone screen appeared in my peripheral view. Two more screens popped up. God bless the social media addicts and their thirst for likes and follows. I could always count on them for maximum exposure.

Mark glanced at the lunch monitor and hesitated, clearly torn between whether to kick my ass now or wait until later.

He needed a push.

"What?" I taunted. "You got nothing to say to me?"

His jaw tightened.

"You're just gonna sit there?" I asked. When he didn't move, I pulled out the big guns and called him a girl.

That did it.

I grabbed Mark's tray and dumped its contents just in time for him to charge me. As predicted, he led with his right shoulder. I dodged left and tripped him, sending him face-first into a pile of his own fries. His head snapped up, his cheeks red with rage. And ketchup. I knew he wouldn't stay down for long, so I held the tray in front of me like a shield. Luckily, the cafeteria had replaced Styrofoam trays with heavy-duty reusable plastic. Safe for the environment, safer for me.

Mark pushed to his feet and charged again, making the same mistake of leading with his right shoulder. Part of me wanted to coach him, but an even bigger part wanted to smack him upside the head. So I darted aside and gave him a wallop as he stumbled by. That enraged him, exactly as I had intended. Anger made people sloppy.

Mark turned and swung at me with his—you guessed it—*right* fist. When I ducked, he shifted his weight and lowered one shoulder in a telltale sign of an uppercut. Based on the direction of his gaze, I knew he was aiming for my crotch. (See? Bullies don't fight fair.) I was prepared for a low blow. I figured the molded plastic between my legs would hurt Mark more than it would hurt me, so I stood firm and let his knuckles connect with my cup.

Oh, my god, that was the worst idea I've ever had.

A thump sounded. I felt pressure around the cup, followed by a sudden weightlessness as the force of the blow lifted me off my feet. I grabbed Mark's shirt to steady myself while pain radiated from my groin to my stomach. I fought the urge to heave, swallowing a mouthful of half-digested Gatorade. The cup must have slid against my boxer shorts and racked me, because I had never hurt so badly, not even in seventh-grade gymnastics, when I had slipped and lost my virginity to the balance beam. I could feel Mark gearing up for another punch, but I wasn't strong enough to dodge it. I couldn't even breathe. So I panicked and did the first thing that came to mind. I poked him in the eye.

Not my finest moment, but "desperate times" and all.

Mark flinched and brought both hands to his face. His distraction gave me a beat to recover. I drew a breath and turned the tables by jabbing him in the windpipe. He doubled over in a coughing fit. I saw my chance to send him down for the count, so I took it, elbowing him in the kidney.

Mark dropped to the floor and curled up in the fetal position. On the other side of the cafeteria, Coach Bollard waded toward me through the crowd of onlookers. I knew I didn't have much time, so I lowered my mouth to Mark's ear and got right to the point.

"Listen," I hissed. "I didn't want to get suspended. That's why I took your shit. But I don't care anymore. If you come at me again, I *will* tag you back, no matter what it takes." To drive my message home, I squeezed the delicate spot between his wrist bones. "Are we clear?"

He cried out something resembling a *yes*.

"And I want my stuff back," I said. "All of it. By the time I get home, there'd better be a bag on my front porch."

"Mm-kay," he grunted.

I released him and stood up, flashing both palms in surrender at Coach Bollard. I didn't wait for the coach to order me to report to the office. I backed away and told him, "Yeah, yeah, I know. I'm going."

I turned and strode across the cafeteria with my head held high—not easy, thanks to my aching crotch. But I wanted to give Josh a dignified exit, and in my opinion, I nailed it. As a bonus, I even made it all the way to the bathroom before I puked. I considered that a double win, since an empty stomach meant more room for food.

Now I could reward myself with lunch at the Sparky Spoon. After what I had been through, I deserved the best chili dog in town . . . coincidentally served up by my ex.

Chapter Three

INSTEAD OF REPORTING TO THE OFFICE LIKE I HAD planned, I ducked out the side door and jogged to the bus stop in time to catch the 12:30 shuttle to town. I hated to ditch. I knew the school cameras had caught Josh sneaking out, and that he would pay for it with a longer suspension. But I had no choice. I'd forgotten that Josh didn't drive. His parents would insist on picking him up as soon as the school called, which meant no binge-fest for me at the Sparky Spoon. And that was simply out of the question. Besides, I still had to return to my shed to switch our bodies back, and I couldn't do that under Fenske house arrest. So the way I saw it, I could sneak out of school now, or sneak out of Josh's house later. Either way, he was super grounded, so I took the direct path—the one that led to chili dogs.

Sorry about that, Josh.

But not *that* sorry.

Because now I had the whole afternoon to walk around downtown. Main Street wasn't my usual scene, but a couple of years ago, the mayor had launched this huge "beautification" project full of so much adorable, clichéd small-town decor that it now reminded me of a theme park. Something about the combination of brick-paved sidewalks, green-and-white-striped awnings, and streetlamps adorned with hanging flower baskets put me in my happy place, so I made it a point to come downtown once in a while and de-bitch.

The sun warmed my shoulders as I walked through the town square, breathing in the weirdly pleasant scent of honeysuckle mixed with car exhaust. I couldn't see the Sparky Spoon yet, but it wasn't much farther, just a few blocks beyond the courthouse and the government buildings. I loped along at an easy pace, exchanging nods with the guys I passed and trying not to make eye contact with the women. I always hated it when a man's gaze lingered on me for too long, and I didn't want to creep anyone out.

I noticed people reacted to me differently as a boy. Even though I didn't smile at anyone, nobody told me to "cheer up" or "be happy" the way strangers did when I wore my own skin. During my entire walk to the Sparky Spoon, nobody talked to me at all. It was nice for a change. The silence almost made up for the aching balls.

I paused outside the Sparky Spoon and peered through the front window, bracing myself for my first glimpse of Nash. I had blocked him on social media last summer after he'd dumped me, and I had carefully avoided him ever since. So I had no idea what he looked like now. I figured college had changed him. Maybe he had grown out his hair and wore it in a man bun, or sprouted some silly poser beard, or even better, maybe he had lost his washboard abs.

I spotted him coming out of the kitchen, and my stomach dipped into my sweatpants. All it took was one glance to tell me he hadn't changed, at least not by much. He had grown an inch or two, and the angle of his jaw had sharpened, but he still wore his hair the same:

short enough to clear his collar and long enough to form a thick black swoop over his forehead. His face still belonged on a magazine ad—straight nose, high cheekbones, cleft chin, and a pair of thick, full lips made for kissing. His white T-shirt still highlighted his dark skin, fabric stretched tight across his broad chest and his rounded biceps. His jeans still hugged him in places I didn't want to notice . . . but I noticed.

So much for the freshman fifteen.

He delivered an order to a table of women and then backed away with a grin that probably doubled his tip. But it wasn't the real thing. His smile didn't draw out the dimples in his cheeks or crinkle the skin around his eyes. That smile was lethal. Or it used to be. I hadn't seen it in a while. Maybe it had lost its power over me.

A girl could hope.

He must have sensed me watching, because he met my gaze through the window, and instinctively I froze, holding my breath as if he'd busted me. Then I remembered what I looked like. Not even Nash would recognize me in this body.

I pushed open the door and chose a booth all the way in the back. A television was mounted high on the opposite wall. I sat facing the screen, feigning interest in a news story about a cell-phone scam while I tracked Nash in my side view. I saw him pick up his order pad and head toward me. I pretended not to notice him, but the closer he came, the harder my pulse ticked. By the time he reached my table, I had to wipe my sweaty hands on my pants. I kept ignoring him, even when he stood right beside me with his pencil at the ready.

He cleared his throat to get my attention.

"Oh," I said, blinking at him. "Sorry, man. Didn't see you there."

The tight set of his lips told me I had annoyed him. Which gave me a thrill.

"No worries," he said. "Can I start you off with a drink while you look at the menu?"

"No, I'm ready to order." I used my fingers to tick off each item as I spoke. "I'll have two chili dogs, all the way, an order of cheesy fries, a side of jalapeño cheddar grits, a soft pretzel with extra butter—don't skimp on the salt—a slice of pecan pie, a chocolate malt, and a peanut butter fudge sundae."

He snickered. "Is that all?"

"And a large Coke."

He glanced up from his pad and gave me a real smile, dimples and crinkly eyes and all. My innards turned a cartwheel. "You got it."

Ten minutes later, the chili dogs arrived, and all thoughts of Nash vanished as a swirl of savory steam wafted up from my plate. The spicy scent of chili made my mouth water. I lifted a soft, warm bun to my lips and held it there, savoring the anticipation until I couldn't wait any longer, and I took a massive bite.

Flavor burst across my tongue, rich and bold and salty. The taste was so exquisite that I had to block out my other senses, closing my eyes and tuning out the noise of the television. I groaned and stuffed in another mouthful. Each bite tasted better than the last. I wanted to take my time and savor every morsel, but I couldn't wait long enough to chew and swallow before shoving a french fry past my lips.

Oh, god.

I might have spoken out loud. I wasn't sure. I didn't care.

Until Nash whispered in my ear, "Hey, T."

My eyes snapped open. I whipped my head around and found him grinning at me with a signature spark in his eyes. It was a look I recognized from a hundred quiet moments we had shared in the hallway at school, on the sofa at home, in the front seat of his car, in the *back*seat of his car.

I never should have told him about my ability.

He slid into the booth across from me. "Don't bother denying it," he said. "I would know you in any body. No one makes love to a footlong like my girl."

I jabbed a fry at him. "I am not your girl!"

I hadn't meant to say it so loudly—or in Josh's deep voice. We drew a few curious glances from the next table. Nash dismissed them with a wave.

"Fair point," he said. "Still, it's good to see you, T."

I rolled my eyes and slurped my chocolate malt, which was so damn delicious I could barely contain a moan.

"Listen," he added, leaning toward me. "I've been wanting to talk to you about something. I texted you a bunch of times, but you didn't answer."

"I answered."

"Random emojis don't count."

"They do if you speak the language."

He pulled his phone from his pocket and showed me our thread: a cartoon face, a skull, a flame, a rose, and a grave. "Enlighten me."

"Go die in a fire," I translated for him.

"Real mature."

"Hey, I'm not one of your college girls," I argued. "I don't have to be mature." I scooped up a bite of pecan pie, flinching when a car backfired outside. I slid the bite into my mouth and closed my eyes to savor the perfect blend of sweetness and spice. I chewed with deliberate slowness and ignored Nash. He could wait. Pies before guys. After I finished my bite and scooped up another one, I glanced at him and added,

"But since I'm here, you might as well tell me what's so important."

Nash opened his mouth and closed it again. Something seemed to catch his attention. He turned slightly and looked at the television screen, squinting for a moment, until his brows shot up and his eyes flew wide.

"Uh, T . . ." he said, still staring at the television as he slowly stood from the booth. "Where did you leave your body?"

His words turned my skin cold. "In my shed. Why?"

I didn't wait for him to respond. I followed his gaze to the television and did a double take . . . a triple take . . . maybe even a quadruple take, before I believed what I saw. A shaky video showed *me*—well, my body—standing inside what appeared to be the lobby of a government building. One of my hands was raised in surrender. The other held a pistol. In the pit of my gut (Josh's gut), I felt the odd, familiar tugging that told me my body was near.

I stopped breathing as I read the bottom of the television screen. In bold lettering, a headline reported ACTIVE SHOOTER INSIDE THE COURTHOUSE. ONE VICTIM CONFIRMED DEAD. I watched in disbelief as the Tia in the video placed her gun on the marble floor, lowered to her knees, and laced both hands behind her head. A moment later, police cuffed her, and the video ended.

"What the—" I blurted while trying to stand up.

Nash shushed me and pushed me back down before I could make a scene in front of the whole diner.

I looked up at Nash. Our eyes locked and held. Neither of us moved or spoke. Had I actually been arrested for murder? The question was too absurd to ask it out loud. Suddenly, it occurred to me that I hadn't heard a car backfiring. I had heard a gunshot from the town square. A gunshot that had killed at least one person—by my hand.

By my hand, but not by *me*.

Chapter Four

IT TOOK A LOT TO SHAKE ME, BUT WATCHING MYSELF get arrested did the trick. I felt suspended in time, fuzzy and muddled, paralyzed with a french fry in one hand and a forkful of pecan pie in the other.

Nash snapped his fingers in front of my face and broke the trance.

"How?" I whispered to him. How had someone taken control of my body? How had someone gotten into my shed or even known that I was there to begin with? I had only told a handful of people that I was an immersionist, and none of them would have betrayed me.

"I don't know," Nash said. "But, T . . . what are you gonna do?"

My legs instinctively twitched to run to the courthouse so I could proclaim my innocence, but I stayed in my seat. There was no way the cops would believe me, at least not at first. I would have to prove my identity, which would be an actual nightmare because I hadn't joined the national registry. Then there was the minor issue that anything I said in public would out Josh to the entire town, and I wanted to keep him out of the dumpster if I could help it.

I had to calm down and think, not an easy thing to do in panic mode.

Taking a deep breath, I started by pinpointing what I knew for certain: Whoever had hijacked my body was also an immersionist. That meant *their* body was out there somewhere, empty and defenseless, just like mine had been. And since the hijacker had found me in my shed, maybe they had left their body there. If so, I could clear my name before dinner.

I held out a palm to Nash. "I need to borrow your car."

"Of course." He dug in his pocket and gave me his keys. "Want me to come? I could close up real fast and call someone to cover my shift."

I shook my head. No matter how quickly Nash could box up his customers' food and get them out the door, it was longer than I wanted to wait. I shoveled in one bite of pie and made for the back door to the employee parking lot.

Nash's car was exactly the same as I remembered: a 1980s harvest-gold Plymouth that he had bought at a sheriff's auction. It looked like something a geriatric pimp would drive, but it packed a surprising punch under the hood. I slid behind the wheel and noticed that even the interior smelled the same—like aged leather and bad choices.

The engine fired up easily, and as I inched out of the lot, I craned my neck toward the courthouse to find the street barricaded by police. I turned in the opposite direction and navigated a different route home. At the next stop sign, I sent my dad a quick text.

I'm in a client's body. It wasn't me. I'm safe.

The message would make sense to him later. I didn't bother trying to call. My dad worked security at a power plant, and he had to keep his phone in a locker until the end of his shift. I figured the police would contact him as soon as they identified "me" as the killer, and then he would check his messages right away.

I found a local news station on the radio and listened for details. So far, they hadn't told me anything new. An unidentified assailant had murdered one victim whose name couldn't be released until police had notified their next of kin. But then I remembered that the rules of journalism didn't exist on social media. I checked Twitter while I stopped at a red light. Just as predicted, the attack was trending under #CourthouseShooting, with district attorney Ben Mitchell named as the victim.

"Ben Mitchell," I said to myself. I had never heard of him.

When I finally reached my house, my (Josh's) unusually long legs were so wobbly that I jumped the curb. I threw the car in park and ran across the lawn into the backyard. My heart sank when I spotted the shed door left open, but I kept going until I reached the entrance. There, all of my hopes drained away, and I let my arms hang limp by my sides.

The shed was empty.

I should have expected as much. Anyone smart enough to commit murder in someone else's skin would know better than to leave their own body behind. Still, I scanned the shed for clues. All that remained of my body was an indentation on the futon cushion. Glancing at the floor, I noticed a trail of black scuff marks, most likely left by the ankle boots I had worn that morning. Judging by the skidded path from the futon to the doorway, it looked like the killer had dragged me out of the shed.

But to where?

I turned and looked outside. On the grass by my feet lay the severed remains of my lock, cut cleanly in half by bolt cutters. Just beyond the metal fragments, I could make out a pair of tracks. I crouched down and noticed the faint imprint of tire marks on the lawn. Someone had driven into my backyard. From there, they had cut the padlock and dragged my body into their car—all in broad daylight.

Ballsy.

I glanced at our next-door neighbors, wondering if they could have seen anything through the massive, leafy oak branches that stretched between our homes. I doubted it. But if I was lucky, maybe the house across the street had caught the killer's license plate on their doorbell camera. I made a mental note to ask them later.

My phone buzzed with a text from Nash.

You okay?

Fine, I told him. Came home to check the shed. It's empty.

I could've told you that.

I frowned. How?

Called a friend with a police scanner, he said. The shooter was taken to county hospital five minutes ago in a coma.

In a coma. That perfectly described what an empty immersionist looked like. It seemed the killer had left my body and returned to their own. But for the life of me, I couldn't imagine how they had pulled it off—while handcuffed and under arrest. Their body would've had to be close to mine, and even then, the transfer would have left them weak. The process of head-hopping was exhausting for all immersionists.

Or so I had assumed.

Maybe I didn't know as much about my own kind as I'd thought.

* * *

Needless to say, I didn't clear my name before dinner. But I did have a chance to sit down with my father and his lawyer friend Stan and strategize a way to prove my identity to the police. Stan couldn't practice law anymore. He was more "lawyer-adjacent" than an actual attorney. He had been disbarred a few years ago for giving himself an interest-free loan by way of a client's trust fund, which was a huge no-no, even though he put the money back. Anyway, I might not trust Stan with my savings account, but he was smart and well connected and free, and that was the only kind of representation I could afford.

Stan cashed in a few favors and got us a private meeting that night with the chief of police and the lead investigator for the shooting. A few hours later, the five of us—or six, if you counted my comatose body—crammed into my hospital room to discuss the bizarre details of my case.

While Stan explained everything, I snuck glances at myself on the hospital bed, my skin pale, my dark hair disheveled, both wrists restrained by thick leather straps. Next to the bed, a heart monitor beeped a steady rhythm, and with each audible pulse, I felt an ever-increasing force drawing me back to where I belonged. I couldn't wait to wear my own skin again. I had never left my body for this long, and I had to resist the urge to dive headfirst onto the bed and smash myself back together.

The lead detective cleared his throat to get my attention. He had introduced himself with a generic last name that I'd already forgotten, but his features were so unique I could easily pick him out of a crowd. Sharp amber eyes peered at me through a set of corrective lenses, his glasses held up by a crooked nose. He was bald, much like my dad, and about the same age. I definitely wouldn't call him attractive, but he had an interesting face.

"So you're a head-hopper," he said.

"Immersionist," my dad corrected for me. He folded his muscled arms and cocked his head, somehow managing to look down at the much taller detective. At five feet, seven inches, my dad's height had never held him back. He was the youngest of seven Jersey boys, so he'd grown up tougher than a two-dollar steak.

"And where is Miss Dante's mother?" the detective asked.

Ooof. My dad hated that question.

"I don't have one," I said. And before anyone could ask if I had hatched from an egg, I added, "She died when I was born."

My mother had technically died *before* I was born, but that was a long story, and telling it would make my dad even more defensive than he already was. My dad would rather chew glass than talk about my mother. He had told me her name was Maria, that they weren't married, and that during her eighth month of pregnancy, she'd suffered a blood clot to the heart and died instantly. I had only survived because it happened at the hospital during one of her well checks. If the doctors hadn't cut me out of her in time, both of us would be in the chrome urn that my dad kept on a shelf in the back of his closet. Sometimes I felt guilty for not asking more questions about Maria. But the truth was I didn't know my mother, and all the stories in the world wouldn't change that.

The detective returned his gaze to me. "So, you're an immersionist. Why didn't you register?"

"I was getting around to it," I lied.

He gestured at the ankle-length raincoat, fedora, and oversize sunglasses I had worn to disguise Josh's identity. "And what's all this? You look like Inspector Gadget."

"Inspector who?" I asked.

"You know," he said, waving an arm above his head. "'*Go-go, Gadget arms.*'"

I had no idea what he was talking about.

"It's a cartoon," he added. "From the eighties."

I shrugged. "I don't watch boomer shows."

At the same time, he and my dad cringed.

"Millennial, not boomer," my dad murmured.

Whatever, same difference. I touched the brim of my fedora and explained, "It's protection for my client. He didn't do anything wrong. He deserves his privacy."

The detective snorted and hooked a thumb toward the parking lot, where half a dozen news vans had camped out to wait for juicy tidbits about the case. "Privacy?"

"My client's a minor," I reminded him. "That has to count for something."

He blew out a long breath and pointed at Josh's head. "So you're telling me there are two of you in there?"

"Yes and no," I said. "It's kind of like having multiple personalities. Both of us can't be aware at the same time. I'm in control right now. My client has no clue what's going on, and he won't remember any of this when he wakes up."

The detective traded glances with his chief and then studied me for a beat, sucking his teeth and probably wondering if this was a prank. "Why should we believe you?"

"Glad you asked," I said, and handed him a small Post-it Note pad and a pen. "Write down something that no one knows about you."

"Like what?"

"I don't know, security question stuff. Your grandma's maiden name. The street you grew up on. Your third-grade teacher. Your first crush."

"Want my banking password, too?"

"How about this," I suggested. "Write down your favorite line from your favorite TV show. Pretty sure I can't steal your identity with that. Just make sure no one sees it but me."

He nodded thoughtfully for a moment, and then faced away from the group and wrote down his answer. When he turned around again, he discreetly showed me the notepad. I glanced at the response and committed it to memory.

"Okay, I'm going to transfer out of my client's body and wake up there"—I pointed at my sleeping form—"and tell you what you wrote."

Because Josh and I wouldn't both fit on the narrow bed, I dragged over a chair and sat down close enough to reach through the bed rails and hold my own hand. I sat back as far as I could and leaned my head against the edge of the mattress, then closed my eyes and did my best to relax under the weight of four stares. I had never transferred bodies in front of an audience before, and it took a few minutes longer than usual to slow my heartbeat and sharpen my focus enough to picture the imaginary room inside Josh's mind.

Once inside the room, I knocked on the closet door and called to Josh, "You can come out now."

The door opened a sliver, and Josh peeked out.

"All done," I said, brushing my palms together.

"But that was so fast!"

"I told you it would be over before you knew it."

He peered at me tentatively. "Did it go okay?"

"Better than okay. The whole lunchroom watched you kick Mark's ass. There's even video online. No one's going to mess with you anymore." I paused. "That's the good news."

Josh's smile fell. "Does that mean there's bad news?"

I couldn't sugarcoat the truth, so I got straight to the point and gave him the condensed version of events. By the time I finished, Josh resembled a taxidermied deer.

"You don't need to worry," I assured him. "I dressed you up so no one would recognize you. The police don't even know your name. As soon as you wake up, my lawyer will drive you home, and no one ever has to find out that I fought Mark for you."

Josh lowered his brows. "Mark? That's why you think I'm freaked out?"

"Well, yeah."

"Tia, I'm worried for *you*."

"You don't have to be."

"The whole world just watched you kill someone!"

"Not the *whole* world," I argued.

"Not yet." He leveled a gaze at me. "But, Tia, when people find out what you are . . . what you can do . . ."

I held up a finger to stop him. I didn't need to hear any more. I had already seen the shitstorm in the forecast. Even if I convinced the district attorney not to charge me with murder, the police would have to give the public an explanation for the shooting. Soon the police would out me as an immersionist, and that would open up a next-level can of worms for legal systems everywhere, because how could a prosecutor prove that someone else had shot Ben Mitchell when I was the one caught on camera pulling the trigger? To my knowledge, this had never happened before. It was an evidence nightmare that might change the way crimes were tried forever.

The whole world would definitely be watching.

I licked my lips and told Josh, "I'll see you on the other side."

I walked to the imaginary door, braced myself for the chaos to come, and strode out of Josh's mind. With my next breath, I awoke to the sensation of stiff leather around my wrists and a pillow beneath my aching head. I blinked and swallowed in a dry throat, then peered around the room for the lead detective.

"'Curse your sudden but inevitable betrayal,'" I croaked, quoting the detective's favorite line from his favorite TV show, *Firefly*. I watched his eyes widen. He showed his chief the notepad, and then the two of them peered at me like I was a calculus problem they didn't know how to solve.

"So," I said, grinning weakly. "Does this mean I can go home?"

Chapter Five

I HAD NEVER BEEN ARRESTED BEFORE, SO MAYBE IT was a little ignorant on my part to assume the detective could simply wave his hands and un-arrest me. As it turned out, un-arresting a person wasn't a thing. Once the criminal process began, it kept on going like a Hula-Hoop rolling downhill. Now it would take a judge to send me home, and since judges didn't work nights, I had to stay in the hospital until we could schedule a hearing the next day.

Josh gave a sworn statement to the detective and then rode home with Stan. After the detective removed my wrist restraints, he coordinated with my dad to send a forensics team to my shed in the morning to collect evidence, and then he posted two guards outside my door and left with his chief. My dad offered to stay the night with me, but I convinced him to go home and ask the neighbors for their doorbell camera footage before the police beat us to it. Besides, my dad snored, and I would have a hard enough time sleeping as it was.

The next morning, my best friend, Val, came to visit me and offer her assistance the best way she knew how: with a tarot reading.

"Wow," she said, raising a blond eyebrow at the card she had placed on my bedside table. She released a low whistle.

I leaned over and frowned at a skull-faced grim reaper. "Uh-oh."

"No, this is good."

"You sure about that?"

"Yeah, the card doesn't mean death. It signifies change—the end of one part of your life and the birth of something new. It symbolizes growth. And power. *Big* power. Combined with these," she said, pointing at the other cards, "I can tell the universe loves you."

I snorted out loud. "Love hurts, I guess."

"I mean it," she insisted. "The universe is trying to teach you something. Impulse control, maybe, based on the Suit of Wands card. You need to show patience and restraint, and then your path will open up for you."

"Cool," I said, and then I called out to my phone, "Hey, Siri, today at noon, remind me to learn how to control my impulses."

Val huffed and folded her arms. "You never take me seriously."

I couldn't argue with her. There were plenty of reasons I didn't take Val seriously. For starters, she called in sick to school whenever a planet was in retrograde. She would rather date a sociopath than a Sagittarius. And she had enrolled in an online course to become a certified pet psychic because her spirit guide had told her to. But I liked Val. She had a good heart. Plus, she was a lot tougher than people gave her credit for. Over the summer, she'd filed for emancipation from her junkie parents and now lived in a conversion van she had outfitted by herself. She was the coolest person I knew.

"I'm sorry," I told her. "I just don't think impulse control is my problem." And to prove it, I chose not to remind her that she believed dreams were alien downloads.

"Hey, resist the cards all you want," she said. "It'll go easier if you listen. But fate will make sure you learn your lesson, no matter how long it takes."

Speaking of time, I glanced at the clock on the wall to make sure Val wouldn't be late for school. Nearly perfect attendance was one of the conditions of her emancipation. "It's almost first bell."

"No worries." She shrugged but started gathering up her tarot cards. "I have Office Aide first period. It's not even a real class."

"Hey," I said right before she left. "I hate to ask you this, but . . . you didn't tell anyone about me, right?" I twirled a finger by my head. "About what I can do?"

"Not a soul," she promised.

I believed her. Val always kept my secrets. But this time I almost wished she had told someone, because then I would have a starting point for figuring out how the killer found my shed—how they'd even discovered I was an immersionist in the first place. The only people who knew the truth were my dad, Val, Nash, and a handful of clients who had every reason to take my secret to the grave.

Clearly someone had talked. What I didn't know was *who* and *why*.

A few hours later, my dad brought me a respectable change of clothes to wear to court. My hearing had been scheduled for mid-afternoon, and since Stan couldn't represent me, he had hooked me up with a "more or less competent" public defender. Stan's description of my attorney didn't fill me with confidence, but he told me not to worry, that the lead investigator had met with the acting district attorney and recommended dismissing my charge. They had even looped in the judge and made her aware of my condition.

Maybe the universe did love me.

Chapter Six

THAT AFTERNOON, I SAT IN JUVENILE COURT NEXT
to my public defender, Wally, a fresh law school graduate who didn't
look old enough to buy his own beer. At the table to our right sat
Shane Douglas, the acting district attorney, who was riffling through
a stack of paperwork. Shane hadn't spoken to me or made eye contact,
and the way he shuffled his papers without really seeing them hinted
that he was nervous. I guessed I couldn't blame him. Overnight he
had gone from Ben Mitchell's assistant prosecutor to taking over Ben's
entire caseload *and* solving his murder.

A judge named Karen Simmons sat ahead of us on the bench.
With a gray bun perched on top of her head, she could have been
someone's granny. But there was nothing grandmotherly about her
shrewd, dark eyes as she narrowed them and surveyed the courtroom.
When she brought the session to order, she spoke in a command-
ing voice that made me sit up straighter and suck in my stomach.
She started by reading my case number and then made a formal
note of everyone in attendance. Since the hearing was closed, that

included me, my lawyer, the acting DA, and my dad, seated a few rows behind me.

"Mr. Douglas," the judge said to the district attorney. "I understand you've learned some new details about the defendant that might affect the charges in this case. Is that correct?"

"Yes, Your Honor," he told her.

"How does the State wish to proceed?"

"To begin with, Your Honor, the State charges Tia Dante with failure to register with the National Security Service as a person of interest, a class C misdemeanor."

I expected a slap on the wrist for that, but a bigger part of me hoped the new DA would empathize with a young girl afraid to join a government watch list. Looked like I had set the bar too high for him.

"Additionally, Your Honor," he added, "we charge the defendant with operating a business without a license, a class B misdemeanor."

"*What?*" I blurted.

"Miss Dante," the judge said. "I'll ask the questions."

"Sorry," I told her.

Shane Douglas ignored me and addressed the judge. "Miss Dante admitted in her sworn statement to police that she enters the minds of her peers in exchange for financial compensation."

"Oh, my god," I muttered a bit too close to the microphone on my table.

"Miss Dante," the judge chided. "Wait your turn."

I clamped my mouth shut and exhaled hard through my nose. My side hustle was no more of a business than dog-walking or mowing lawns during summer break. The DA was just being petty now. Did he want my ninth-grade babysitting money, too?

"However," he said, "we're willing to expunge those two charges from Miss Dante's record in exchange for community service and repayment of court costs."

The judge glanced at my lawyer. "Is that acceptable to you? Court costs and . . . let's say twenty hours of volunteer work?"

Wally looked to me for an answer. I nodded, and he accepted the offer.

"Now," the judge said to Mr. Douglas, "let's discuss the charge of murder in the first degree. Considering what we know about the defendant's condition, I assume you no longer have the means to prove malicious intent beyond a reasonable doubt."

"That is correct, Your Honor," he said. "But . . ."

But? The way he said it raised the hair on the back of my neck.

"Miss Dante's ability to transfer her consciousness does not absolve her of responsibility for her body." He held up a sheet of paper. "There's plenty of legal precedent to hold her accountable in this case. *Klein v. Lake County*, for example."

I turned to Wally for an explanation.

"It's a ruling from a couple of years ago," Wally whispered to me. "A weapons retailer sold a gun to a man without running his background check. The man used the gun to kill his coworkers, and the retailer was found liable."

Oh, no. I didn't like where this was going.

The district attorney continued, "Miss Dante had a legal and moral obligation to remain in control of the body she was born with. But she recklessly abandoned her responsibilities for illicit financial gain, and that decision contributed to Ben Mitchell's death."

I shook my head in disbelief. He couldn't be serious.

"Therefore, the state charges Tia Dante with criminally negligent manslaughter," he said. "A felony in the third degree."

The judge went silent for a long moment, mirroring my surprise until she nodded appreciatively and murmured, "Interesting."

Interesting? More like *disturbing as hell*, because not once had the district attorney made a reference to the real shooter. There had been no mention of finding the person who actually took Ben Mitchell's life. I began to see that the DA wasn't petty at all. He was desperate. He knew full well that he couldn't prove who had killed Ben, so instead of admitting failure, he intended to throw me under the bus and close the case for an easy win.

I scoffed at him. "This isn't fair, and you know it."

He refused to look at me.

"The real killer is out there," I went on. "Does that matter to you?"

"Miss Dante," the judge warned. "Control yourself."

Wally elbowed me in the ribs and shushed me.

"You may continue, Mr. Douglas," the judge said.

He lifted his chin. "We also request that the defendant be tried as an adult—"

"Of course you do," I mumbled.

"—based on the close proximity of her eighteenth birthday."

"I will consider your request," the judge told him. She tilted her head at me. "Miss Dante, how do you plead to the charge of criminally negligent manslaughter?"

"Not freaking guilty," I spat.

"*Not guilty* will suffice."

I resisted the urge to roll my eyes.

"Now, as for the matter of bail," she said, and slid down her bifocals to read from an open file on her bench. "It looks like the defendant has no prior offenses—and despite her questionable behavior today—is an honors student with strong ties to the community. I see no reason to hold Miss Dante until her trial. Bond is set at ten thousand dollars. The defendant may be released into the custody of her father."

"Thank you, Your Honor," Wally said.

I didn't know why he was thanking her. My dad and I didn't have an extra ten grand lying around for bail.

"In the meantime," the judge told Wally, "I suggest you counsel your client on the importance of self-restraint. I won't be so patient with her when we reconvene."

Restraint—wasn't that the lesson the universe wanted me to learn?

The universe could suck it.

* * *

My dad and I had just enough time to make it home before the district attorney held a press conference, and the media descended on our neighborhood like a swarm of locusts. I peeked through the gap in the living room curtains at dozens of journalists and camera crews, their vans lining the street. If the neighbors didn't already hate me, this would clinch it.

My dad tossed a thick packet onto the coffee table, the paperwork he signed to guarantee my bond.

"Thanks, Dad," I told him.

"What, for that?" he asked, flapping a hand at the documents. "That's nothing. Just do me a favor and don't skip town. The court will take the house, and I'll have to go live in that old, raccoon-infested camper on your uncle Vinnie's lawn."

"Thanks for that," I said. "And for not saying *I told you so.*"

"Oh-ho-ho," he chuckled without humor. "I sure as hell told you so." He wagged a finger toward the shed in the backyard. "What did I always used to say, Tia Marie?"

"Don't stick Cheerios up your nose," I droned.

"No, the other thing."

"Stay in my own lane."

"Exactly. Nothing good comes from getting up in other people's business. But did you listen? No. You saw drama, and you crawled right up into its brain." He tapped his temple. "You meddled in strangers' heads. What did you expect to happen?"

I expected to help people, grow my savings account, and eat chili dogs without going into anaphylactic shock. And I accomplished all of that, thank you very much. But there was no point in arguing with my dad, so I rested a hand on his forearm and told him, "Well, I'm glad you have my back."

He covered my hand with his own. "Always, little bee."

My childhood nickname made me cringe. "If the court can try me as an adult, you can stop calling me little bee."

"I can, but I won't." He flashed a grin. "Just do me one favor."

"What?"

"Quit leaving your body lying around like an empty shoe."

He didn't have to worry. I wasn't trying to get body-snatched again. "I promise."

"So no more dirty deeds done dirt cheap?"

"My deeds are done at fair market value, but yes. I'm taking a break. Hey," I said, changing the subject. "Did you have any luck getting the footage from the doorbell camera across the street?"

"That depends on your definition of luck."

He flipped open his laptop and set it on the coffee table. A few clicks later, a black-and-white video played on his screen. I sat on the sofa and leaned in to study the footage of a dark, sleek Audi pulling up in front of our house. The car did a three-point turn and then backed into our yard until it disappeared from view. I replayed the footage and watched it again in slow motion. The tinted windows concealed the driver, but I could easily read the license plate: L8 4 CRT.

"We got him!" I told my dad, pausing the video.

Dad gave me a consoling smile. "Yeah, I thought so, too. Then I had a buddy of mine run the plate."

"And?"

"It belongs to Ben Mitchell."

"The murder victim?" I asked. I reread the license plate and realized what L8 4 CRT stood for. *Late for court.* "All right, so maybe the Audi was registered to him, but he bought it for someone else to drive. Like my car—it's titled and registered in your name, but I'm the one who uses it."

Dad shook his head. "I checked with the courthouse. It was his daily driver."

"Crap," I said. "So you're telling me the same person who shot Ben Mitchell also stole his car?"

"It looks that way."

"What about the cameras at the courthouse? Maybe there's video of whoever stole it."

"I already asked Detective Roberts when he came over this morning with the forensics team."

"Detective who?"

"Inspector Gadget."

"Oh, right."

"He said there's no footage of Ben's Audi in the parking garage on the day of the shooting. Ben must have parked it somewhere else that morning."

"Crap," I repeated. "So we have nothing?"

"Sorry, bee." Dad patted my shoulder. "I wanted an easy fix, too."

"What about forensics?" I asked. "Did they find anything in the shed?"

"I'm sure they found plenty," he said. "They were out there long enough, bagging up little bits of lint and hair. But evidence takes time. It's not like the movies, where the detective calls the lab an hour later and gets a DNA report."

Then I would have to start from square one.

I began by sending a text to my former clients, asking if they told anyone that I could head-hop. "I promise I won't be mad if you did," I assured them in hopes of getting the truth. "I just need to know."

All of them responded right away, swearing that they stayed silent. If anything, they seemed worried that *I* might spill the beans about what I had done for them. I couldn't know for sure whether they were lying, but my gut told me my clients weren't the problem. I also knew Val had kept my secret, and so had my father.

That left Nash.

I sent him a text. Can you talk?

He replied about twenty minutes later, probably between classes. I've been trying to call you. Are you home? Yeah, we def need to talk.

I'm ready when you are.

Give me an hour, he said. I'll come to the back door.

An hour later, a knock sounded on my bedroom window, aka the "back door." I slid it open, and Nash shimmied through, just like he had done a hundred times before, back when I was younger and dumber and thought we would be together forever.

I hid a smile as he banged his ankle on the window ledge. "Careful."

"It's nuts out there," he said, jutting his chin toward the front of the house. "I parked two streets over and cut through a bunch of backyards to get here, but I'm pretty sure a drone camera caught me sneaking in."

"Well, now my reputation is ruined," I said. "Thanks a lot, Nash."

He leaned down and studied me, his dark eyes moving over my face with concern. His closeness made my insides flutter, so I retreated a step.

"I saw the press conference," he said. "You okay?"

"As okay as a national scapegoat can be."

"That charge is bullshit. It'll never hold up."

"I hope you're right, but I'm not leaving it to chance," I said. "I'm trying to figure out how the killer knew about me. Did you ever tell anyone?"

"No one," he answered immediately.

"Are you sure?" I asked. "Maybe you drank too much one night at a Sigma Pi kegger, and you let something slip?"

"I don't get drunk, I don't go to frat parties, and I don't snitch on the people I care about." He reached out as if to cup my cheek, but seemed to think better of it. "Especially you. We have a lot more in common than you think, T."

I huffed a laugh. "I hope this isn't your way of saying you gave me a disease."

"I'm an immersionist."

He had blurted it out so abruptly that I could only stare at him.

"That's what I've been trying to tell you for so long," he went on. "You wouldn't speak to me until yesterday, and then we got derailed before I had the chance."

"You're serious?"

"Completely."

"Prove it," I said. I couldn't help myself. I didn't believe him.

Nash didn't miss a beat. It was almost like he had expected me to ask for evidence, because he pointed at the bed and told me, "Lie down and close your eyes."

"Why? What are you going to do?"

"I'm gonna try to breach your mind," he said. "I won't make it very far, but you'll feel me. I guarantee it."

And he was right. As soon as my head hit the pillow, I felt a wall of electricity pressing against my skull. I mentally pushed back against the force, but not before I heard the echo of Nash's voice calling my name from inside my own brain.

"You *are* serious," I said, sitting up and trying to shake off the eerie sensation of having been mentally probed. "How long have you known?"

Nash took a sudden interest in his shoes. "A little over a year."

"What?" I asked. "But that was . . ."

"Yeah." He nodded, still avoiding my gaze. "A few weeks after you found out you were one."

I thought back to the weeks after my fateful discovery with Val at the Chick-fil-A. Nash and I had still been together then. I had told him first, before my own father. I had trusted Nash with my deepest secret, but he hadn't trusted me with his. A dull pain spread through my chest. It was a familiar ache that reminded me—once again—of how much more Nash had meant to me than I had meant to him. But I would drag my naked body over two miles of gravel before letting him know he still had the power to hurt me.

"So," I said coolly while smoothing a wrinkle from my T-shirt, "why bother telling me now? Solidarity?"

"I mean, yeah, kind of," he said. "Your case affects all of us. We have to look out for one another."

"I don't need a support group, so you can go now." I used both hands like a flight attendant to direct him toward the exit. "Buh-bye."

"Tia, I know people who can help you."

"Duly noted," I said, repeating the gesture.

He held both palms forward. "Okay, I get it. I should have told you as soon as I found out."

At least he wasn't *completely* clueless.

"You have every right to be pissed at me," he added.

For some reason, that made me snap.

"Gee, thanks for validating my feelings, Nash. I can't tell you how much that means to me. Oh, wait. Yes, I can." I stood up and flipped him the double bird. "*This* much."

He turned his eyes to the ceiling. "I can see I'm wasting my time."

"And yet, here you are."

"Fine," he said, and headed for the window. "I'll go. But when you calm down, call me. We can help each other. I'm not your enemy, T."

I practiced stellar impulse control by choosing not to kick him on his way out. But as I stood there with my chest heaving, I couldn't tell who I hated more: Nash for breaking my heart and walking away from me, or myself for wishing he would turn around and come back.

Chapter Seven

IN THE DAYS THAT FOLLOWED, MY DAD AND I
learned the hard way that our contact information wasn't as private as
we had thought it was. Someone had leaked our cell numbers to the
press, and after the thousandth spam call, my dad threw in the towel
and bought us a pair of burner phones. That helped a lot, but it didn't
stop a flood of emails from drowning my inbox, or my social media
apps from being so clogged with notifications that I had to delete my
accounts and make new ones.

I had predicted a nuclear-level can of worms, and there it was,
slimy and bursting at the seams. Right after my story went viral, at
least twenty inmates from prisons across the country asked for their
convictions to be overturned, citing an out-of-body experience as their
defense. Not that I could blame them for shooting their shot, but the
influx of fake claims had started a national debate about the implica-
tions of my case. The words "slippery slope" came up so often that I
could use them in a drinking game.

At least I didn't have to deal with anyone at school. My principal, Mr. Morrison, had agreed to let me learn remotely. He didn't want my drama on campus any more than I wanted to bring it there, but staring at my bedroom walls for two days had almost made me miss the paint-peeled cinder block, the slamming lockers, and the smell of teen spirit from Harvey Davis High School.

I seriously needed to get out of the house.

I found my dad in the kitchen, talking on his burner phone while holding a lit cigarette out the open window. I stalked over to him and tried to smack the cigarette out of his hand. He quit smoking ages ago, and I wasn't about to let him start up again because of me. He flicked the butt into the grass and made an apologetic face.

"Stress," he whispered around his phone.

"Whatever," I hissed. "Deal with it like a normal person and day drink."

While I fanned the air, my dad finished his call.

"Well, that was interesting," he said, setting his phone on the table.

"What?"

"I just talked to an old buddy of mine from my bouncer days at the Tropic Thunder. He heard that a certain recently deceased district attorney was on the take."

My eyes flew wide. "No way! Ben Mitchell was dirty?"

"That's the rumor."

"*How* dirty?" I asked. "Are we talking dust on his shoulders or poop on his wingtips?"

"More like hazardous waste from head to toe," my dad said. "Dirty enough to get involved with Constantine Romanovitch."

"Who?" I asked.

"He's an enforcer for the Russian mob, handles collections and whatnot for their gambling ring. The kind of guy who breaks knee-caps, not someone you associate with on accident."

Romanovitch. The name sounded familiar. I couldn't help thinking I had heard it or read about it somewhere. Maybe I had come across the name yesterday when I read the public records of Ben Mitchell's former cases.

"Did Ben prosecute him?" I asked.

"No, not him. His son, Blade." My dad snorted. "*Blade.* What kind of asshole names his kid after a shaver?"

Now I remembered. I asked myself the same question when I came across Blade Romanovitch in the list of Ben's cases. "So what did you hear?"

"Supposedly, Blade got picked up a while back for doing something stupid," Dad said. "Loitering or public intoxication, I don't remember. But whatever it was violated his probation, and he had just turned eighteen, so Constantine paid Ben to bury the case. They say Ben took the payoff and then threw the book at the kid anyway."

"Whoa," I said. "Double-crossing the Russian mob. Bold move."

"If by *bold* you mean *idiotic*, then yeah."

"That would give Constantine a motive for murder."

"Not just Constantine," Dad said. "Blade did six months in prison. And get this . . . he was released a week ago."

A week ago? Convenient timing. So Blade had motive and opportunity. But what about means? "I don't suppose your old bouncer friend mentioned if Blade can head-hop?"

"No idea."

Then I would have to find out for myself. I pulled up the public criminal records and scrolled through them until I found Blade's case.

He had been released on parole and was ordered to perform twenty hours of community service.

Twenty hours . . . what a coincidence.

"Hey, Dad, do you mind if I go out for a while?" I asked. "I think I'll start my community service today."

*   *   *

Local delinquents like me and Blade had three basic options for court-mandated volunteer work: we could serve soup and save souls at the Hellfire Baptist Church, clean up roadkill with the Department of Public Sanitation, or sort donations at Saint Valliant's thrift store. I figured anyone in their right mind would choose door number three, and I was correct.

I spotted Blade as soon as I turned into Saint Valliant's parking lot. He was impossible to miss at six feet tall and built like a tank. A tracking cuff encircled his ankle, one of the conditions of his parole. He tossed garbage bags full of clothing out of the donation bin and onto the pavement, occasionally pausing to push back his jet-black hair, giving me a glimpse of a colorful tattoo on his bicep.

Kind of hot, if you were into self-sabotage.

I got out of my car and walked toward him, holding up my service sheet. "Excuse me," I called. "Can you tell me where I should go to get this signed?"

Blade glanced at me and wiped the sweat from his forehead. Recognition sparked in his piercing blue eyes, and he unleashed a crooked smile that had probably dropped a thousand panties. "Hey, I know you."

I returned his grin. "Sorry, no autographs."

"That's too bad, because you're my hero."

"Your hero? You might need better role models."

"You might be right," he admitted. "I'm Blade."

I shook his hand. His grip was callused and strong, but not over-bearing. So far he didn't fit the profile of a guy capable of committing murder, but profiles had been wrong before.

"I'm Tia," I said. "But you already knew that."

"Yeah, I think everyone knows that." He shaded his eyes and peered at the parking lot, where a caravan of news crews had followed me from my house. "Come on," he said, thumbing at the store. "I'll take you to meet the supervisor. She's cool. She'll sign your court slip, and then we can work in the back room. No cameras in there."

He introduced me to a middle-aged woman named Sue, who scribbled a signature on my service form and asked me not to stuff socks down the toilet. An oddly specific request, but I promised to behave myself, and a few minutes later, Blade and I were sorting clothes in a vast storage area at the back of the building.

I had never volunteered at a thrift shop before, and it boggled my mind to see how much garbage people had passed off as charitable giving: broken toys, expired food, dirty towels, pants with stains in dubious places. Call me crazy, but I thought the whole point of charity was to give something that mattered to those in need, not to turn your trash into a tax write-off.

"Gross," I said, using a coat hanger to toss a pair of tighty-whities into the garbage pile. I wore two sets of rubber gloves, but they still didn't feel thick enough. "What kind of psycho thinks he's doing the world a favor by giving away his drawers?"

Blade chuckled. "I've seen worse, believe me."

"Oh, I believe you," I said to avoid hearing the details. "I swear some of these people are just too cheap to pay for garbage pickup."

Blade inspected the tag on a polka-dotted blouse and then stuffed it in a bin labeled MEDIUM WOMEN'S BUSINESS CASUAL. "So, you're a head-hopper," he said. "What's that like?"

I slid a glance at him. That was exactly the kind of question I would ask if I were an immersionist in hiding. "You've never met one?"

"Uh-uh."

"Statistically, you probably have. There are a lot of us out there."

"You're the only one that I know of," he said, and tucked a pair of jeans into the bin behind him.

I watched Blade's body language for the usual signs of lying— shifting his gaze, fidgeting with his hair, covering his mouth or eyes. So far, nothing stood out. But that didn't necessarily mean he was telling the truth. As the son of a Russian mafia heavy, a guy like Blade Romanovitch would have learned how to lie before he had mastered his ABC's.

"How does that work?" he asked. "Getting in people's heads? Can you really make them do whatever you want?"

I chuckled and lifted a purple lace bra from my pile. "If I could control people's minds, I would be on my own private island, sipping fruity drinks out of a coconut, not sifting through some stranger's underwear."

"Huh," he said, grinning. "I never thought of it that way."

"You and the rest of the world."

"So it wasn't you who shot DA Mitchell?"

"No. I didn't even know the guy."

Blade released a bitter huff. "Yeah, well, I knew him well enough for the both of us. Trust me when I say he was a real piece of shit."

"Is that why you called me your hero?" I asked. "Because you hated him enough to want him dead?"

As soon as the words left my mouth, I knew I had overplayed my hand. Blade froze and cocked his head a fraction to the side, letting me know I had set off his alarm bells.

"Are you wearing a wire?" he asked, his voice low and menacing in a way that left no doubt what he was capable of. "Is that what's going on here?"

I didn't usually give in to panic, but in that instance, my body acted without permission. The next thing I knew, I was lifting the front of my T-shirt and flashing Blade my B-cups. The move seemed to surprise the both of us. He blinked at my chest for a moment, and then the tension broke, and he burst into hysterical laughter.

I lowered my T-shirt, grateful that I had remembered to put on a bra after two days of lounging around the house. "If you're trying to give me a complex, it's working."

He wiped his eyes. "Sorry, I'm not laughing *at* you. . . ."

"You're just laughing *near* me?"

"I didn't see that coming," he said. "You're a trip, Tia Dante."

"So they tell me."

"Listen, sorry that got weird."

"No worries," I told him. "It was a weird question for me to ask."

"Swear you're not working with the cops?"

I raised my right hand. "I'm a lot of things, but a snitch isn't one of them."

"Then I'll tell you this," he said. "Ben Mitchell got exactly what he deserved. Whoever offed him should get free beer for life."

"Any idea who that might be?"

"Listen, half the town would dance on Ben's grave if they thought no one was looking. But here's the thing," Blade said, leaning in as if to tell me a secret. "I grew up around a lot of sketch people, and I can tell you that an asshole in the streets is an asshole at home. I guarantee you Ben Mitchell was a piece of shit in his private life, too. Crime is a lot more personal than you think. Violence is extra personal. *Murder* is as personal as it gets. So if you want to know who killed your boy Ben . . ."

I finished the rest. "Find out who he was up close and personal with."

"That's what I would do," he said. "We always hurt the ones we love."

Blade was right. I didn't trust him any farther than I could drop-kick him into the *extra-large men's* bin, but I agreed with him. Most victims of violent offences knew their attackers intimately. That didn't mean Blade and his father were off the hook. Both of them had motive, and the timing of Blade's release from prison couldn't possibly be a coincidence. But I needed to find out who Ben loved and who loved him—maybe to death. And if I played my cards right, I might find all of Ben's favorite people gathered in the same place at the same time.

All I had to do was crash his funeral.

Chapter Eight

"IS THIS GIVING ME BAD KARMA?" VAL ASKED, mostly talking to herself. She had to know better than to ask me for insight into the cosmos. "It feels wrong."

"It's the opposite of wrong," I told her. "You're helping me find out who took a man's life. If that's not good juju, I don't know what is."

"Juju and karma are not the same thing," Val said, and then she launched into a lecture that I immediately tuned out.

I shifted my focus to my computer screen, where live video footage showed me the dashboard of Val's van. I had decided that crashing Ben's funeral would cause more problems for my investigation than it would solve. Ben's loved ones watched "me" shoot him on camera. I doubted they would want to talk to me about their dirty little secrets. Besides, the media would have followed me to the church and turned the service into a spectacle. So I sent Val to the funeral in my place, wearing a nifty bit of homemade tech.

I had taken an old brooch shaped like a daisy and replaced the center disc with a Bluetooth surveillance device that I ordered online.

The mini camera included a microphone, and even came with an app that allowed me to record the live feed and play it back whenever I wanted. Combined with the discreet earpiece Val was wearing, we were ready to pull off a James Bond–caliber mission.

"Angle it up a little bit," I told Val.

She adjusted the brooch, and it gave me a better field of vision. "How's that?"

"Perfect. Now let's go earn us some karma points."

"Karma points don't exist."

"Then juju points," I told her.

Val released a long sigh and stepped out of her van onto the church parking lot. The video feed shook during her walk to the front doors, but once she made her way inside the sanctuary and took a seat in the last pew, she gave me a perfect wide-angle view of the service.

All I could see were the backs of a hundred heads, and at the front of the aisle, Ben's coffin draped in a lavish floral spray. Val lifted the funeral program for me to view. The front cover read *Celebrating the Life of Benjamin Arthur Mitchell* and showcased a photo of Ben, handsome and smiling from behind his office desk. A poem was printed on the inside of the program, along with the order of events for the service and an address for the cemetery. *Burial to follow*, it said at the bottom.

Val didn't know it yet, but she was definitely going to the burial.

When the priest began the service and led the congregation through a choreography of kneel-pray-stand, kneel-pray-stand, I used my phone to look up Ben's obituary. I learned that Ben had been thirty-five years old, an only child, preceded in death by his father and both sets of grandparents, and survived by his mother, Marjorie Mitchell; his fiancée, Lilith Littler; and his goddaughter, Molly Kazinski.

"Molly Kazinski?" I murmured. I was pretty sure she went to my school.

Val cupped a hand over her mouth and obscured the camera. "What?" she whispered. "Did you say something?"

"Molly Kazinski was Ben's goddaughter."

"Yeah, I know," Val whispered. "She's here."

"How did you know that?"

"Because I'm an office aide."

"Oooooh," I said as the pieces clicked into place. Val worked every day with Sharon Kazinski, the attendance secretary. "She's Mrs. K's daughter, right? Skinny freshman with brown hair?"

"Yeah," Val said. "She's been absent since the shooting. This is the first time I've seen her. She's really torn up. Her mom, too." Val rotated her brooch toward the Kazinskis in the second row. Even from across the sanctuary, I could see their shoulders wracking with sobs, their brunette heads tipped together.

Guilt pricked my stomach. I hadn't done anything wrong, but I was glad I had stayed home from the funeral, and doubly grateful to my principal for letting me take online classes. I couldn't imagine going to school and seeing the pain in Molly's eyes every time she passed me in the hallway and saw her godfather's killer.

"What about the fiancée?" I asked Val. "Her name's Lilith Littler."

"I can't tell who she is," Val whispered. "There are too many people in here."

A middle-aged law professor stood behind the podium to deliver Ben's eulogy, and I took the opportunity to google Ben's intended bride. The results were weirdly predictable. Lilith Littler was a female version of Ben. They had even met in law school. She was an attractive, conservatively dressed, dark-haired lawyer in her mid-thirties who described herself on Twitter as a "self-made woman," even though her family was rich as balls.

"Remember Selma Blair's character in *Legally Blonde*?" I asked.

"Oh, yeah, you mean Vivian," Val said.

"Well, look for the constipated bitch, and you'll find Lilith Littler."

Val stifled a laugh. She angled the camera toward a brunette woman seated at the end of the first pew, as far as the woman could get from the casket while remaining with Ben's family. It was Lilith. I recognized the blunt edge of her haircut. She sat with her arms tightly folded, darting occasional glances at the side exit as if she had somewhere else to be. It was hard to tell from a distance, but she didn't seem to be crying, and there were no streaks of mascara on her cheeks. I made a mental note to ask Val for a close-up of Lilith's face at the burial. If Ben's fiancée didn't grieve his loss, that might be the red flag I was looking for.

As the eulogy wrapped up, I noted that Ben Mitchell had left behind quite an impressive résumé. He had chosen public service over a seven-figure salary at a big law firm. In his spare time, he had given free legal advice to abuse victims at the women's shelter. He'd spent one weekend a month cleaning up nature trails and another weekend mentoring high-risk youth in juvenile detention.

A list of accomplishments to make Mother Teresa proud.

And yet, a salty voice inside my head wondered if the former district attorney didst protest too much. Had Ben Mitchell been a genuine philanthropist, or had he used his prolific good deeds as a way to fool the public and overcompensate for a guilty conscience?

My money was on the latter.

When the eulogy ended, the priest invited members of the

congregation to come forward and share their memories of Ben. No one took the offer at first. Then Sharon Kazinski raised a hand and made her way up the steps to the pulpit. It weirded me out to see the school secretary standing at the head of a church, kind of the same way I felt when I crossed paths with one of my teachers at the grocery store.

"I met Ben in the third grade," Mrs. K. said in a hoarse voice. "He traded me his Twinkies for my nacho cheese Lunchable, and we were friends ever since."

Soft laughter echoed in the sanctuary.

"Ben was brilliant and funny," she continued. "And even as a kid, I knew he would make an excellent lawyer, because I could never beat him in an argument."

More soft laughter.

"Life took us in different directions when we got older." She used a tissue to blot her nose. "But Ben always showed up for me when it mattered. He was there on my wedding day. He came to the hospital when my daughter was born." She drew a deep breath and let it go. "And he was the first person to look me in the eyes and treat me like a human being when my marriage ended."

No one laughed at that.

"Funny thing about divorce," she said. "It will show you who your real friends are. The fake ones will treat you like you're contagious, as though the more time they spend with you, the more failure might rub off on their own marriages." She cut her eyes at the priest. "Then there's unofficial excommunication. Even the church will seem to turn its back on you if your family falls apart."

Damn. Shaming a priest in his own house? Mrs. K. was my kind of petty.

"But not Ben." Mrs. K.'s voice broke, and she paused to clear it. "He was there for me. He was *always* there for me, and now that he's gone, I don't know how to—" She cut off with a shake of her head, and then finished in a rush, "Godspeed, Ben. We miss you already."

So it sounded like Ben hadn't been a total piece of shit. I guessed I could believe that. There was no black or white in the world, no one who was all good or all evil.

Except the person who had framed me. They could rot in hell.

*   *   *

The sun glowed behind the clouds at Ben's burial—ideal lighting that allowed me to pick up details I had missed inside the church. Val made sure to casually rotate her chest and capture everyone in attendance.

I noticed our principal there and learned he had graduated from the same high school as Ben and Mrs. K. I spotted Lilith Littler seated in the first row of chairs facing Ben's grave. As I had suspected, her flawless makeup and clear, bright eyes confirmed that she hadn't shed a tear for her lost love, at least not recently. But more unusual was the fact that she didn't seem to be playing the grieving fiancée. I had expected *some* performative sadness out of her: a few fake tears, a sniffle or two. But aside from tossing a single white rose onto Ben's casket as it lowered into the ground, she just sat there checking her phone. Either Lilith had an unhealthy way of dealing with loss, or she gave zero shits about Ben Mitchell and didn't care who knew it.

On the other end of the spectrum, Molly Kazinski sat slumped back in her chair, as limp as a rag doll. She looked nothing like the girl I knew from school. Dark circles shadowed her lifeless eyes. She wore a bulky black cardigan, despite the May heat, and even though her mom rubbed her back for comfort, Molly stared blankly ahead as though her spirit had left her body.

"Wow," I said to Val. "You weren't kidding. Molly's taking it hard."

"I should say hello," Val whispered. She walked over to the Kazinskis and told them, "I'm sorry for your loss."

Mrs. K. blinked at Val as if noticing her for the first time. "Oh, Valencia. I didn't realize you knew Ben."

"I didn't know him well," Val said. "I spent a lot of time in court last summer when I was going through the emancipation process."

Val recited the excuse exactly the way we planned. I had expected someone to question why she was at the funeral. Val hated to lie, so we came up with a simple truth that might imply she and Ben had met, even though they hadn't.

"He seemed like a nice person," Val added.

"He could be," Mrs. K. said. "He was fierce in the courtroom, but he took care of the people he loved."

Molly swiveled her vacant gaze to Val. "Like me. He loved me."

The flatness in her tone gave me the shivers.

"That's right, baby," Mrs. K. said, wrapping her arm around her daughter. "He took good care of us, didn't he?"

Molly nodded and then buried her face in her mom's shoulder to cry.

I could practically feel Val's awkwardness. She backed away and strode to the fringes of the crowd. "Can I go now?" she asked.

"Almost," I said. I remembered what Blade Romanovitch had told me: that half the town would dance on Ben's grave if they thought no one was watching. "Can you hide out in your van for a while?"

"I guess so. Why?"

"I want to see if anyone comes to the dance."

"You're an odd duck," Val told me, but she unfastened her brooch and positioned it on her dashboard with the camera facing the gravesite.

About half an hour later, the site cleared out. The cemetery maintenance crew came to remove the folding chairs and the canopy shade, until all that remained of Ben's burial was a pair of horseshoe-shaped floral arrangements and a mound of earth waiting to be shoveled back into the ground.

Another few minutes passed . . . and then my patience paid off.

Two people strode into the video frame, a man and a woman approaching Ben's grave together. I recognized Lilith Littler at once. The man, not so much. He had concealed his entire face by wearing an oversize hoodie. I knew he hadn't attended the funeral. I definitely would have noticed him. He was impossible to miss . . . at six feet tall and built like a tank.

I jerked my gaze to his ankle. He wore a cuff.

Blade?

How did Blade Romanovitch and Lilith Littler know each other?

I watched Blade toss a small object onto Ben's casket. While I squinted at the screen and wondered what he had thrown down there, Lilith leaned over her fiancé's grave and promptly spat on it.

"Holy shit!" I said. "That's better than dancing!"

"What did you say?" Val asked.

"Did you just see that?"

"See what?" she said. "I'm in the back doing homework."

"Stay there for now," I told her. I didn't want Blade or Lilith to notice her. "But then I need you to do me a *reeeeeeeeally* big favor."

"Bigger than spending my only day off stalking a funeral?"

"Slightly bigger than that. But I'll owe you one."

"You already owe me one."

"Then I'll owe you two."

"All right," she said. "But it's going to cost you a weekend in the woods."

I cringed from the pit of my soul, because a weekend in the woods meant a whole lot more than camping. For ages, Val had been raving about this crunchy holistic emotional-healing retreat she wanted to register for, but she didn't want to go alone. I weighed my options: one weekend of sound baths and feelings circles and mood affirmations in exchange for evidence that might clear my name. "Fine. It's a deal."

"What do I have to do?"

"Nothing major," I said with a grin. "Just some light grave robbing."

Chapter Nine

THANKS TO VAL'S PERSISTENCE, I LEARNED THAT THE object Blade had tossed onto Ben's casket was a folding knife—a *blade*, to be exact. A little on the nose, if you asked me, but I sealed the knife in a Ziploc bag to protect it from evidence contamination. Then I threw myself down the rabbit hole of Lilith Littler's online history.

Slightly disturbing fun fact: everything we do on the internet is tracked, gathered, and sold as a commodity. Our internet searches, our social media engagement, our private messages, certain juicy key words and phrases captured by cell phones that aren't supposed to be listening (but totally are). Companies purchase our web data to run advertising campaigns that target us, but regular folks like me can get their hands on it, too. In addition, all it takes is a credit card number to order a background check that includes every minor brush a person has ever had with the law.

Privacy really was an illusion, and by violating Lilith's, I was able to discover some juicy secrets about her past. During her senior year in college, she had been taken into custody for trying to buy ADHD meds from an undercover cop. Her father had made the charges disappear with a generous donation to the Fraternal Order of Police. Then, when Lilith was in law school, her father had worked that same magic to get her off the hook for cocaine possession. *Abracadabra!* But aside from a low-key stimulant dependency, Lilith seemed to lead a very basic kind of lifestyle. Her internet searches mostly consisted of investment strategies, vacation destinations, fashion trends, and how to grow a bigger butt.

I had to dig deeper.

Lilith had several social media accounts, all private, but she only posted to one of them on the regular. I could tell from the disproportionately higher following on that account compared with the rest. So I created the username *Lawyer Up!* and uploaded the logo for Harvard Law School as my profile picture. After adding a bio and a dozen pictures of the Harvard campus to my fake profile, I sent Lilith a follow request and waited for her to approve me.

It didn't take long to get my wish.

I dove right into Lilith's account and started scrolling. She had uploaded years of photos, but as I traced my way through them, I noticed all of the recent uploads were memes. The newest one showed Kermit the Frog sipping a cup of tea, surrounded by the text: "Cheating isn't a mistake, it's the result of your intentional, selfish choices . . . but that's none of my business." The next picture showed a gray-haired man reading from a piece of paper: "You claimed to be an honest man, but the lie detector test said you're a cheating piece of garbage." On and on it went, one meme after another. My favorite was a picture of a pan of acorns over a campfire. It read: "When he's lying to your face, but you're about to roast his nuts over an open screenshot."

That was a good one.

So Ben had cheated on his fiancée. That sucked for Lilith, but it matched what Blade had told me about Ben: Assholes in the streets didn't behave any better at home. Ben's cheating explained why Lilith had spat on his grave and also gave her a solid motive for his murder.

But something bothered me.

I tried to put myself in Lilith's shoes and imagine how I would feel if the love of my life had betrayed me with another girl. Nash popped into my head. Not that he was the love of my life or anything, but when I pictured him proposing to me and then sleeping with some sorority bitch behind my back, white-hot rage rose up inside my body, and I fantasized about taking a Louisville Slugger to his soft parts. I wouldn't really beat anyone with a baseball bat, but mentally, I wanted Pretend Nash to suffer as much as he had made me suffer.

That was why violence was personal. When someone caused us pain, it was natural to want to hurt them back. Not *acceptable*, but natural. Most of us had enough self-control to ignore the urge to pick up a bludgeoning object, and instead go for symbolic revenge, like tossing an ex's picture into the fireplace. But for scorned lovers who had no self-control, revenge tended to look . . . messy.

That didn't describe Ben's death. The shooter had put a single bullet in Ben, quick and efficient, almost businesslike. There had been zero suffering, not even a few words of emotional taunting beforehand. The murder reminded me of an assassination, not the work of a jilted fiancée lashing out in pain. Even if Lilith was secretly an immersionist, I had a hard time believing she pulled the trigger.

But what if she had hired Blade to do it?

I would believe *that* all day long.

Lilith had plenty of money and a track record for using it to solve her problems. Blade had plenty of beef with Ben and probably would have whacked him for free. It was a match made in . . .

"Shit." I realized a hole in my theory.

Blade wore an ankle monitor as one of the conditions of his parole. If he had jacked Ben's car and driven it to my shed, his parole officer would have noticed. I supposed Lilith could have stolen my body and delivered it to Blade's house. But to make the reverse transfer, Blade still would have had to position himself close enough to the courthouse to exit my body.

Actually . . . that sounded doable. A trip to court would have seemed perfectly legit to Blade's probation officer. Criminals were in and out of court all the time. If I could prove that Blade had been in close proximity to Ben Mitchell during the shooting, maybe the DA would take a closer look at him and quit gunning for me.

Now to get my hands on Blade's tracking information.

I had no idea how to swing that. I paced around my room to brainstorm. I was halfway through my third lap when my dad knocked on the door and let himself in.

"Someone's here to see you," my dad said, jutting his chin toward the front of the house. "A lady from the military. Corporal something-or-other."

I tilted my head in confusion. What did the military want with me? "I didn't join the Marines and forget about it, did I?"

"Semper fi," he said. "But no. She's here to do paperwork for the NSA."

"Oh, the registry. I did forget about that."

In the living room, an attractive, twenty-something-year-old woman in a camouflage uniform stood with her hands clasped loosely in front of her, twiddling her thumbs and rocking back and forth on her boots while she gazed at the photos on our wall. I approached her, and she offered me a grin.

"Hi, there," she said. The name tag stitched on her uniform read DIAZ.

As soon as our eyes met, I sensed that something was off. I didn't know how to describe my doubts except to say her vibe was all wrong. She didn't seem like the kind of girl who belonged in combat boots. When I moved in to shake her hand, I paid close attention to her face and noticed a tiny hole in her left nostril and another one above each eyebrow. Last I checked, the military frowned on facial piercings. If my dad would stop being stubborn and admit that he needed glasses, he would have noticed it, too.

"Tell me, Corporal Diaz," I said, "is it illegal to impersonate a soldier, or just a douchey thing to do?"

My dad stiffened beside me. "What?"

"Oh, come on," I said, using a hand to indicate our guest. "If she's a soldier, I'm a debutante. You're slipping, Dad."

To her credit, the woman didn't try to deny it. She smiled in a *you-got-me* kind of way and tipped up her palms. "Sorry. I've been trying to reach you—"

"About my car's extended warranty?" I interrupted. She was obviously a reporter scheming for an interview. Her face had *communications major* written all over it. "No thanks. Go back out there with the rest of the losers and stalk me from across the street."

"I'm not a reporter," she said.

I was about to tell her I didn't care when she added, "Nash sent me."

That got my attention.

"Your friend, Nash Brock?" she clarified, as if I had an abundance of Nashes in my life. "He said he tried to have a conversation with you a few days ago, but . . . it didn't go well."

I folded my arms. "And?"

"And I'm here to continue that discussion. I want to help you, Tia."

"Excuse me," my dad asked. "But who the hell are you?"

"Sorry about that," she said. "I'm Mackenzie McDonald."

"McProve it," he told her. "Let's see some ID."

She produced her driver's license and handed it to my dad, who gave it a once-over and passed it back to her.

"So what do you want?" he asked.

"I'm with the ILO," she told us. "The Immersionist Liberation Organization. We advocate for the rights and liberties of the consciously transferrable."

"The consciously transferrable?" I repeated. "That's a new one. Are you an immersionist, then?"

"Yes, we all are," she said. "Well, not the people we outsource to help the cause, but every member of the ILO is one of us. They have to prove it to join."

"I've never heard of you," I said.

"That's because we just went public this week. We started out as a private network of college students from all over the world. That's how I met Nash. We were chatting on the online boards last summer, and we realized we were going to the same school. We started a local chapter, but we kept it quiet, just a forum to share experiences and compare data."

"Basically a head-hopping Reddit?" I asked.

She laughed. "I guess so."

Jealousy twisted my stomach. I could have used a resource like that when I was just starting out. It also stung to learn that Nash had shared his secret with a group of strangers on the internet but not with me. I hated to imagine him chatting away with Mackenzie, and then meeting up with her in person to talk about all the things he was hiding from his own girlfriend. What else had he shared with Mackenzie? Was she the girl who had replaced me?

I didn't want to think about that. I pushed Nash out of my head. "Why go public now?"

"For you," she said, raising her pierced brows. "When we heard about your story, we knew we had to radicalize and do more."

"Radicalize?" my dad repeated, clearly not liking the sound of that.

"I meant mobilize," she told him.

Sure, I thought. Because those two words were so easily confused.

"We wanted to be more than just online message boards," she said. "We agreed it was time to level up our organization and go from talking to doing. So we pooled our money and collected donations and hired a political activist to lobby for us. Then we got a PR firm to push awareness." She pointed at the television. "Maybe you saw us Sunday morning on *Meet the Media*?"

I shook my head.

"We've been fighting for you in the press," she said. "And on social media. Our PR team is running a positivity campaign in regions where you need support. We want to start a collection for your legal fees, too."

On the surface, that sounded great. But my inner skeptic asked what was in it for them. What Mackenzie had described sounded expensive. No one, not even an organization, parted with that kind of money unless it benefited them in some way.

"What do you want from me?" I asked.

"Nothing. There's no catch. All we would have to do is set up a GoFundMe account and publicize it in our social campaigns." She lifted a shoulder and tucked both hands in her pockets. "We would need your permission, though. And it would help if you joined us. Maybe you could come to a few meetings, get to know us, film a couple of video clips. . . ."

It sounded like the ILO wanted to make me their poster child. I didn't know how I felt about that. I was more of a loner than a joiner. The money sure would help, though. I could afford a lawyer who was old enough to shave.

"Let me think about it?" I asked.

"Of course." She handed me a business card. "Call or text me anytime."

I glanced at her card. A logo of two overlapping heads was printed at the top, followed by *Mackenzie McDonald, Director of Operations, Immersionist Liberation Organization.*

"By the way," she said as she was leaving, "Nash told me a lot about you. All good things, of course. It's nice to finally meet the legendary Tia Dante."

I matched her smile and waved good-bye instead of telling her what I really wanted to say, that Nash hadn't mentioned her to me a single time. It was almost like he had tried to hide her. I couldn't help but wonder if I had just been scoped out by his new girlfriend.

Chapter Ten

THE NEXT DAY, I DROVE TO THE POLICE STATION TO visit Inspector Gadget. I hoped that between the folding knife I had recovered from Ben's gravesite and the video of Blade Romanovitch throwing it in there, the police would agree to test the knife for evidence and give us clues we didn't have before. Plus, I figured the cops would want to take a closer look at Lilith Littler's alibi after they watched her hock a loogie on her fiancé's grave.

I took the last parking spot in front of the police station and gave a single-finger salute to the media vans that had followed me there. After making my way inside the building, I emptied my pockets for the security checkpoint and then placed my purse on the conveyor belt. My bag was halfway through the X-ray machine when I remembered the weapon inside it.

"Oh, wait," I said, pointing wildly. "There's a switchblade in there."

The cop behind the machine gave me the stink eye. He waited

for my purse to exit the other end of the machine and then retrieved the Ziploc baggie.

"It's evidence," I explained. "I'm here to give it to Inspector . . . uh . . ." No, *Gadget* wasn't the guy's name. "Detective . . . Smith, maybe?" I gave up trying to guess. "Whoever's in charge of the Ben Mitchell shooting investigation. I'm Tia—"

"Yeah, I know who you are," the cop interrupted. He turned his face toward a walkie-talkie clipped to his shoulder. "Can you tell Detective Roberts to come out to the lobby? Tia Dante is here to see him, and she brought a knife with her."

I scoffed at him. "When you say it like that, it sounds bad."

He pointed at the floor by my feet. "Stay there."

I waited for a couple of minutes, and then Detective Roberts—I seriously needed to remember his name—met me at security. He took the Ziploc baggie from the guard and left it sealed as he studied the switchblade inside it.

He turned the plastic over in his hands. "What's this?"

"Evidence," I explained again.

"Miss Dante, this isn't how evidence works."

"But I watched Blade Romanovitch throw it on Ben Mitchell's casket after the burial service," I said. "I figured you would want to see it. I have video, too."

The flash in his eyes told me I'd had him at "Romanovitch." He waved me through security and handed me my purse, minus the Ziploc bag. After leading me through a maze of cubicles, he stopped at his workstation and pulled up an extra chair for me.

I sat down and glanced at his desk space. Unlike the other cubicles, there were no photographs tacked to the dividing walls, no mini potted plants, no coffee mugs or leftover napkins or vending machine snacks competing for his attention. A single manila file folder rested beside his keyboard. He had tucked an insulated lunch bag behind his computer monitor, and next to his mouse stood a tall stainless-steel water bottle, buffed to an impeccable shine. I could tell a lot about a person from their workspace, and the detective's cubicle told me he thrived on order, cleanliness, and routine. In other words, he was a massive control freak.

Not that I judged. The world needed nerds.

I placed my purse on his desk and dug out the thumb drive containing the video footage of Blade and Lilith. I gave the detective the video file and summarized my thoughts about how the pair could have worked together to steal my body and murder Ben Mitchell.

When I was finished explaining my theory, the detective sat back in his chair and rubbed a hand over his bald head. "Wow. That was a lot of speculating, Miss Dante."

"But it makes sense," I pointed out. "They both had motive. Did you know that Ben Mitchell cheated on Lilith?"

"Yes."

"Oh." My shoulders sank. I hadn't expected that. "But I bet you don't know *who* he cheated with," I added, giving him the impression that I had already found out the answer, which I hadn't. It was an old trick my dad had taught me. Sometimes people would slip up and give away information if they thought you already knew the truth.

"Yes, Miss Dante," the detective said in a patronizing voice. "I'm well aware of Ben's weakness for young blond paralegals. It wasn't the nation's best-kept secret."

"Okay, but what about his friend Sharon Kazinski?" I asked. I didn't have any reason to think that Ben and Mrs. K. had hooked up. Mostly, I was just being nosy and fishing for bonus information. "They seemed close."

"They were close," he agreed. "And platonic."

"Completely platonic?" I asked. "They never dated? Not even in school?"

"No," he said.

"How do you know that?"

"Because it's my job to know, Miss Dante. And believe it or not, I'm good at it." He tapped the file on his desk. "I interviewed every human being who ever looked twice at Ben Mitchell. I even interviewed the cashiers at his grocery store. I can tell you how many pounds of grapes he ate in an average month."

"Cool," I said. "But can you tell me who stole his car?"

Detective Roberts shot me a look.

"I'm just saying," I told him. "Until today, did you have any idea that Lilith and Blade were hanging out together?"

"No," he admitted.

"So maybe we can help each other."

"Except we can't," he said. "You've been charged in Ben's death. Even if you weren't a minor *and* a civilian, I couldn't involve you in my investigation. I'm already crossing the line having this discussion with you."

"What about the forensics from my shed?" I asked. "I'm entitled to that information for my defense."

"Yes, you are. And as soon as the report comes back, I'll call you."

"But what about the murder weapon?" I asked. "What does it tell us? I know you recovered the gun, because I saw the killer give it up when they surrendered."

He retrieved a pen and a sticky pad from his desk drawer and jotted down some notes. Then he peeled off the top note and stuck it to the desk space in front of me. "Here's what the murder weapon tells us."

I read his scribbles: *Glock 19 Gen 3, 9 mm.* "This means nothing to me."

"Exactly. That's the point."

"That I'm ignorant about guns?"

"That the gun doesn't tell us much," he said. "It's the most common nine-millimeter on the market, unregistered, and with no fingerprints except for yours. Whoever chose this pistol did it deliberately and used it in a way that couldn't be traced back to them. They knew what they were doing."

"Oh."

"I wish I could give you more, Miss Dante."

I bounced my heel against the floor. I didn't want to leave, but I sensed he was about to give me the boot. "Just do one thing for me," I said. "And then I'll go."

"No promises. But what is it?"

"Look up the tracking information for Blade Romanovitch's ankle monitor. See if he was at the courthouse the day Ben was shot." I faked a *no-big-deal* shrug. "What have you got to lose? If Blade wasn't there, you can eliminate my theory."

The detective considered for a moment or two, and then curiosity seemed to get the better of him. "All right, fine. But I'm not going to tell you anything."

We would see about that.

He angled the screen away from me and did some typing and clicking. When he found what he was looking for, he leaned in to peer at the screen. A trio of lines wrinkled his forehead.

"That can't be right," he muttered.

"Why?" I tried leaning in, but he fended me off. "What does it say?"

He clicked the mouse as if refreshing the page. He shook his head in confusion, continuing to mutter under his breath.

"What does it say?" I repeated. "Was Blade at the courthouse?"

"That information is none of your business, Miss Dante."

I very much disagreed, but I doubted he would see it from my perspective. So I thought fast and acted faster. I discreetly tapped my phone to open the camera in forward-facing mode. Then I reached for my purse while "accidentally" knocking over the detective's water bottle. He bent over to catch the bottle before it hit the floor, and I darted out an arm to snap a picture of his computer screen. It was lightning fast—he never noticed a thing.

Whether the picture was legible remained to be seen.

"Okay, well, a deal's a deal," I told him, standing from my chair. "I'll leave you alone to solve Ben's murder without me. No pressure or anything."

"Thank you for coming in, Miss Dante." He minimized his screen before I could peek at it. "Do you need me to walk you out?"

I assured him that I could find my own way, and then I strode back toward the front of the building. I had nearly reached the lobby doors when I heard a familiar voice that stopped me in my tracks.

It was Mrs. K., the secretary from my school. She sat across the desk from a young male intake officer, wringing her hands and fidgeting in her seat.

"Our custody hearing is next week," she said to the officer. "That's the reason he's doing this. He's desperate. He knows he's going to lose, so he's trying to scare me into backing down because he doesn't want to pay child support. The father of my child threatened to *kill me* over three hundred and fifty dollars a week!"

"I hear you." The officer made a *calm-down* motion. "I can send someone to talk to your husband—"

"Ex-husband."

"Your ex-husband," he corrected. "But without proof that he threatened you—emails from his account, or texts or voicemails from his phone number—it's your word against his."

"What about this?" She pulled her cell phone from her bag. "I used the voice memo app to record our last conversation. This was two hours ago." She tapped the screen, and a man's voice yelled through the phone, *"I swear to god, Sharon, I will fucking end you! I will put you in the ground if this doesn't stop!"*

Whoa. There was no misinterpreting that.

Or so I thought. The officer shook his head and splayed both hands. "There's no way for me to prove whose voice that is. Unless you think your ex will admit to it."

"Of course he won't admit it."

"Then my hands are tied."

"You're telling me there's nothing you can do?" she asked.

"I don't have grounds to arrest him," he said. "I can send an officer to talk to your ex-husband. And you're free to file for a temporary protective order with the court of common pleas, but I warn you, they'll want evidence, too."

She stuffed her phone back into her bag and stood up, pointing at the paperwork on the officer's desk. "But you'll document this, right? If anything happens to me, I want you to know it was Mike Kazinski."

"Yes, ma'am," he assured her. "I already registered your complaint."

At that moment, Mrs. K. must have sensed me watching her, because she abruptly turned her head and met my gaze. Her eyes widened in surprise, and she clutched her purse to her chest like a shield.

I tried not to take her reaction personally. "Hi, Mrs. K.," I said.

She recovered with a nervous smile and strode over to meet me. "Well, hello, Tia. I didn't expect to see you here."

"I was just dropping off some evidence for Ben's case," I told her, thumbing toward the labyrinth of cubicles behind me. "I'm sorry for your loss, by the way. I heard you two were friends."

"Oh, yes." Tears welled in her eyes. "He was my last real friend in the world."

"I didn't kill him," I said, glancing at my shoes. "I want you to know that."

"Oh, honey, of course you didn't." Briefly, she touched my arm. "You're a victim in all of this, too. No one blames you for what happened."

"I wouldn't say *no one*," I told her. "But I'm trying to find out who killed Ben. I already have a lead."

"Please be safe. One loss is already too much."

"I'm being careful," I assured her. "But what about you? Are you okay? I wasn't trying to snoop, but I overheard that stuff you said about Molly's dad."

"I'm sorry you had to hear that." She blotted her eyes and released a long, heavy breath. "Never get married, Tia. At least not to a man. Men are the worst."

Divorced people always said things like that. But actually, she might have a point. All of my problems, at least the recent ones, traced back to men. Starting with the former and current district attorneys and ending with Nash. The reason for all my stress: guys.

Coincidence? Didn't seem likely.

After saying good-bye to Mrs. K., I returned to my car and thought about what she had told the intake officer, and more specifically, what it meant for Ben's shooting.

I didn't know the private details of her divorce, but I assumed Ben Mitchell had helped Mrs. K. with the legal process. Ben had been her closest friend and Molly's godfather. He would have used his influence as the district attorney to help them. And he definitely wouldn't have let Mike Kazinski threaten Mrs. K, or take Molly away from her. I fully believed that if Ben were alive today, he would have pulled whatever strings necessary to get a restraining order against Mike and to keep him from winning custody of Molly.

But Ben wasn't alive to protect Molly and her mother.

How fortunate for Mike Kazinski.

I wondered if Detective Roberts had interviewed Mike and checked out his alibi. Knowing the detective, he probably had. But it couldn't hurt for me to take a closer look at Mike. The man had as much motive to kill Ben as Lilith and Blade combined.

Blade. I had almost forgotten about taking a picture of his tracking data. I whipped out my phone, hoping the photo wasn't blurry. I couldn't believe my luck. The image was crystal clear. All I had to do was zoom in to read the words on the detective's monitor.

Department of Corrections location history: Blade A. Romanovitch. I skimmed through a list of dates. They all said the same thing: *Data unavailable.*

Data unavailable?

At first, I thought there had been a problem with the connectivity between the probation department and the police station. A temporary glitch that could be fixed by now. But then I continued reading the log and noticed another message toward the bottom of the screen, dated and time-stamped the same morning of Blade's release from jail: *ankle monitor location services suspended.*

"No," I whispered. I swore under my breath.

There was no glitch. Blade's tracking device had either been hacked or deliberately turned off the entire time. That explained why his data was missing. But it didn't explain why multiple weeks had gone by without anyone noticing, especially Blade's probation officer. No one was that lucky. I didn't know what was going on behind the scenes with Blade, but one thing was certain.

I had underestimated him.

Chapter Eleven

THE NEXT MORNING BEGAN WITH A TEXT FROM
Nash, which used to be my favorite way to start the day. Back then,
our morning ritual had been truly nauseating. We started each day
by exchanging kissy-face selfies and describing one new trait that we
liked about each other. (And the trait had to be non-physical, so boobs
didn't count.) I had to admit, I'd enjoyed learning to appreciate something new about myself every morning. But that seemed like a decade
ago. Now I scowled at my phone and wished I hadn't given Nash my
new number.

ILO meeting tonight, he said. You should come.

Will there be snacks? I asked sarcastically.

Actually, yes, there will be.

The kind *I* can eat?

The delay in his response told me the answer.

Yeah, that's what I thought, I said. Hard pass.

I'll make you a deal, he replied. If you come to the meeting, I'll
swap minds with you and let you eat donuts in my body.

I gasped—out loud. Nash couldn't possibly know how much his offer tempted me. The ILO could take a long walk off a short pier for all I cared, but donuts . . . oh . . . to plow through a box of donuts was one of my top ten ultimate fantasies, right below eating my way through a bathtub-size chocolate lava cake.

As many as you want, he added. I'll bring an extra dozen just for you. Assorted jellies, creme filled, fudge glazed, a bunch of eclairs. Those are the ones you always wanted to try, right?

Damn him. He *did* know.

7 PM at the student union building, he said. I'll come with an empty stomach.

I told him I would think about it, and then I spent the rest of the morning trying to forget about donuts. Not an easy thing to do, but it helped that I had a lot to distract me. I worked on school assignments until lunchtime, taking occasional breaks to creep on Mrs. K.'s ex on social media. It turned out Mike Kazinski didn't have many surprises for me. His main account was private, but like most middle-aged knuckle draggers, he quickly accepted a friend request from the fake "hot girl" account I created. All it took was a picture of a random Instagram model copied and pasted from the internet.

Catfishing shouldn't be this easy.

Had no one heard of a reverse Google image search?

Anyway, Mike Kazinski struck me as a suburban male stereotype. He lived in a two-story home in a neighborhood that regulated how tall the grass was allowed to grow. He drove a Ford F-150 pickup truck with a DON'T TREAD ON ME! bumper sticker. His main interests included watching sportsball, drinking beer, and grilling bratwurst—and he had the gut to prove it. In the looks department, I rated him a solid three, although I could have gone lower if I had deducted points for his thinning brown hair or the socks he wore with his sandals. Mrs. K. definitely could have done better. How this man had convinced her to procreate with him was beyond me, but I did see a resemblance to Molly in his eyes.

Mike had listed Quantum Total Lawn Care as his place of employment. Scrolling though his posts, I gathered that he worked in the office side of the business: sharing deals and promos, soliciting new clients, customer service, that sort of thing.

I looked up the contact information for Quantum Total Lawn Care and dialed the number for human resources. A woman named Brenda answered.

"Hi, Brenda," I told her. "I was in your office a couple of weeks ago, and I spoke with one of your sales reps about taking over my company's lawn care contract. I have a follow-up question, but I can't remember who I talked to. Maybe you can help me narrow it down by looking at the schedule to see who was working that afternoon?"

"I can transfer you to our sales department," she said. "Anyone there can help you. They share accounts."

"No, no," I told her. "I really want to talk to the same person."

She hesitated.

"It's important," I added. "We talked about something specific. He's the only one who can answer this question for me."

She huffed into the phone and asked, "All right, when was your meeting?"

I gave her the date and time of the courthouse shooting.

After a few keyboard clicks, she said, "Several of our reps were in the office that day."

"What are their names?" I asked. "Maybe that will ring a bell."

"Let's see . . ." she began. "Bill Jones, Rick Vasquez, Mike Kazinski . . ."

"Mike Kazinski," I told her. "I think that's him. But it was a lunchtime appointment. Can you confirm he was there during lunch hour?"

"Oh, the guys never leave to eat," she said. "We have food trucks come in. The sales reps buy something out front and then they eat in their offices."

"Oh, okay."

"Would you like me to transfer you?" she asked.

"Yes, thank you," I told her, and then I hung up as soon as Mike's phone rang.

Well, that wasn't the answer I had wanted. Mike Kazinski had an alibi. I supposed he could have hired someone to kill Ben Mitchell, but so could anyone else. From Ben's jilted fiancée to the hundreds of criminals he had convicted, there was no shortage of people who wanted him dead. Then there were all of the upcoming cases on Ben's schedule—the people he hadn't had a chance to prosecute before he died.

I hadn't looked into Ben's open cases, but maybe I should. According to what I had read, Ben had held the record for the highest conviction rate in three decades. Anyone on his schedule would have good reason to be nervous. More than nervous, terrified of going to prison and losing everything they had built in life. That was a definite motive for murder, especially for someone already comfortable with breaking the law.

Of course, a new lead meant even more unpaid work for me.

No rest for the wicked.

• • •

Two hours later, I finished downloading all the open criminal cases that were set to go to trial in the next few months. My eyes burned and threatened to cross themselves. Since I couldn't take any more screen time, I decided to drive to Saint Valliant's to work off a couple of community service hours.

On the drive to the thrift store, I noticed an addition to the news vans trailing me. An obnoxiously loud motorcycle roared in the background, the kind of noise that rattled my teeth. I heard the bike long before I could see it, but each time I glanced into the rearview mirror, the rider seemed to have passed another news van until he was right behind me. Even though he wore a black helmet with a shield that concealed his face, I recognized his muscled frame and the ankle monitor around his riding boot.

Blade had decided to join me . . . and he'd followed me from my house.

That didn't bode well.

I chose the most visible spot in the parking lot when I pulled in, making sure Blade would have an audience for whatever he had in mind. I doubted he would hurt me in public when he could easily wait until dark and ambush me where I slept, but no need to tempt fate.

He whipped into the spot beside me so quickly he left tire marks on the asphalt. No sooner had I turned off my ignition than my passenger door swung open, and Blade plopped onto the seat. He unfastened his helmet and tugged it off, and then he faced me, breathing hard, his nostrils flaring.

Oh, he was *big* mad.

His index finger appeared an inch from my nose. "You said you weren't a snitch. But I don't know why I believed you, because that's exactly what a snitch would say, isn't it?"

"I'm not a snitch," I told him calmly. "Snitches work for the cops. I don't inform for them or anyone else."

"Then explain this," he said, pointing at his ankle monitor. "A brand-new probation officer who I've never met before showed up at my house, banging down the door at the ass crack of dawn because my old tracker wasn't working, and he wanted to replace it."

My pulse thumped, but I didn't let it show. "What's that got to do with me?"

"Tia, Tia, Tia." He tilted his head to the side and flashed a cold, knowing smile. "You're a good liar. Even better than I am . . . but not good enough."

I let go of a breath. There was no use trying to bullshit him. He obviously had an inside source that had told him about my visit to Detective Roberts. "All right. I might have let some information slip, but it's not what you think."

"What should I think?" he demanded. "Because here's the deal, Tia. I *really* liked my old probation officer. I liked him a lot. His name was Chip. My man Chip was a nice guy with a gambling problem. Chip and I had an understanding. I paid off his debts to his bookie, and in return, he let me live my life in peace. It was a win-win. But not anymore, Tia. Now, thanks to you, my man Chip is unemployed, and I have a new PO who doesn't understand me at all. So enlighten me: What should I think about those loose lips of yours?"

I turned in my seat to face him and abruptly asked, "How come you didn't tell me that you and Lilith Littler know each other?"

His lips parted, his expression blank.

"Ben Mitchell's fiancée," I added.

"What does that matter?" he said.

"It matters because I saw you with her at Ben's grave."

"And you thought what?" he asked with a humorless laugh. "That I killed Ben for her? That I would risk going back to prison for *her*?"

Yes. That was exactly what I thought. "Someone framed me," I reminded him. "Can you blame me for wanting to find out who?"

"What I blame you for is interfering in my business."

"You didn't explain how you and Lilith know each other."

"There you go again," he said, "getting up in my business."

"Why can't you just tell me?"

"Because I don't owe you anything, Tia! We're not friends!"

I folded my arms as heat rose into my cheeks. If I had the power to help someone clear their name, I would do it . . . unless the truth implicated me in the crime. More and more, it looked like that was the case with Blade.

"How about this?" he said, pointing back and forth between us. "Quid pro quo. I'll help you if you'll do the same for me."

"I'm listening."

"I'll tell you everything you want to know about me and Lilith," he said. "And in return, you owe me a favor."

I scoffed. An open-ended favor? Owed to the son of a Russian mafia heavy? Did this guy think I was born yesterday? I had seen all the Godfather movies, even the crappy third one.

"What *kind* of favor?" I asked.

"Any kind I want."

"No," I told him.

"All right, all right, fine, nothing illegal," he said. "Whatever I ask for, it will be fully legit and guaranteed not to get you in trouble. How's that?"

"Better," I said. "But how do I know you'll tell me the truth about Lilith?"

He lifted his phone for show. "Because I have receipts."

He said the magic word. I loved receipts. I bit my lip and considered his offer. It didn't take me long to decide. Lucky for Blade, he had caught me on a day when answers tempted me even more than donuts.

"All right," I told him. "One favor in exchange for all the tea."

We shook hands.

"Now spill," I told him.

"Okay, exhibit number one." He held up a photo of Ben Mitchell and a professionally dressed blond woman approaching Ben's Audi in a remote corner of a parking garage. Blade swiped to the next picture, showing Ben and the woman climbing into the backseat. Then the next picture, a close-up of the woman straddling Ben's lap. "Exhibit B," Blade said, and showed me another series of photos, same car, same backseat, different blond. "And last but not least, here's my favorite, exhibit three." Again, Ben in the backseat with a *different* blond woman who was clearly double-jointed.

I made a face. There was no un-seeing that. Then I remembered *my* body had been stuffed into that same backseat, and I felt the sudden urge to strip naked and run back and forth through a steaming car wash.

"My dad had these taken while I was in lockup," Blade said. "He hired one of his guys to follow Ben and wait for him to trip over his own dick. It only took a day."

"Why would your dad go through the trouble of catching Ben cheating?" I asked. "Why not bust Ben for taking bribes or doing something that's actually illegal?"

"Who says he didn't?" Blade countered. "When it comes to blackmail, there's no such thing as too much dirt." He pointed at the location of Ben's Audi. "Anyway, the dude thought he was so slick. He always parked right here, every single time."

"Security camera blind spot?" I guessed.

"Yep," Blade said. "Amateur. As if that's the only way to get caught."

Maybe Ben had wanted to get caught. Not *caught* in the actual sense of having to face the consequences of his actions. No man wanted that. But I would bet that deep in the kinky recesses of Ben's heart, he had liked feeling exposed. Otherwise he would have gone to a motel room or to the other woman's house to cheat. Instead he chose the backseat of a remotely parked car—private enough to avoid an arrest for lewd conduct, but public enough for a thrill of danger.

"Okay, so Ben was a freak," I said. "What does that have to do with you and Lilith?"

"Because I'm the one who told her."

"You?" I asked. "That's how she found out he was cheating?"

"I sent her an email. I told her I had photos of her boyfriend fooling around, and if she wanted to see the evidence, she would have to pay. At first, she told me to piss off. But a few days later, she changed her tune." He waggled his eyebrows and curled one muscled arm behind his head. "I made five hundred bucks *and* blew up Ben's love life. It was a good day."

"Let me see," I told him.

He pulled up the email thread and showed it to me. The messages read much like he had described, except that Lilith had used stronger language than *piss off*.

"So you met up with her and gave her the pics," I said. "And then what?"

"And then nothing."

"Until you showed up at Ben's burial . . . together," I reminded him.

"We weren't *together* together," he said. "She was already there when I showed up. We saw each other, we talked some shit about the dead, and we went home."

"And the timing? Am I supposed to believe that was a coincidence?"

"No. It wasn't a coincidence that we both waited until the gravesite was empty before we desecrated it." He rolled his eyes. "That was on purpose."

"You know what I mean."

"What do you want me to say?" he asked. "She hated Ben. I hated Ben. That was all we had in common. I didn't plan to see her there that day. And I'm not banging her, if that's what you're asking. She's not my type."

"Okay, so why'd you throw a knife on the casket?"

"It was a blade," he corrected. "Something to remember me by."

"A calling card?" I asked in disbelief. "Not very original."

"Sorry to disappoint you. I'll try to be more poetic when my next enemy dies." He flung a hand in the air. "Are we done now?"

"One more question," I said. "Your ankle monitor wasn't working the day Ben was shot. There was no way to prove your alibi."

"That's not a question."

"Where were you that day?"

Blade flicked his gaze to the left as a wall went up behind his eyes. I could tell my question had triggered something in him. His response was so clear that anyone would have noticed it. But having studied body language, I picked up on something else that the average bear would have missed. People usually glanced in one direction or the other when they were thinking about or recalling details from the past. For Blade, it was to his right. But this time, he glanced to his left. That meant he was engaging a different part of his brain—active processing instead of memory recall. Whatever he told me next, I couldn't trust it.

"I was with my dad," he said flatly.

"Doing what?" I asked.

"None of your business."

I opened my mouth to argue, and he delivered a burning glare that had me clamping my lips shut. There was an unspoken boundary in his eyes that I knew better than to cross. But his reaction, his *over-*reaction, gave away more than it should have. I had touched a major nerve. Whatever Blade was hiding, I would bet that it either shamed or scared him. That pretty much guaranteed I wouldn't stop digging until I found out what it was.

"We had a deal," he said, his voice throaty and quiet, almost a whisper. "And it didn't involve my father. I told you everything I know about Lilith. My part is done."

I didn't argue with him.

He pocketed his phone and tucked his helmet under one arm. Right before he left, he reminded me, "You owe me now. Be ready when I call to collect."

Chapter Twelve

BLADE DIDN'T JOIN ME DURING MY SHIFT, NOT THAT I had expected him to. He rumbled away on his motorcycle, and I sorted donations for the next couple of hours. The work was mindless, and while I was separating T-shirts into bins according to size and color, a thought occurred to me.

Ben Mitchell had chosen a security camera blind spot for his hookups—that was how his backseat shenanigans had gone undetected for so long. But what if Ben had parked there *every* day, not just on the days when he had planned a tryst? That would make sense for two reasons. First, it would have maximized his odds of getting lucky; and second, more importantly, it might explain why the police hadn't found any camera footage of Ben's car from the day of the murder. If the cops had only skimmed the footage of parked cars, not the vehicles in motion, they would have missed the mobile motel room otherwise known as Ben's Audi.

I called Detective Roberts and left a voicemail asking him to rewatch the security video from the courthouse parking garage.

"I know there are a ton of cameras," I added. "Maybe you already thought of this, but you could start with the ticketing kiosk cams at the entrance and the exit. That way we'll have people's faces, too."

After that, I sorted clothes for a while longer, until my stomach growled and reminded me of Nash's offer to let me eat donuts in his body. I checked the clock. The ILO meeting would start in one hour, plenty of time for me to drive to the university if I left soon. I would still have to feed my actual body, but I could grab a to-go vegan, non-soy protein bowl from the restaurant next door and eat it in the car on the way to the student union.

The decision made itself.

Donuts won. They always would.

I texted Nash while I waited for my protein bowl. He warned me that campus parking was an actual nightmare, so he sent me the address to a private lot, along with a promise to meet me there and walk me to the student union building.

About an hour later, I finished the last bite of my tasteless excuse for a dinner and pulled into the parking spot beside Nash's gold Plymouth.

I stepped out of my car, inhaling a deep breath of honeysuckle and grass clippings mingled with the faint, smoky scent of grilled meat from the restaurants in the distance. The late-spring sun had slipped close to the horizon, but with no sign of setting anytime soon. The days were growing longer, and I loved the lingering brilliance in the sky, the illusion of bonus hours added to my (albeit bonkers) life. The way I looked at it, if I had to face a bogus manslaughter charge and the scrutiny of the entire world, I would rather do it during springtime. Winter made everything worse.

I joined Nash at his trunk, where he retrieved a slim cardboard box festooned with pink and white polka dots. The logo on the box lid read SWEET CHEEKS, a local bakery famed for its decadent treats made twice daily from scratch. Nash had unlocked a new level of respect from me. I would have been happy with a dozen donuts from a grocery store or a big-chain drive-through, but he had raised the bar and sprung for gourmet.

"Impressive," I told him.

"I aim to please."

I jutted my chin at the box. "Let's see the goods."

He lifted the lid and displayed a dozen sweet dreams come true. There were no rejects inside, no squashed edges or missing bites or splotched glaze. Each donut was fluffy and flawless, as if hand selected, and so fresh that I could smell the scents of sugared cake and chocolate from three paces away.

My mouth watered, and I moved in closer for a whiff.

Nash snapped the lid shut, barely missing my nose. "Not until the meeting."

"No way," I objected. "We have to trade bodies and do this now. I don't want to eat in front of an audience." I gazed at the polka-dotted box and felt the kind of longing that a therapist would probably consider unhealthy. "I'm gonna do things to those éclairs that no civilized human being should have to watch."

His brows pinched together. "Damn, T. Sometimes I worry about you."

"Worry about me later," I said. "Right now we need to turn that pretty mouth of yours into my own personal donut hole."

Instead of laughing at my joke, he swiveled the box out of reach. "Uh-uh. You have to come to the meeting. That was the deal."

"Are you serious?" I asked, splaying a hand over my heart. "Do you really think I would trade bodies with you and then go back on my word after I'm done eating?"

"That's exactly what I think you'll do."

He was smarter than he looked. "Fine. Let's go."

The college campus stood at the top of a tall hill, and naturally, our parking lot was situated at the bottom of it. Nash led the way toward a steep residential road lined on both sides by parked cars. The homes along the road were mostly old, dilapidated two-story Colonials that had been built too close to the street to allow for sidewalks. Judging by the Greek letters nailed to the wood siding and the beer cans littering the lawns, we had found fraternity row. Strangely, all was quiet on the hill. Nash and I hiked side by side up the middle of the street with no front porch onlookers that I noticed. Maybe everyone was indoors studying, or at the campus dining hall for dinner.

"I'm glad you changed your mind," Nash said. "I didn't know if you would."

"You used the right leverage," I told him.

"Yeah, but still . . ." He glanced at me and paused, delivering a half grin. "I'm glad you came. I was afraid you wouldn't talk to me again."

Maybe I had imagined it, but there seemed to be an apology in his tone, the kind of genuine remorse that I never expected from Nash. I didn't know how to feel about it. He had certainly done a lot to be sorry for. But part of me didn't want his apology. Because if Nash would keep playing the role of my asshole ex-boyfriend, I could keep pretending that I was better off without him. But if he showed remorse—if he gave me hope that he could learn from his mistakes and finally stop hurting me—then the scab on my heart might reopen and make me raw again. And that was dangerous.

"Hey," I said. "Can I ask you something?"

"Sure."

"I want you to be honest, though."

"Okay," he told me. "I will."

"What's the real reason you broke up with me last summer?" I asked. "I know it wasn't because you wanted to focus on school."

Nash blew out a long breath. "Yeah, it wasn't."

"You wanted to see what else was out there, didn't you?" I asked.

He shrugged a vague *yes*.

That was what I figured. I had never heard of a high school couple surviving all four years of college. Everyone hoped their relationship would be the exception, but the dating pool at universities was more like an ocean, or even better, like a stocked pond that had been filled to the brim with fish from every hatchery in the world. And who didn't want to catch the biggest fish they could? So if a college freshman like Nash wanted to cast his line back into the water, first he had to release the totally awesome, shiny rainbow trout he had caught in high school. Not that I saw myself as a trout. A barracuda, maybe. But anyway, he could have just told me the truth.

"At least you didn't cheat on me, I guess," I said. "So congrats on doing the bare minimum. But you didn't have to lie to me."

"I know," he admitted. "I didn't want to hurt your feelings."

I laughed without humor. If protecting my feelings was his goal, he had failed miserably. In fact, his fake excuse had made our breakup even worse, because it showed me just how little he thought I knew about him. Maybe I was being dramatic, but I still felt like his lie had been an insult to our relationship.

"There were other reasons, too," he went on. "But for what it's worth, I was wrong about all of them. I should have appreciated you more. It didn't take very many dates for me to see there's no one else like you, T."

Hearing that made my heart flutter, but I didn't respond to him. I didn't know how to respond. I stared straight ahead and marched up the street, trying my best to turn my thoughts away from what-ifs and possibilities and the nearness of Nash's body. I counted backward from one hundred to zero. I matched my breathing to the rhythm of my footsteps. I recited song lyrics in my head. I did such an excellent job of distracting myself from Nash's presence that I didn't notice the electric car silently speeding up the road behind me.

Nash glanced over his shoulder, and then several things happened in a flash. He tossed the box of donuts in the air while grabbing my arm with both hands, and then with a mighty tug, Nash heaved our bodies onto the hood of a parked car just as a black-matte Tesla plowed through the space where I had stood a nanosecond earlier.

No sooner had I righted myself and touched one foot to the ground than the Tesla came careening at me again, this time in reverse. I drew back my leg before the car could hit me, but the side-view mirror clipped my shoe hard enough to knock it off. Nash gripped my wrist and pulled me across the hood of the parked car until it stood between us like a barrier. We both crouched behind the front fender, bracing ourselves for another attack.

"What the hell?" I panted as I peeked over the hood.

Nash grabbed my arm and yanked me back down. "Don't!"

We waited there for a while longer, catching our breath. Then we scanned the street, but the Tesla was gone. When it seemed the threat had passed, we inched onto the asphalt to retrieve my shoe. All that remained in the street were a set of tire marks and a twice-crushed box of donuts.

"Oh, no, not my donuts," I whispered as I worked my foot back into my shoe. I must have been in shock, because even though I knew ruined donuts were the least of my problems, I couldn't tear my gaze away from the strawberry jelly and vanilla crème oozing out of the box and onto the pavement. "I knew it!" I said to Nash. "I knew we should have changed bodies in the parking lot and eaten there. I told you! You never listen to me!"

Nash ignored my ranting and locked eyes with me. "Tia, that wasn't an accident."

"Well, no shit it wasn't an accident!" I yelled. I had kind of picked up on that when the driver put the car in reverse and tried to run me over a *second* time.

Nash settled a hand on my lower back and guided me to the grass. He gripped my shoulders and spoke to me like a parent to a child. "Someone tried to kill you."

Logically, I didn't need the reminder. But hearing him say it out loud sobered me. I glanced again at the crushed box of donuts lying in the road and realized that it could have been me. If Nash hadn't pulled me out of the way in time, I would have been crushed and oozing on the pavement. The sight of bright red strawberry jam hit differently now that I imagined it as my blood.

My heart pounded. Someone wanted me dead.

"And they almost succeeded," Nash added, his grip tightening on my upper arms. "That was so close, T. You could have *died*."

"But I didn't," I reminded him. I gently freed myself from his hands and put a more comfortable distance between us. "I'm still here."

He swallowed hard and raked a hand through his hair.

"Listen, thank you," I told him. "You saved my life. I owe you."

"I don't want you to owe me," he said, his eyes going wild. "I want you to be okay. I want you to walk down the street without getting run over by a psycho!"

"I wasn't paying attention," I told him. "*At all.* I was completely zoned out, and I know better than that. I should have heard that car coming."

"It didn't make a sound. Electric cars are silent."

"They make some noise. You heard it."

"Not until it was right on top of you."

"And that's because I was distracted," I said, hoping to calm Nash down. It wouldn't help either of us to spiral into panic. "I'll be on high alert from now on. No one's getting the jump on me again, I promise. Next time, I'll be prepared."

"Next time?" he asked in disbelief. "Do you hear yourself? There shouldn't *be* a next time! There shouldn't have been a *this* time!"

So much for calming him down.

"I'm calling the police," he said, and pointed at the grass. "Do me a favor and try to make yourself less of a target until they get here."

I sat on the lawn, and while Nash dialed the cops, I called my dad's cell phone and left a voicemail telling him not to worry about me . . . just like I had done after the courthouse shooting last week.

Déjà vu all over again.

"I promise not to make a habit out of this," I added at the end of the message, but there was no way my dad was letting me out of the house anytime soon.

Two squad cars arrived and blocked off the street, and then, a few minutes later, Detective Roberts pulled up in an unmarked sedan. He shook his head when he saw me, as if *I* was the source of all his problems.

"Hey, I didn't ask for this," I said when he joined us on the lawn. "Just like I didn't ask for someone to steal my body and use it for a murder. I'm the victim here."

"Yes, you are," the detective agreed, but in a patronizing sort of way. "A victim *and* a common denominator, but never mind that. Go ahead and tell me what happened."

Nash and I took turns explaining the attack. Detective Roberts took notes while we talked, and then he asked us a *ton* of questions— an obnoxious amount—sometimes reframing the same question in a different way as if to catch us in a lie. I didn't appreciate his suspicion toward me, but I reminded myself that he was just doing his job. And to be fair, he did seem invested in the truth, and that mattered more to me than my pride. After he finished taking our statements, he instructed the beat cops to go to every house along the street and ask if anyone had witnessed the attack.

"See if they have doorbell cameras," he added. Then he turned his focus back to me and asked one final question. "Can you think of anyone who would want to kill you?"

A couple of weeks ago, I would have said no. But since then, I had gained the world's attention and pissed off a few sketchy people. The first one that came to mind was Blade Romanovitch, and by extension, his mob boss father. But my confrontation with Blade had ended in a truce of sorts. I doubted he would talk me into owing him a favor and then whack me a few hours later. Besides, his ankle monitor was working now, so he couldn't drive around in stealth mode anymore. It was possible an extremist nut job had watched me on the news and then decided to hunt me down. But to me, the most likely suspect was the person who stood to benefit more from my death than anyone else.

"Ben Mitchell's killer," I said. "If I die, there's no way to prove who stole my body. They'll get away with murder."

"Two murders," Nash corrected.

Two murders.

Again, the truth sobered me. Because finding Ben's killer was no longer about clearing my name and avoiding jail time. Now my future was a zero-sum game—winner take all. A game I couldn't afford to lose.

Chapter Thirteen

AS I HAD PREDICTED, MY DAD FREAKED OUT AND instituted a full household lockdown. He installed alarms on the doors and the windows. He mounted a motion-activated security camera in the living room. He "borrowed" a very large and very ugly dog from a vacationing friend. And at the present moment, he sat at the kitchen table cleaning and oiling his many guns.

I decided my dad's love language was *overkill*.

And he wasn't the only one.

In the days following the attack, Val and Nash barely left my side. Each of them came over in the afternoon as soon as their classes ended, and they stayed until the dinner leftovers had long turned cold on the stove. We spent most of our time going through the list of Ben Mitchell's open criminal cases and ranking them in order of sentencing severity if the defendants were convicted. So far, we had flagged three suspects with the motive and the means to commit murder. Now we were checking their alibis for opportunity.

"Cross this guy off the list," Val said. She reached over from her spot next to me on the bed and pointed at the top name scribbled on my notepad. "He didn't make bail. He's been in jail the whole time."

I marked through his name. "One down."

From the other side of the room, Nash raised his pencil. He sat with his back against the wall, his long legs crossed at the ankles, wearing a pair of athletic shorts that gave me a perfect view of his muscular thighs. I tried not to look at him, but I kept failing. Ever since I learned that he regretted breaking up with me, I couldn't stop having dirty thoughts about him. It was seriously annoying, because the truth didn't change what he had done to me. Nash's regret didn't rewind time and un-break my heart or restore my trust that he would never hurt me again. I needed my brain to stop seeing him as someone safe to fantasize about. I didn't even know if he had a girlfriend.

"Make that two," Nash said. "I just found out that Mickey Jones, the guy on trial for beating up his pregnant girlfriend, choked to death on a hot dog he stole while he was robbing a Circle K."

I made an appreciative face. "Maybe there is some justice in this world."

"The universe balances," Val agreed.

"So now we're down to Richard Franco," I said. The man was a real prize. He had already served five years for wire fraud, and then approximately one hot minute after his release from prison, the cops busted him for holding his senile grandma hostage in the basement of her home and funneling her Social Security checks into his bank account. But despite the fact that Franco was a whole dumpster full of rancid assholes, he wasn't a violent offender, so I hadn't picked him as my top suspect. "I called the halfway house where he's living and pretended I was checking his references for a job. They wouldn't give me much, but they said he didn't have any infractions at the house."

"That doesn't mean a whole lot," Nash said. "Just that he's passing his drug tests and he comes back to his room before curfew. If you want to check his alibi, you need to call his boss. Do you know where he works?"

I shook my head.

"He has to be employed," Nash told me. "It's one of the conditions for staying at the halfway house."

"How do you know?" I asked.

"I'm taking a criminal justice class," he said. "The professor's an adjunct who works part-time as a parole officer."

I raised an eyebrow. "A parole officer could come in handy."

"Yeah, I was thinking the same thing." Nash scratched his jaw and went pensive for a few beats. "I might have an idea for getting him to help us."

Any help was better than none, but what I really needed was a way to get back in the game—to gather intel outside the house without making myself an easy target for Ben's killer. I knew I could ask Val to pin on the surveillance brooch and do my spying for me, but I didn't want to put her at risk either. I was still thinking about it when a familiar buzzing noise hovered outside my window—the sound of a hornets' nest in motion—and an idea came to mind.

"What about a drone?" I asked.

Val glanced at me and then at the closed window blinds that blocked the media from their constant efforts to spy on me. "It can't see us."

"No, not that one," I said. "I'm talking about a drone for us to use.

If we could get our hands on a good one, not the recreational kind, but professional grade or something like that, I could do surveillance right here without leaving my room. I could follow Richard Franco from the halfway house and find out where he works."

Nash let out a dry laugh. "Sure, all we need is a military connection who has access to a ten-thousand-dollar piece of equipment. *And* who's willing to risk a court-martial for loaning it to a bunch of civilians. Should be a piece of cake."

"Actually . . ." Val said, trailing off to sheepishly bite her lip.

"Aw, come on, you're screwing with me," Nash told her. "You don't actually know anyone like that."

Val tipped up a palm. "I've been dating this guy for a while, just casually, nothing serious because he's not my usual type. He's a . . ." She cringed, cupping one hand around her mouth and leaning forward to whisper, "Gemini," like it was the most vulgar word in the English language.

I gasped and clutched a set of imaginary pearls. "No! Not that! Anything but that!"

"Say it ain't so!" cried Nash, pretending to swoon.

Val slanted me a dirty look. "I don't expect you to understand."

"So how come I'm just now hearing about this guy?" I asked.

"Because you had more important things going on. I didn't want to bother you."

"Uh-huh," I said, rolling my eyes. I knew Val better than that. She shared everything with me, with one exception. Val had this oddball belief about the power of the spoken word. By her logic, talking about something would make it substantial, and conversely, silence would make it irrelevant. I kept trying to tell her that reality didn't work that way, but apparently, she knew better than I did.

"You're ashamed of him," I said.

Her cheeks turned bright pink.

"He's your dirty little Gemini secret," I teased, glancing at Nash and wagging my eyebrows so he could join the game.

"You're using him for his dirty Gemini body, aren't you?" Nash added. "Shame on you, Val. The universe is crying a fat tear right now. Unless Mercury is in Gatorade. . . ."

"Don't be silly, Nash," I said. "Mercury's not in Gatorade. It's Uranus that's the problem, and we have to get to the *bottom* of it."

He nodded in mock-serious agreement. "True. The only way to get to the bottom of Uranus is to send a probe and plunge it really deep."

I snorted a laugh, unable to contain it anymore.

"All right, that's enough," Val said. "The only reason I brought him up is because he used to work at a military surplus store, and while he was there, he bought a couple of drones that were decommissioned."

That sounded perfect. "How much does he like you?"

"Enough to loan you one?" Nash added.

"I think so," Val said. "I'll see if I can persuade him tonight."

"Want me to give you some pointers?" I asked with a teasing elbow nudge. "I know a few powers of persuasion that would work on any sign, even a Gemini."

Nash pointed at me. "That's facts. She's hard to say no to."

Val glared at each of us. "Are you two having fun?"

Yes, I realized. I was having fun . . . for the first time since the shooting. It felt good to smile again, to trade silly jokes, to feel the weightlessness of laughter in my chest. I had almost forgotten the sensation.

I wanted to hold on to it, but that wouldn't be fair. The sun had set, and I knew Val and Nash had other things to do besides playing detective with me. So I walked them to the front door and disabled the alarm, and then I passed the rest of my nighttime hours focused on Richard Franco.

Something about Franco's situation bothered me. I didn't understand how a repeat offender, freshly released from prison, had broken the law *yet* again and then made bail so quickly after his arrest. Even if he wasn't a flight risk, the bond would have been super high. I was a first-time offender, and my bond was so expensive that my dad had been forced to use the equity in our house to cover it. What assets did Franco have that allowed him to walk around a free man until his trial?

It took me an hour of digging to find the answer.

Franco had a baller lawyer. Her name was Morgan Stokes. I had never heard of her because she didn't advertise. But according to what I had read online, she was seriously connected, the kind of attorney who made massive campaign donations to judges and not-so-coincidentally received a lot of rulings in her favor. Stokes charged a bazillion dollars an hour and was so elite that she didn't take clients without a referral.

So how had Franco snagged her? And who was paying the bill?

• • •

The following afternoon, my friends came bearing gifts.

Val wheeled a tow-behind, hard-shell suitcase into my bedroom. Before I could open my mouth to speak, she lifted an index finger and warned, "I don't want to hear a single word or a single question asking me how I convinced him to loan it to us." She narrowed her eyes. "Not one word."

I made a zipper motion across my lips and then pretended to lock my mouth and throw the key into the air behind me.

Nash arrived about half an hour later. Val had just finished unpacking the drone and was familiarizing herself with the remote control while I watched over her shoulder.

"Don't ask how she got it," I told him.

He held up a hand. "That's okay. I don't want to know." He set his backpack on the floor and rummaged through it until he retrieved a bright yellow sticky note. "You probably shouldn't ask how I got this either."

I squinted at the note: two lines of letters and numbers written in ink. "What is it?"

"My professor's login and password to the police database."

My jaw dropped.

"He had office hours this morning," Nash said with a shrug. "I stopped in and asked about my grade on the last exam. While he checked his computer, I noticed that he keeps his login and password on a teeny tiny printout taped to the top of his mouse."

"And you read it?" I asked. "Upside down while he was using it?"

"Nah, I took a picture when he wasn't looking." He flashed a smile. "Twelve megapixels for the win."

It struck me then how lucky I was to have friends like Nash and Val in my life. To be honest, I didn't think I would ever consider Nash a friend again, not since the heart breakage. But I couldn't deny that he was acting like one. He and Val weren't simply there to support me. They were putting their necks (and in Val's case, other body parts, too) on the line to help me clear my name. If there was ever any evidence that the universe loved me, it was the two of them.

"Nice," I told Nash, extending a fist to bump because that was the only form of bodily contact I could handle from him without blushing. "I don't know what's in the database, but I bet it's a gold mine."

"We should download a VPN blocker to your laptop before you go digging," Nash said. "I know a good one that's cheap."

I nodded in agreement. I didn't know as much about computers as Nash did, but I figured any government database would have security software that flagged logins from new or unusual IP addresses. A VPN blocker would allow me to hide my real location and make it look like I was using a computer in the same campus building as Nash's professor.

Val piped up, still staring at the drone remote. "We need to install some video software on your computer too, and pair you to the drone so you can see what it sees in real time."

After Nash installed a free trial of Sneaky Stonewall Surfer on my laptop and then paired it with the drone, the three of us moved to the backyard to experiment with our new toy. Val insisted on going first, which was only fair. When she finished, I took the next turn. The drone was surprisingly easy to maneuver, a hundred times more stable than the cheap toy model I had gotten for my thirteenth birthday . . . and then wrecked into a tree an hour after unwrapping it.

"Wow," I said, admiring the drone's flawless rotation, the way it stopped on a dime in midair. It seemed to disobey the laws of physics. "This thing is the real deal."

"Just don't crash it into a tree," Val begged.

I glanced at Nash, who sat cross-legged on the grass with my open computer on his lap. "How's the footage?" I asked him.

"Way better than it should be," he said. "I zoomed in on a reporter across the street, and I could almost see what he was texting on his phone."

"No way," I said.

"*Way*," he told me. "After this, I'm buying a privacy screen for my cell."

I slid a glance at Val. "What exactly does your Gemini do with these drones?"

"He's not *my* anything," she said. "But he records stock footage and sells it on the internet. It's mostly nature stuff, like short clips of flying over trees or going over a cliff. People pay to use his clips in their videos."

"So he uses it responsibly?" I asked. "Borrring."

"There's good money in it," she said, defensively enough that I could tell she was catching feels for her boy toy. "Way better than minimum wage."

I smiled at her. Val and I were different in every possible way, but falling for the wrong guy was a common unifier for us both. I handed the remote control to Nash, and for a moment too long, I let my gaze linger on the slope of his jaw, and then the soft curve of his lips. I looked away, but the image stayed put, repeating on a loop inside my brain. Whoever Val's mystery man was, I hoped her heart stayed whole in the end. More than mine had, anyway.

"Don't worry," I told Val. "I know how important this is." I wasn't talking about the drone, and I could tell that Val knew it. "I won't ruin anything for you. I promise."

Chapter Fourteen

EVERY ONCE IN A WHILE, LIVING IN A SMALL TOWN didn't completely suck.

Like today, for example. I mapped the halfway house where Richard Franco was staying and discovered it was only four miles away from me, easily within drone range. Now I crossed my fingers and hoped his daily activities didn't take him more than another mile in the opposite direction.

I started bright and early, watching on my laptop screen as I navigated the drone to the halfway house. The weather was sunny and clear, perfect for the occasion, with full visibility of the shabby four-story brick building. I hovered the drone high above the roof until I saw a man who matched Franco's description walk out the front door. Using the zoom function, I compared the man to Franco's mug shot—tall and wiry, bulbous eyes, thin nose, light brown buzz cut— and confirmed that I had the right guy. Then there was nothing to do but sit back and wait for him to show me something interesting.

Which took a while because he rode a bike.

Richard Franco didn't strike me as the environmentally friendly type, and the lit cigarette dangling from the corner of his mouth hinted that he wasn't into fitness, so I could only assume he couldn't afford a car, which made me wonder for the hundredth time who was footing the bill for his high-powered lawyer.

He pedaled to the corner convenience store and stopped in for a Red Bull and a king-size Snickers bar—the standard breakfast of champions. Then he rode to a nearby cell phone store and walked out with an armload of burners, which he stuffed into his backpack before continuing to his next stop. In the hour that followed, he biked all over Hell's Half Acre, stopping at two more convenience stores, one hole-in-the-wall bar, and a combination massage studio/tattoo shop inside a half-abandoned strip mall. But the one place he didn't lead me to was an employer. I didn't know what Franco had told the halfway house about the nature of his work, but his job didn't seem like the legitimate kind to me.

Not at all shocking.

Until his next stop . . .

Franco wheeled his bike into an alleyway between a pair of low-income apartment buildings. He propped his bike against a dumpster and stood there with his hands tucked into his pockets, rocking back and forth on his heels as if waiting to meet someone. Less than five minutes later, a familiar motorcycle turned into the alleyway, and none other than Blade Romanovitch showed up. Blade motored close enough to the dumpster to hand Richard Franco a thick white envelope. Franco took the envelope and tucked it inside his backpack, and then Blade backed out of the alley and sped away.

Richard Franco had finally shown me something interesting.

He was working with the Russian mob.

That explained who paid for his lawyer. But not necessarily *why*. I was no expert when it came to the inner workings of the Russian mafia or how they compensated their workers, but I seriously doubted they offered platinum-level legal coverage as part of their standard benefits package. Movies and TV shows had taught me that low-ranking gangsters kept their mouths shut and did their time when they got arrested. The grisly threat of death was enough to stop them from snitching or flipping sides and working for someone else. But the top-tier guys, the big bosses with enough status to make the Feds sit up and take notice—not to mention offer them a sweet witness protection deal in exchange for defecting—those were the guys rescued from jail by slick attorneys.

Maybe I was speculating, but I bet Richard Franco was no ordinary loser.

* * *

I navigated the drone to my backyard and brought it inside to charge. Franco hadn't done anything else of interest. He'd made a few more stops and then pedaled out of range. I wasn't sure what to do with the information I learned about him, so I shifted my focus to exploring the police database.

Nash had told me his professor's teaching schedule, but I texted Nash anyway to make doubly sure the guy was in class and not in his office. If I tried to log in as someone who was already online and in the system, it would trigger the security software and prompt the user to change his password.

We didn't want that.

Nash confirmed that class was in session and would end in

forty-five minutes, so I got right to work. A few keystrokes later, I logged in as parole officer Hector Gonzalez.

"Thanks, Hector," I murmured, scanning the landing page to orient myself.

The layout was seriously old-school, way less intuitive than I was used to, and I had to waste a couple of minutes figuring out how to access the main menu. I eventually found it, but then it took me another fifteen minutes of trial and error to learn which sub pages had any information worth reading. Maybe parole officers didn't have the same access to information as the inspectors, because there were no forensics data or any photos of crime scenes. But I did find my name under citizen complaints, along with some details about the Tesla incident that no one had told me about.

The police officers who canvassed fraternity row for witnesses and doorbell camera footage had turned up quite a treasure trove of information. None of the residents had seen the attack in person, but their combined video footage captured several images of the driver, who was described as a person of medium height and build, wearing a dark hooded sweatshirt, black leather driving gloves, and a latex Hillary Clinton mask that covered their entire face and head. Because the driver had concealed every inch of their skin, the police hadn't been able to determine the suspect's race, age, or gender, but they did trace the Tesla's license plate back to a local rental office that had reported the car stolen that same day. But best of all, an asterisked footnote at the bottom of the report mentioned that a suspect matching the same description had been filmed driving Ben Mitchell's Audi out of the courthouse parking garage on the day of the shooting.

"Well, well, well," I said with a smug smile. It looked like Detective

Roberts had taken my advice and rewatched the security footage from a different vantage point. But he hadn't said *thank you* or shared his findings with me, and he probably hadn't given me credit either.

Rude.

But that clinched it. The same person who killed Ben Mitchell had tried to kill me, too. I already suspected as much. Now that my suspicions were confirmed, I had one more data field for filtering out suspects. To eliminate anyone as the killer, they would need an alibi for not only stealing Ben's car and shooting him, but also for stealing the Tesla and murdering my donuts with it.

That should narrow down the pool of losers by a lot.

•　•　•

On the subject of losers, I replayed the drone video of Richard Franco later that evening when Nash came over. Val canceled on us, claiming that her boss had asked her to pick up an extra shift at work. I didn't know if I believed Val or if she had just ditched us to hang out with her Gemini boy, but either way, she deserved a break from my drama.

The only problem was the vibe.

That old saying "Two's company and three's a crowd" didn't apply when ex-boyfriends were in the mix. I didn't realize how much I relied on Val as my human buffer until she was no longer there to sit next to me on the bed and take up half of my attention. Now every sound in the room was amplified. Every shift of Nash's body seemed exaggerated. With him beside me on the mattress instead of Val, the space felt bigger . . . and somehow infinitely smaller at the same time.

It was like suffocating in pure oxygen.

"Hmm," Nash said. He sat cross-legged, tilting his dark head to the side, his eyes narrowed on my laptop screen. He licked his lips, and my whole body went hot. Did he know? Was he doing that on purpose? He paused the footage of Richard Franco pedaling on his way to his last stop. "You know what it looks like he's doing?"

I shook my head and covertly put another inch between us.

"It looks like he's making dead drops," Nash said.

The term sounded familiar, but I couldn't place it. "What's a dead drop?"

"It's when people pass things to each other without meeting face-to-face."

"Oh, right," I said. "Like in the first Godfather movie, when someone hid a gun in the bathroom so Michael Corleone could show up unarmed to the restaurant and whack the mob bosses."

"Yeah, or in spy movies, where one person tapes a note to the bottom of a park bench and the other person comes and gets it later." Nash pursed his lips in consideration. "But I guess in this case, it's technically a live drop, since Franco is making trades in person instead of using hiding places."

I thought about what Richard Franco might be dead (or live) dropping for the Russians. If he worked for Blade's dad, then it probably had something to do with the gambling side of the business. "I wonder if he's collecting bets for his boss."

"I think those get called in."

"That might explain the burner phones," I pointed out. "Maybe Franco rides around to each stop to collect bets *and* money, and then he delivers the cash to his bookie."

"But he didn't hand off anything to Blade."

That was true. Instead, Blade had handed Franco what appeared to be an envelope stuffed to the seams with cash. "Maybe Blade was giving Franco money to pay the winners. That would make sense, if Franco takes care of the bets and the payouts, too."

"Could be . . ." Nash said, trailing off with an unspoken *but*.

"You don't think so?"

"It's just . . . an unprotected skinny dude on a bicycle doesn't seem like the smartest choice for a money runner. He could have gotten jumped by anyone who weighs more than a hundred pounds."

Nash was right. If money meant everything to the mob, which it probably did, then they would send teams of armed heavies to move big cash, like the gangster version of an armored truck. "So what do you think he was moving?"

"Information?" Nash guessed. "He could have been passing messages around that his boss didn't want to put in writing or get traced back to his phone."

"Again, that would explain the burners," I said. But Nash's theory didn't feel right. It didn't make sense to me for the mob to pay a lawyer like Morgan Stokes to spring Franco from jail, only to use him as a messenger boy. "He has to be more important to them than that."

Nash nodded slowly. "Yeah, I think so, too."

"I just don't see *how* he's important," I said.

"Me neither."

"Then I guess we're back to square one."

"Not square one," Nash said. "More like two and a half."

"Oh, well, that's much better," I quipped, sliding him a dirty look. "Thanks for keeping it in perspective for me."

"That's what I'm here for." He unleashed one of his lethal smiles, the kind that lit up his eyes, drew out his dimples, and made the inside of my chest go light and tingly in a way I didn't appreciate at all. "Someone has to look out for my girl."

I drew a breath to remind him for the tenth time that I wasn't his girl, but the wrong words came out, and instead, I found myself blurting a question that I had been too afraid to ask until now. "Why didn't you tell me you could head-hop when you found out last year?"

His smile fell.

"I want to know," I pressed. I wasn't afraid of the answer anymore. Whatever he told me, however much the truth hurt, I needed to hear it so I could stop driving myself crazy wondering what had gone wrong, what I had done to make him stop trusting me. Because, clearly, he had, and I couldn't see why. I could kind of understand why he had broken up with me to date other girls. It sucked, and he was an idiot to think he could replace me, but most high school couples broke up when one of them went to college. It was practically inevitable. But for him to stop trusting me while we were still together? That didn't track. "Why did you keep it a secret? Did you think I would tell on you? Because if you thought for one second that I would snitch on you, then you never knew me at all."

"It wasn't that," he said. "I swear."

"Then what?"

He wet his lips and pulled in a long breath. "Because . . ." He paused, splaying one hand as if trying to magically summon the right words. "Because of the way I found out. It was unusual."

I wrinkled my forehead. "What does that mean?"

"I didn't find out like you did, on accident."

"So . . . you're saying you found out . . . on purpose?"

"Basically, yes."

I shook my head and tipped up a palm, more confused than ever.

Nash raised his face to the ceiling and groaned in frustration. I didn't understand what his problem was. All he had to do was tell me the truth. I hadn't asked him to explain advanced calculus to me.

"Just spit it out!" I ordered.

"I can't!"

"Yes, you can." I pointed at my mouth. "You open this thing and you make the words come out. It's not rocket surgery!"

"Rocket science," he corrected. "Or brain surgery."

"Damn it, Nash!" I shouted as my temper bubble burst. "Are you *trying* to piss me off? Because if so, you're doing a really good job. Five stars!"

"No!" he shouted back. "I'm trying to tell you that the secret wasn't mine to tell!"

"So what?" I demanded. And then I let out everything I had kept bottled up inside me. A truth of my own. The real reason his silence had bothered me so much. "You shouldn't have had secrets from me, especially not that one! I was an immersionist, too . . . *and* your girl-friend! Your loyalty should have been to *me*, not to anyone else! It was supposed to be you and me against the world! We used to be a team, Nash, and then you screwed it all up by shutting me out, even before you dumped me to date other people!" My eyes welled with hot tears. Tension built in my throat. I knew my voice would crack if I spoke again, but I didn't care. I wanted him to hear it. "I used to love you," I told him. "I loved you, and I trusted you, and you ruined everything!"

There was just enough time for hurt to register in Nash's gaze, and then my bedroom door swung open, and my father stood at the ready, assessing the situation while holding his borrowed attack dog by the collar.

"What's all this?" my dad asked, narrowing his eyes at Nash.

I wiped away my tears and said, "Nothing."

We all knew that wasn't true, but no one argued with me. My dad burned a glare into Nash's skull, a silent form of communicating that he hadn't forgotten the last time Nash had broken my heart, and that it had better not happen again. Though it already had. If my dad knew that this was Heartbreak 2.0, an attack dog would be the least of Nash's problems.

Nash mumbled something about needing to get back home to study, and then he hastily packed up his backpack and inched past my dad, who was still partially blocking the exit. On his way out the door, Nash patted our guest dog on the head, and in response, the dog licked Nash's hand and wagged its stumpy tail.

"Traitor," I said. I was talking to the dog. But if Nash overheard me, then that worked, too. He was the worst traitor of them all.

Chapter Fifteen

AS IF CHEATING DEATH AND DODGING A THIRD-degree felony wasn't stressful enough, I woke up the next morning and realized I had forgotten about my college-entrance exam, which was scheduled to take place two hours later at the high school. I had already taken the exam in the winter, but I wanted to try again for a higher score, and this was my last chance. Thankfully, the principal called to remind me that he'd arranged for a special proctor to administer the test for me in the conference room, otherwise I would have blitzed on the whole thing and ruined my shot at fall enrollment.

Assuming I wasn't in prison by then. Or in the afterlife.

So with zero prep time and my dad as my personal shadow for the day, I arrived at Harvey Davis High School and waited for the front office to buzz us in.

Mrs. Kazinski greeted me from her desk with a smile and a wave. "Hi there, Tia. Good to see you again, hon."

"You, too," I said, returning her grin. I felt a prickle of guilt, because I had also forgotten that Mrs. K. had gone to the police for help last week after her ex-husband had openly threatened to kill her. I meant to check in on Mrs. K. and her daughter to see if they were all right, but after confirming Mike Kazinski's alibi, I deleted him from my brain to focus on other suspects.

"How are you doing?" I asked. "Are you and Molly okay?"

"Oh, well, you know," she said in a fake positive, singsong tone, "we're taking it one day at a time. That's all any of us can do, right?"

For me, it was more like one minute at a time, but I nodded.

I found my dad a spot to hang out, and then I left him sitting outside the principal's office like an oversize troublemaker while I strode to the conference room to take my exam. Two hours and forty-five minutes later, I emerged, yawning and stretching, and feeling a little more confident in myself than not.

"How'd you do?" my dad asked.

I excitedly balled my fists. "I got the highest score in my class!"

"Really?" he asked.

"No, of course not." I shook my head at his gullibility. The results wouldn't come out for weeks. Plus, he should know me better than that. I had never brought home the highest score in any class, ever. When it came to school, my motto was *Cs get degrees.*

"Wiseass," he mumbled. "How do you *think* you did?"

I didn't know why he insisted on asking me that after every big test, as if my gut reaction were a Magic 8 Ball that could predict test scores. But I humored him. "I guess I did okay," I said. "The math section was hard, but I knew it would be, so that was no shock. . . ."

I trailed off as someone caught my eye.

A student had just walked into the office from the hallway. Whoever it was, they reminded me of the Unabomber, who we learned about in history class, or maybe a depressed ninja, draped from head to toe in a massively oversize black fleece hoodie and sweatpants, slumped over and dragging their scuffed-up sneakers toward Mrs. K.'s desk. The student walked with a slightly feminine sway in their hips, but underneath all that fleece, I couldn't make out who it was. It wasn't until they plopped down onto the chair next to Mrs. K.'s desk and lowered their hoodie that I realized the student was Molly Kazinski.

Holy shit. I blinked and did a double take.

Not to be mean, but Molly looked like fresh hell. Or rather *stale* hell, because there was nothing fresh about the greasy curtains of hair hanging in limp strands around her face. The shadows beneath her eyes had darkened a few shades since the day of Ben's funeral, and when she sensed me watching her and met my gaze, there was no spark behind her eyes. She simply regarded me for a few beats and then swiveled her gaze back to her mother. She didn't seem to recognize me at all, even though I was (allegedly) the person who had shot her godfather on live television. Maybe she had taken Ben's death harder than I'd thought.

"My stomach hurts," Molly droned to her mother. "Can I go home?"

Mrs. K. rested a hand on Molly's forehead. "You don't feel warm. Did you take anything? Tums or Pepto?"

"I took some Tums. They didn't help." Molly implored, "Please, I want to go home. Don't make me stay here."

"Of course, love," Mrs. K. told her. She glanced over her shoulder as if looking for someone. "None of my office aides are here today because of testing. Let me find someone to cover my desk, and I'll take you home."

"We can drive her," I volunteered, and tossed a glance at my dad. "Right? We don't have any plans after this. We're just going home. We can drop off Molly on our way."

"Sure," my dad said. "Not a problem."

Mrs. K. froze in hesitation for a long moment. I could tell from the pained expression on her face that she was trying to think of a polite reason to say no. Maybe I shouldn't have offered to help. To most of the outside world, I looked like a killer or a head-hopping freak. Just because Mrs. K. was nice to me didn't mean she trusted me. If our roles were reversed, I probably wouldn't want me spending time with my kid either.

I was thinking of a way to backpedal when Mrs. K. finally spoke up.

"Thanks, that would be great," she said, practically forcing the words past her teeth. She turned to Molly and asked, "Do you remember where the extra key is?"

"Uh-huh," Molly said. "Under the yellow flowerpot."

"That's right. Call me when you get home."

Molly agreed. Mrs. K. gave her daughter a list of instructions—replace the key under the flowerpot, lock the dead bolt, don't answer the door for anyone, eat some saltine crackers, and go straight to bed. Then she kissed Molly on the head and sent us on our way.

I figured Molly would feel more comfortable by herself in the backseat, so I rode shotgun while my dad drove to the address Mrs. K. had given him. Molly barely made a sound as the miles passed. She stared out the window for most of the ride, and then out of nowhere, she piped up and said, "Hey, Tia?"

I turned around to face her. "Yeah?"

"Can I ask you something?"

"Of course," I said. "What's up?"

"Do you still take clients?"

Her question shocked a smile out of me. I hadn't seen that coming. "Uh, no, not really. Not right now, at least. I'm taking a break until things calm down."

"I get it," she said, and returned her gaze to the window. "The last time you head-hopped, it didn't go too well for you, did it?"

"No, it didn't," I told her.

My dad snorted in agreement.

"I used to hear rumors about you," she went on. "I mean, not about *you*. I never knew your name. No one did. But people talked for a long time about a head-hopper who went to our school and did jobs for people, on the cheap."

On the cheap? I had considered my rates fair, but clearly I had undersold myself.

"I wanted to find you," she added. "But I didn't know who you were."

"Well, I'll make you a deal," I told her. "If I'm ever ready to get back in the business, you'll be at the top of my list. I'll even give you my old rate."

"Mm-kay, thanks," she said, and then she went silent for the rest of the trip.

We pulled up alongside a small but tidy brick Cape Cod with an immaculate lawn and flower beds teeming with colorful blossoms. On the front stoop stood three flowerpots, one of them yellow. Molly thanked us for the ride, and then she shuffled up the sidewalk to the yellow flowerpot, retrieved the key from underneath it, and let herself inside the house.

"Strange kid," my dad said as we drove away. "Wonder why she wanted to hire you."

"Yeah," I told him. Now that he mentioned it, so did I.

. . .

That afternoon, Val and I kicked back on my bed with two bowls of popcorn, and I filled her in on everything she had missed, including the biking adventures of Richard Franco, the details I learned about the Tesla driver, and my epic blowout with Nash.

"Wow," she said, her eyes wide. "I was only gone for a day."

"I know, right?" I told her. "You got to keep up if you want to hang with me. Time moves at warp speed in my world."

"It really does," she agreed. "The universe must be fast-tracking your education."

"Sweet! Now I can finally say I'm in an accelerated class."

She laughed. "Too bad it won't count toward college." It sounded like a joke, but knowing Val, she was being serious. "So," she said, switching gears with a heavier tone, "how did you leave things with Nash?"

"Ugh." I shoved in a mouthful of flavorless homemade popcorn, the only kind I could eat. I'd break into hives if I added anything to make it taste good. I cast an envious glance at Val's bowl and tried to pretend I was chewing her salted, buttery snack instead of mine. It didn't work. "Nowhere," I said. "He walked out, and that was that."

"No texts?" she asked. "No DMs or anything?"

"Nothing." I picked up a piece of popcorn and let it fall back into the bowl. "But I didn't expect him to. What's he going to say?" I deepened my voice and did my best Nash impersonation. "'Hey, girl, sorry I made you fall in love with me and convinced you we were a

super-solid power couple, and then stabbed you in the back by protecting someone else's feelings instead of yours . . . and then dumping
you to date random college girls, like you're totally replaceable and
what we had was never even special at all. Anyway, here's a free cou-
pon to punch me in the dick.'"

Val giggled. "Yeah, I can't picture him saying that."

"Me neither."

There were two light knocks at the door.

"Come in," I said, expecting my dad.

But instead of my father, Nash walked in, wearing a ball cap and
an awkward grin, a faint stain of color darkening his cheeks. "You can
punch me if you want," he said. "But keep it above the waist. My dick
isn't the bad guy here."

At the sight of him, my heart thumped with a mixture of emotions,
some of them good, some of them . . . uncomfortable. I couldn't label
exactly what I was feeling, and I had no idea what to say to him except
"You were listening."

"Well, yeah, it's hard not to," he told me, and closed the door
behind him like this was any other day. "You're loud talkers. Take it
down a decibel or two the next time you want to have a conversation
about my junk."

Val and I traded a glance, and in an instant, a wordless conversation passed between us. Nash wanted to pretend like nothing had
happened. That meant I could either accept his olive branch and
sweep yesterday's fight under the rug. Or I could do what I really
wanted to do: shake out the rug and smack him in the face with the
tassels. Not my best metaphor, but I was done pretending with him.

"I'm surprised you came," I told Nash. "After what went down
yesterday."

He blew out a hard breath and slanted me a look, finally dropping the oblivious act. "You yelled at me. I deserved it." He flung a hand in the air. "Big deal. It changes nothing. You need my help, and I'm not going to turn my back on you just because we had an argument. Give me some credit, T. I'm not a total asshole."

"Just a partial one?" I asked.

He pressed his lips together and clenched his jaw for a beat or two. "Yeah," he finally said. "A partial one." He turned his gaze to the floor. "Look, I know I screwed up. I would take it back if I could. I would take it *all* back if I could. I might be twenty percent asshole, but the other eighty percent wants to make it up to you." He glanced at me just long enough to reveal a hint of tenderness in his deep brown eyes. "Is that enough?"

Honestly, no, it wasn't enough. Not even close. I wanted more—the answers to my questions, an explanation for why he hadn't trusted me with the truth, whose secrets he was still protecting, some sort of understanding that would make *me* feel safe enough to trust *him* again. But when he looked up and peered at me beneath the fringe of those dark lashes, he unraveled every argument on my tongue.

I couldn't tell him no. So I nodded.

After that, the mood was awkward as hell.

Nash sat in his spot on the floor and unzipped his backpack while Val and I fidgeted with our popcorn bowls and avoided each other's eyes. None of us spoke. I remembered how weird the vibe had felt yesterday without Val there to defuse the tension between me and Nash. Now that the three of us were together again, the situation seemed worse. With Nash in the room, I couldn't relax and have fun with Val. And with Val in the room, I couldn't hash things out and clear the air with Nash.

Luckily, my phone buzzed with an incoming call. I checked the screen and found *unknown number*. I didn't usually answer junk calls, but at the moment, I would take any distraction I could get.

"Hello?"

"Hey, it's me," said a deep male voice. "Blade."

Blade Romanovitch? My life really was full of surprises today.

"How'd you get my number?" I asked.

"Does it matter?"

"No, I guess not. What do you want?"

"The favor you owe me," he said.

"Seriously?" I asked, my voice raising an octave. "You're cashing in now?"

"That's what I just said, isn't it?"

"Hey, don't be salty," I chided. His timing sucked, but I kept that detail to myself. Maybe the favor would be something easy that I could do from home. "Just tell me what you need."

"I can't talk about it on the phone. Someone might be listening."

"But it's legal, right?"

"Yes, oh my god, it's legal. Don't be such a prude. I'll tell you about it when you get here. I'm texting you my address."

"To your house?"

"No, to Disney World," he said sarcastically. "I want to ride the teacups."

"Forget it," I told him. I had no intention of ending up on a *Dateline* episode anytime soon. "You can come here."

"Seriously, grow up, Tia," he told me. "If I wanted you dead, your severed body parts would already be stuffed inside a garbage bag and sinking to the bottom of the lake."

"As charming as that sounds," I said, "it doesn't make me feel better."

He released a growl through the phone. "You're a real pain in the ass, Tia Dante. Has anyone ever told you that?"

"Nope," I lied. "Not one person."

"I don't believe you."

"That's not my problem."

He swore under his breath. "Fine, we can meet in public. Half an hour in the parking lot behind Saint Valliant's. Don't be late."

"You don't get it," I told him. "I can't leave the house. My dad has me on lockdown because the same person who killed Ben Mitchell is trying to—"

"That's not *my* problem," he interrupted. "You owe me a debt, and now you're going to pay up. I expect to see you in half an hour. Figure it out."

Before I could argue with him, he hung up.

Chapter Sixteen

I WHISPERED A SWEAR. "CAN THIS DAY *GET* ANY worse?"

"Don't ask that!" Val held up an index finger. "Never ask that! You're inviting trouble into your life."

Too late. Trouble had already invited itself . . . and brought along a few friends named Danger, Anxiety, and the Possibility of Ending Up Inside a Hefty Bag at the Bottom of the Lake. I explained the situation as briefly as I could to Val and Nash. If nothing else, talking about my newest crisis broke the tension in the room.

"Ooof," Nash said, making a face. "Promising a favor to a Russian mobster was *not* one of your better ideas, T."

"You think?" I quipped. "Criticize me later. Right now, I need solutions."

"All right, first things first," he said. "Is it possible Blade is lying to you about calling in your favor? Do you think he's luring you into this meeting so he can make you disappear or something?"

I shook my head. Blade had known my address and studied my

movements for long enough to "disappear" me a dozen times by now. He was plenty capable of murder, but I doubted he would kill me in the Saint Valliant's parking lot, or even at his house. He was smart— too smart to commit a crime anywhere the cops could place him. Plus, his ankle monitor tracked his movements, assuming his new parole officer hadn't taken a bribe and disabled it.

"I really believe he wants something from me," I said. "I just don't know what it is." I checked the time on my phone. "And I have twenty-seven minutes and ten seconds until I'm supposed to meet him."

"What if you just don't go?" Val asked. "Or call him back and tell him he has to wait for his favor? Do you think he'll actually hurt you if you don't show up?"

I wanted to say no. Blade had never hurt me. But I also wanted Santa Claus to be real and for climate change to be a hoax. "It's possible, but I'd rather not take the risk if I can help it."

"Then there's only one thing to do," Nash said. "You have to meet him."

"But how?" I asked. "Even if I can sneak past my dad, I won't get very far before he hears me start my car and chases me down the street."

"And then there are the reporters," Val pointed out. "And the news vans."

"And their drones," I added. "There's no outrunning them."

"But they don't follow me," Val said. "We could take my van. If no one sees you get in, you could hide in the back until we're far enough away that you're out of range. Then I can drive you to the meeting."

"That could work." There was only one snag. "But I'm pretty sure Blade wants me to come alone."

"So I'll drop you off around the corner," she suggested. "And hang out and wait for you to text me when you're ready to be picked up."

"All right, that's enough," Nash said, waving dismissively at us. "I'm gonna stop you both right there. You're *way* overcomplicating this. There's an obvious solution right in front of you. All you have to do is open your eyes."

"Well then," I said. "Enlighten us, oh great one."

"It's easy." He tipped up his palms. "Trade bodies with me."

I blinked for a moment. I had never considered going to the meeting in a different body.

"Think about it," he said, and began ticking items on his fingers. "Your dad won't bat an eye when I leave. He low-key hates me."

"High-key," I corrected. "Medium at best."

"Okay, he medium- to high-key hates me," Nash said. "My point is he'll be happy to watch me walk out the door. The press doesn't give two shits about me, so you can take my car, and no one will follow you. And the best part is you won't have to worry about some psychopath stealing your body and taking it for another joyride, because you won't be empty. I'll be inside you." His mouth slid into a lecherous grin, his eyebrows waggling. "Again."

"But this time for longer than two minutes?" I asked.

Val snickered.

Nash made a wounded sound and clapped a hand over his heart. He grinned at me because we both knew that duration had never been a problem for him. "Just admit it, T. You can't wait to use me for my body."

I refused to add any more fuel to Nash's ego by telling him he was right, but his idea checked every box. Still, I held up a palm in a *let's-be-serious* motion, because I didn't know if Nash had considered the possible consequences of his idea. Trading bodies was always a risk, and in this case, Nash would carry the risk alone. My body would stay safe and protected right there in my bedroom. But his would go out into the night to do whatever sketchy mystery errands Blade had in mind.

"Before we commit to anything," I said. "I want you to really think about it. What if something goes wrong while I'm in your body? What if I get killed or I don't make it back? You would have to live as me forever. You'd be trapped in my body for the rest of your life. Are you okay with that?"

"Well, it *is* a bangin' bod . . ." he teased.

"I mean it, Nash," I told him. "You're not just loaning me your car. This is a big deal, and I need to know that you're really okay with it."

"Yes, T, I'm cool with it. I swear." His smile softened into something akin to a promise. "I keep trying to tell you. Someone has to look out for my girl."

An unexpected wave of flutters broke out in my chest. I wished Nash would stop calling me his girl. It hit me every time, and I had a feeling he knew it, which was why he kept pushing my buttons. Kind of like a little boy tugging on a girl's ponytail to get a rise out of her. But what annoyed me most of all was that I kept falling for it. The fact that my body gave him a reaction was proof that part of me wanted to be his girl again, and that made me feel like a loser, because *he* had dumped *me*. He had taken me for granted, and according to the law of Bad Bitches, I should have had my glow-up a long time ago and left his memory in the dust.

"I'm not your girl," I corrected him. And then I warned, "I'm picking up a box of donuts on my way to the meeting. You don't know it yet, but there's type 2 diabetes in your future."

"Do your worst," he dared.

"Challenge accepted."

I glanced at the time. Donuts or not, we would need to hurry. I went through my usual mental checklist for preparing to leave my body and realized I needed to take a bathroom break. I made a quick trip to the restroom and then returned to Nash and Val.

"See this bladder?" I asked Nash, pointing at my lower abdomen. "It's one hundred percent empty. That means there's no reason for you to remove these shorts after I leave. Or any other articles of clothing." Another possibility occurred to me, and I told him, "And no playing with my boobs!"

"You don't have to worry, T," he said. "I won't fondle your goods."

"I'll make sure of it," Val promised.

"I won't fondle yours either," I said to Nash.

"Oh, you can feel me up all you want." He winked. "I give you consent."

I rolled my eyes and held out a hand for his car keys. He tossed them over to me, and I added, "Your phone, too. We need to trade, or else our facial recognition won't work. I'll text Blade about the body switch when I'm on my way."

At that, Nash's playful smirk fell. "Why can't we keep our own phones? We can go into security settings and add a passcode for each other. Or a new face ID."

"There's no time for that," I said. I had less than five minutes to leave the house if I wanted to make a stop for donuts first—which I absolutely did. I rested my phone on the nightstand and made a *gimme* motion for his. "Come on. Give it up."

He hesitated.

"Seriously?" I asked. "You're cool with me borrowing your body to do errands for a Russian gangster, but you draw the line at letting me use your phone?"

Val and I shared a glance. He was probably hiding nudes of college girls.

"And you tell *me* to grow up," I said to him. "Just give me your phone, and stop being a baby about it."

"All right, fine, just a sec." He unlocked his phone and made a couple of swipes and taps, obviously deleting whatever incriminating evidence he hadn't wanted me to see. "There," he said, shoving it back in his pocket. "You'll have it when we switch. Knock yourself out."

I wondered if he realized there was no such thing as truly erasing his activity from a device. I knew half a dozen ways to retrieve deleted files, pictures, messages, and apps from his hardware and his cloud account. If I wanted to, I could dig up every gritty molecule of dirt that Nash had tried to hide from me. The question was: Did I want to?

I would think about that later.

For now, I leaned back on my side of the bed with my head resting against my pillow. Nash settled beside me while Val stood at the foot of the bed and peered at us with interest. I had never traded bodies with another immersionist. I assumed it would work the same way as it had with my clients. I would enter the room inside Nash's mind and then send him . . . into the closet? No, that wouldn't work. That would keep him in there. Maybe he should enter a room inside *my* mind. But then what?

"How are we gonna do this?" I asked him. "I've only shared a body. I've never swapped one out."

"I've done it both ways," he said. I waited for him to elaborate on who he had shared and traded with, but he didn't. He reached out for my hand, and I clasped it. "It's super easy. We're going to count down from three to one, and then at the same time, you'll move your mental energy into my head, and I'll move mine into yours. It's that simple."

I wasn't sure I believed him.

"Really," he insisted. "And if we don't get it right the first time, it's no big deal. The worst thing that can happen is both of us end up inside the same head. Then one of us will push the other out, and we'll try again."

"Okay." I pulled in a deep, calming breath. "Val, will you count us down?"

"Sure," she said. "Are you ready?"

"I'm ready," I told her.

"Me, too," Nash said.

"Okay, switch on 'one,'" Val reminded us. "Three . . . two . . . one."

I concentrated on Nash, imagining myself leaving my mind and traveling into his head. My fingertips tingled, the usual sign of disconnect, and then my skin went numb as I floated out of my body. The resistance that sometimes pushed against me when I entered a client's mind didn't exist now. I drifted into Nash effortlessly, as if his body wanted me there. A moment later, my limbs felt several pounds heavier than before, and I recognized the sensation of soft bedding underneath me. When I opened my eyes, I found myself on the other side of the mattress. The hand I lifted in front of me belonged to Nash.

"Wow," I said, startling myself with the low timbre of his voice. That would take some getting used to. So would the faint tugging that drew me to my own body, though that would fade with distance. "You weren't kidding. That was easier than I thought."

"You're welcome," he said. The sound of my voice seemed to startle him, too, because he grimaced. "Okay, that's freaky." He made another face and then sat up and scanned my body. He used one hand to pat me down as if frisking me for a weapon. "Why does everything hurt?"

"What do you mean?" I asked.

"I mean it hurts in here," he complained. "My stomach, my lower back, my neck." He rotated his (my) head and massaged one shoulder. "Damn, T, your traps are like bricks. Do you ever stretch?"

I tipped up both palms. "Nothing was wrong with me before we switched."

"Are you telling me you always feel like this?"

Val smiled at him. "Congratulations, Nash. You're a woman now."

"Oh, right," I said, remembering where I was in my cycle. "I get, like, one good week out of the month, and this definitely isn't it. I'm hard-core PMSing. That's why you have cramps. They start early for me."

"In my back, too?" he asked.

"Yeah. You'll get used to it."

"Awesome," he said flatly. Then he jutted out his lower lip and whined, "I really want a donut."

I burst out in laughter. Finally someone understood my struggle. I sat up and lightly socked him in the upper arm. "Sucks to be you!"

"Ouch!" He rubbed his bicep. "Watch it. You're punching outside your weight class."

"Oh, is this the part where I'm supposed to say I don't know my own strength?"

"Whatever," he muttered. "You're the one who's gonna have a bruise tomorrow."

Val swept her hand toward the door in a reminder to get going.

I stood up from the bed faster than I should have and stumbled over my massive feet before righting myself. I took a moment to bounce up and down on my sneakers and pump both arms, acclimating myself to the power in my new limbs. The energy was incredible. Each muscle movement propelled me into the air with barely any effort at all. I felt like I could parkour to the meeting. Whatever Nash had eaten that day, it was really paying off.

It almost made me want to skip the donuts.

Almost.

On my way out the door, Nash pointed at me. "Hey, I have a new appreciation for that body," he said. "Take care of it, will you?"

"I'll do my best," I promised, and added a wink. "If you're lucky, I might even give it back to you."

Chapter Seventeen

VAL MIGHT HAVE BEEN ONTO SOMETHING WHEN she had warned me not to ask the universe how my day could get any worse. Because as I drove Nash's mammoth pimp wagon across town, every single one of my donut detours led to failure. A power outage had shut down the Krispy Kreme. The town's fancy bakery, Sweet Cheeks, had closed at 5 p.m. The local coffee shop only stocked "artisan pastries" for hipsters who were too pretentious to eat real food. In a last-ditch effort, I even tried the grocery store bakery, but I struck out there, too. And because I had spent so long looking for donuts, now there was no time for me to stop for a backup treat like a cupcake or a brownie sundae.

I whimpered as I turned onto the employee parking lot behind Saint Valliant's. Maybe I could reward myself with a milkshake on the way home. McDonald's stayed open late. Though with my luck, the ice-cream machine would probably be broken.

I spotted Blade standing beside his motorcycle with his mus-cled arms tightly folded across his chest, his booted feet planted in a defensive stance. He eyed the Plymouth warily and reached one hand for the weapon that was doubtlessly hidden beneath his leather riding jacket. I kept my distance and parked on the opposite side of the lot, far enough away that Blade couldn't identify me. I tried texting and returning his call to let him know about the body switch, but the number he used didn't work. So for my first trick, I had to convince him that the tall, dark stranger lurking behind the steering wheel was actually me.

Preferably before he fired any shots.

I rolled down the window and held up both hands. "It's me," I hollered in Nash's baritone. "Tia Dante."

Blade cocked his head aside and shouted, "Bullshit." Then he told me to go do something to myself that was equal parts vulgar and anatomically impossible.

"I mean it," I said. Keeping both hands visible, I stepped out of the car and used my hip to shut the door. I approached Blade slowly, as though he were a wounded animal. When he reached for his gun, I stopped. "This is my friend's body," I explained. "I had to borrow it to get out of the house. Remember I told you my dad put me on lockdown? Plus, the news vans follow me everywhere. This was the only way to meet you on short notice with no one trailing me."

Blade pinched his eyebrows together in consideration.

"I'll prove it," I told him. "Ask me something that only I would know."

"All right." He moved his hand away from his holster and gripped his hips. "Tell me about the time we were filing papers in Samantha's office and you bent over in your short skirt and flashed me your bare ass."

I grinned at him. "You wish."

"What?" he asked innocently.

"As fun as that sounds for you, we both know it didn't happen," I said. "First of all, our supervisor is Sue, not Samantha. And we weren't filing papers in her office. We were sorting gross clothes in the back room. I wasn't wearing a skirt, and I didn't moon you. I lifted up my T-shirt to prove I wasn't wearing a wire. And nothing was bare. I was wearing a bra, thank you very much." I pointed at him, remembering the best part. "And you laughed! You looked at my boobs, and you actually laughed!"

He chuckled and scratched the back of his neck, regarding me with a fresh gaze. "I wasn't laughing at you. You surprised me, is all. Your boobs are . . . pretty nice."

"Pretty nice?" I quipped. "Please, Blade, enough with the flattery. You're gonna make me blush."

"Oh, yeah, that's definitely you in there."

"I'm glad you believe me," I said. "Now we can get down to business, and you can tell me what *totally legal* favor you want me to do."

A pair of lines creased his forehead, and he exhaled hard as if gearing himself up for an unpleasant task. Even though we were alone, he scanned the parking lot twice before he spoke. "It's big, this thing I need from you. Really big. I'm trusting you not to screw it up."

"You're trusting me?" I had no idea why. He barely knew me. "Not a lot of people do these days."

He lifted a massive shoulder. "I can tell you're a good person." He jabbed a finger at me and clarified, "*Annoying* . . . but good. I've been around enough ugliness to tell when someone has it in them and when they don't. You don't. I knew it the day we met."

That almost sounded like a compliment. His praise caught me off guard, and then I noticed something about Blade that I had missed before. It was his eyes, as vivid and blue as ever, but now filled with a hint more vulnerability than cunning. That small difference made me notice other changes in him, too. Somehow the angles of his face had softened, even though he wore the same straight nose and high cheekbones as the last time I had seen him. I knew logically that Blade's features hadn't changed, but he seemed different to me now, more human, less Terminator.

"Thank you," I told him.

"Yeah, well, I'm not saying I trust you to keep your mouth shut to the cops." He lifted his jean hem to show me his ankle monitor. "I already know you have snitch tendencies. I'll just be careful what I tell you."

"Oh my god, I'm not a snitch," I objected.

"Yeah, you kind of are, but that doesn't matter," he said. "What matters is I need you to have my back tonight."

"I'll do my best," I told him. "But I have no idea what that looks like."

He licked his lips in a beat of hesitation. "Okay, so, you probably know what my dad does for a living."

"I've heard rumors."

He flashed a palm. "I'm not saying what you heard is true."

"How would you know what I heard?" I asked. "I didn't tell you."

He huffed a laugh. "All right, so tell me, smart-ass."

"Well, word on the street is . . ." I leaned in, cupping a hand around my mouth. "Your dad runs a pizza shop."

Blade's laughter deepened and filled the air, and then he flashed me the first real smile I had ever seen on his face. "Yeah, that's right. You nailed it. He works in a family-owned pizzeria that specializes in extra-spicy Russian side dishes."

"Okay," I said. So now that we had established a metaphor to describe the Russian mafia's illegal gambling ring, we could talk about Blade's dad without openly acknowledging him as a criminal. But I wondered what gambling had to do with me. "I hope you're not asking me to work in your dad's pizza shop, because I won't do it."

"No, no." Blade shook his head. "You would make a lousy cook. You don't know the secret family recipe."

"Okay . . . so what's the issue?"

"The issue is I *do* know the recipe," Blade said. "And my dad expects me to take over the shop for him so he can move down to Florida and set up a new pizza place. Old folks love eating pizza. It's one of the few things they can do anymore. They can't get high or have wild sex, and none of them can handle their liquor. Pizza's the only vice they have left. Old fogies will sit around on their scooters or in their adjustable beds and blow their kids' inheritance on . . . uh . . . anchovies . . . and extra cheese. Anyway, there's a high demand for pizza in the retirement villages down south. Lots of cash to be made."

"Huh," I said. Elderly folks loved to gamble? Who knew? "Seems like a solid business plan."

Blade picked at his cuticles. "I guess. If you're into pizza."

"You're not?"

"Would *you* be?"

"No," I said. "But I didn't grow up baking dough and cooking marinara sauce. You've been making pizza since you were a kid. I figured you liked it."

"I don't." A shadow seemed to pass over his face. "The sauce is messy, and it stains my shirts. And grinding pepperoni sausage is the worst. I've only done it a few times, but I know I'll never get used to it. I hate that part. I don't want to do it ever again."

I cringed, and with tremendous effort, resisted the urge to ask him if grinding pepperoni had anything to do with sunken garbage bags at the bottom of the lake. I didn't want my suspicions confirmed. "Okay, so, from what you're telling me, it sounds like you don't want to take over the family business."

"I don't."

"What do you want to do instead?"

He patted his motorcycle seat. "I want to work on bikes. Harleys, mostly, but I can fix just about any small engine. I took a class in prison, and I was good at it. I want to learn the business side of things, too, how to go legit, so I can run my own garage someday."

"Good for you," I said, and I meant it. "That's way better than making pizza."

"Yeah." Blade scratched the back of his head. "But my dad doesn't know."

"You haven't told him?"

He shook his head.

"Why not?" I asked. "Are you afraid you'll, uh, get the 'pepperoni experience' if you try to leave the business?"

Blade drew back. "Jesus, Tia. How can you even ask me that? He's my dad. What kind of monsters do you think we are?"

"I keep telling you I don't know anything about pizza!"

"Okay, well, we don't *pepperoni* our own!"

"Fine. Then what's stopping you from talking to your dad?"

"It's complicated," Blade said. "That's where you come in."

I shook my head. I didn't follow.

"Because you're a head-hopper," he added.

It took me another beat or two to figure out exactly what he wanted from me. Then realization struck, and my eyebrows jumped up my forehead so fast they might have left track marks.

"*That's* the favor?" I asked in disbelief. "You're too scared to tell your dad the truth, so you want me to do it for you?"

Color flooded Blade's cheeks. He dropped his gaze, and I instantly wished I could take back what I had said, or at least the way I had said it.

"I'm sorry," I told him. "I didn't mean for it to come out like that. It's just . . . you can practically bench-press a car, so I figured . . ." I trailed off before I could make an even bigger jerk out of myself by saying "*You're not afraid of anything.*" Of course Blade had fears. His size and his strength didn't make him a robot.

"I wanted to tell him myself," Blade said. "I tried a bunch of times. But it's like my brain shuts off. Even when I practice what to say, the words won't come out." He fisted one hand and smacked his temple. "I don't know what's wrong with me."

I did. And I should have figured it out sooner.

Ever since I started my side hustle, my most popular job had been delivering news that parents didn't want to hear. At first I hadn't understood why. Whenever I upset my dad, which was a regularly scheduled event, he lectured me about it. And if I *really* pissed him off, he took my car keys or my cell phone, or changed the Wi-Fi password. But that was it. He didn't throw tantrums or call me a bitch. He didn't give me the silent treatment or threaten to kick me out of the house. He didn't chip away at my self-esteem by telling me I was stupid or a failure or a sinner. Even Val's parents, who had once gotten so high they had nearly drowned in a five-gallon bucket, had never bullied her.

But working with my clients had taught me that not everyone had bare minimum emotional safety, and by *bare minimum*, I meant parents who didn't use abuse to control their kids. My definition of decency had set the bar pretty low, and still, people surprised me by bending over backward to limbo under it. The truth was assholes made babies, too—a lot of them—and in those cases, there was no hate like parental love.

Blade didn't feel safe enough to disappoint his father.

I could help with that.

"I'm in," I told him. "I guess I'm going to your house after all."

He dipped his chin in a silent *thanks.* "I won't forget this."

"But first you have to promise me that nothing will happen to my friend's body," I said, indicating Nash's face. "This is a loaner. My friend did me a solid by letting me use it, and I don't feel good about leaving him lying around empty while I'm inside your head."

"He'll be safe," Blade said. "There's no business at the house tonight, and even if someone decides to show up, they won't get past the gate. It's easier to break into Fort Knox than into my dad's place."

I supposed that made sense. "Your dad's not going to hit me, is he? I can take a punch, but I'd rather dodge it if I can."

"Nah," Blade said. "He stopped hitting when I was big enough to hit back."

Charming. "All right. Then tell me everything I need to know."

Chapter Eighteen

TO GIVE US MORE TIME TO TALK, BLADE SUGGESTED we leave his motorcycle in the Saint Valliant's parking lot and take Nash's car to his house. So we piled into the Plymouth, and we headed toward the rich side of town, where Blade lived in a gated compound with his father and their full-time housekeeper, a forty-something-year-old woman named Marta.

During the ride, Blade filled me in on the details I would need to pass myself off as him without raising any red flags. Usually I would insist on budgeting multiple days to learn about my clients and their families, but in this case, I would have to make do. I couldn't borrow Nash's body forever.

"Here, turn right," Blade said, pointing at an unmarked private driveway that led to a wrought-iron gate about twenty yards in the distance. When we pulled up to the security keypad, Blade entered the code, and then we motored through the gateway until the drive split in two directions. "Make another right," he told me. "Keep going until you see the pool house at the back of the property. That's where I stay."

"What's to the left?" I asked in Nash's deep voice, peering out my window at the leafy wall of trees that lined the driveway. The sun had nearly set, but its purple glow lingered in the sky. If I squinted, I could just make out a steeply pitched roof line beyond the trees.

"That's the main house."

"Oh, the *main* house," I mimicked in a bad British accent. "You didn't tell me you live on a whole estate, Bruce Wayne."

"I keep telling you there's big money in pizza."

He wasn't kidding.

I followed the driveway to an Olympic-size swimming pool that stood adjacent to a charming little storybook cottage, complete with its own flower garden and a winding stone path from the parking pad to the front door. A decorative wooden sign staked in the grass read ALL ARE WELCOME, which I doubted was true, but still. The pool house was ripped straight out of a Disney movie.

"This is where you live?" I asked, stopping the car. "Do birds fly in through the window to brush your hair in the morning?"

"Yeah, they do," Blade said flatly. "Then the mice cook me breakfast, and I send out my chipmunk buddies to beat the shit out of people who order pizza and don't pay for it."

"I would choose raccoons for that." I turned off the ignition and added, "Or geese. Have you ever seen one in action? Geese have no chill. They will mess you up."

"Swans are worse."

"Really?"

He pulled down his T-shirt collar and showed me a thin, silvery scar, roughly an inch wide on his upper chest.

"A swan did that?" I asked.

"When I was five."

"That must have hurt."

"Not as bad as it did for the swan," he said. "My dad broke its neck in three places and then fed it to the dogs."

On that chipper note, we made our way inside the pool house.

As soon as I stepped through the door, all traces of fairy-tale enchantment vanished, replaced by the smell of sweaty socks and Axe body spray in the air, dirty laundry and take-out boxes littering the floor, and posters of Harley-straddling bikini babes tacked to the walls. In the center of the room stood a queen-size bed covered in rumpled black linens. Mounted on the opposite wall was a flat-screen TV connected to a gaming system with a steering wheel and assorted controllers strewn about. A snack bar lined with three wooden stools divided the sleeping area from the kitchen. Ironically, the kitchen was the cleanest part of the house . . . or maybe *un*ironically, because Blade didn't strike me as the kind of guy who liked to cook.

"This makes a lot more sense," I said, pointing all around the man cave. "Now I can believe you live here."

He kicked a girlie magazine under the bed. "Sorry, it's not usually this messy."

I didn't believe that for one second. "So do you think your dad will let you stay? After I tell him the truth?"

"I don't know. I hope so. But if not, I'll deal."

"You might want to pack a bag, just in case," I suggested. "I've done this before, and it's not always pretty."

He pulled a duffel out of his closet and stuffed it with clothes, toiletries, and a metal lockbox that he retrieved from some hiding place. Then he brushed his hands together as if to say *All done.*

"Now what?" he asked.

"Now we get comfortable." I hastily made the bed by pulling the comforter over the sheets and pillows. "I'll try not to think about the last time you washed this blanket."

We settled face-up on the bed, much like Nash and I had done, but leaving a lot more space between us. I scooted closer to Blade to make physical contact, but each time I moved toward him, he inched away. I understood the weirdness of seeing me in Nash's body, but if Blade retreated any farther, he would fall off the bed.

"This doesn't make you gay," I pointed out. "I'm still a girl, and even if I wasn't, it's okay for two guys to lie down next to each other."

"I know that!"

"Then get closer to me."

"How close?"

"Close enough for our shoulders to touch," I said. "I need to be able to feel how fast you're breathing and how tense your muscles are so I'll know when you're relaxed enough for me to go inside you."

"Go inside me?" he repeated. "Can you *please* not say it like that?"

"Oh, my god, just get over here."

He inched his way to the middle of the bed, and I made up the rest of the distance until our arms pressed together. His body was clenched tighter than a cinder block, so I told him to close his eyes, and then I distracted him by explaining the process of immersion. My chatter seemed to relax him, and by the time I was finished describing the last step, he had unwound enough to move into the deep-breathing stage. From there, I was able to transfer my consciousness into the imaginary room inside his mind.

I knocked at the pretend door.

"Whoa," he said, his eyes wide as he answered. "You look like you."

"Because I *am* me," I told him, now using my own voice. "That's what I keep trying to make you understand. Even when I'm in a different body, I'm always the same Tia."

"Yeah, sure, I know," he said. "But I like it when your inside matches your outside. It's less freaky that way."

I couldn't argue with that. I pointed at the walk-in closet. "Do you remember what you're supposed to do?"

"Go in there and chill until you tell me to come out."

"That's right," I said. "Are you ready?"

"I guess so."

His answer didn't fill me with confidence. "Are you sure? Is there anything else I need to know before I talk to your dad?"

Blade shook his head. "You should be fine. Just keep it short."

I had planned to.

"And be careful," Blade added, a hint of fear and hesitation in his voice. "This is my life, you know what I mean?"

I knew exactly what he meant. In giving me control of his body, he also gave me power over his heart. Blade's father was the only family he had. That connection mattered as much to him as breathing.

"I'm good at what I do," I reminded him. "I got this."

He backed toward the closet and then gave me a nod good-bye before he opened the door and disappeared inside. All alone inside his mind, I turned my focus to the physical sensations of his body: the heat radiating from his skin, the heavy pulse at his throat, the tight denim gripping his thighs. When I felt firmly rooted in his flesh, I opened my eyes and drew my first breath as Blade Romanovitch.

I sat up, noticing a high-pitched ringing in my ears. Blade had a wicked case of tinnitus, probably from riding his loud-ass motorcycle without using hearing protection. I wondered if the ringing bothered him or if he had gotten used to it.

I wiggled a pinkie finger in my ear and swung both legs over the side of the bed. My left knee ached when I stood up, so I rotated to the side to pop it. As I stretched my massive arms over my head, a few more of my joints popped. I didn't feel the same rush of energy that I had experienced in Nash's body. Blade was more sluggish, similar to me in my own skin. He wouldn't be running any marathons, but the power in his limbs was the closest I would ever come to feeling like a superhero.

Just for fun, I crossed to the other side of the bed and lifted Nash's vacant body off the mattress. The act was effortless, like picking up a textbook. I set Nash back down and straightened his neck and limbs, and then I made a quick detour to the bathroom to flex in the mirror.

Don't judge me.

It was weirdly satisfying to show off for myself. I whistled at the reflection of my rounded, rock-hard biceps and my bulging forearms, and then I tightened my chest and watched my pecs move back and forth in a twitchy little dance. I didn't think Blade would mind if I snuck a peek at his six-pack, but when I lifted his T-shirt hem, I could swear that I counted more than six of them.

"Damn, Blade," I muttered in his voice. "Save some abs for the rest of us."

I smoothed down his T-shirt and ran a hand through his thick black hair to make him more presentable, and then I stopped playing around and got to work. Blade had told me to look for his father in the study, which was located on the first floor of the main house. To get there, I would follow the sidewalk from the pool to the house, and then enter the kitchen through the back door.

That sounded easy enough.

As I strode along the sidewalk, I rehearsed the Russian greeting I would use when I met Blade's dad. Thankfully, Blade didn't speak much Russian, so I only had to remember a few key words and phrases. The trick was getting the accent right. Blade had also prepared me to cross paths with the housekeeper, Marta, who apparently didn't like him and communicated through glares instead of actual language. That was fine with me. One less thing to remember.

The main house loomed ahead, a multistory Swiss chalet-style home that belonged on a ski resort instead of a small-town gated compound. Flowering hibiscus bushes flanked the entrance to a patio of hand-laid stone, while above it, a lattice of wisteria blossoms glowed behind the rising moon. Hidden outdoor speakers played a soothing guitar rendition of "Edelweiss," and I half expected Julie Andrews to twirl around the corner and proclaim that the hills were alive.

Seemed like an odd home for a Russian mobster, but what did I know?

I approached the back door and reminded myself to stay in character. Imitating Blade's body language, I lengthened my stride, relaxed my neck and shoulders, and wiped away any trace of happiness from my face. I had mimicked him perfectly. Or so I thought. I forgot that I possessed the strength of ten elephants, and I pushed open the door with enough force to send it slamming backward into the kitchen wall.

"Oops," I whispered, peering into the kitchen and hoping no one had seen. So far, I was alone. I tried to shut the door behind me, but the knob was buried in the drywall. I gave it a good yank, and white dust fluttered from the gaping hole in the wall to the floor.

There was no covering that up.

I tiptoed through the kitchen, deciding to leave the mess behind. I had nearly made it out undetected when a petite redheaded woman rounded the corner and narrowed her eyes at me.

This must be Marta.

"What was that noise?" she demanded. Before I could respond, she glanced behind me and gasped, and then released a torrent of words in a language I didn't understand.

I muttered, "Sorry," and kept on walking. It seemed like what Blade would do.

I followed his directions, continuing down the hallway to the second room on the left. When I reached the door to Constantine's office, I knocked twice, as Blade had instructed.

"Come," a man's voice replied.

I opened the door and finally met the man who had terrified Blade into submission, the infamous swan-slayer and mobster, Constantine Romanovitch. At first glance, the man didn't intimidate me in the least. He sat in a rolling office chair behind a mahogany desk, a pair of reading glasses perched on the end of his nose as he peered at a stack of spreadsheets. He was older than I had expected, with puffy eyes and a heavily lined face, his thinning salt-and-pepper gray hair slicked back against a receding hairline. His vibe seemed more *grandpa* than *gangster* . . . until he looked up and met my gaze.

In that moment, I understood what Blade meant when he'd said he could recognize ugliness when he saw it. The cold shrewdness in Constantine's eyes made my stomach clench. I drew a breath and reminded myself that he couldn't hurt me.

Probably.

"*Privyet*, Papa," I said, as rehearsed.

He greeted me with a grunt. "What did you do this time to upset Marta?" His accent was thick, but his English flawless. "Hmm?"

"It's nothing," I said. "An accident. I'll fix it."

Constantine made a throaty noise of disbelief.

"I need to talk to you," I said.

I closed the door and considered whether I should sit or stand for what would happen next. Standing would give me the illusion of power, but it might intimidate Constantine and put him on the defensive. I glanced at his workspace: clean, organized desk, free of clutter, no mugs or water bottles, no picture frames or any decorations on display except for a single gold bar stamped TWENTY-FOUR KARATS. That told me Constantine had a need for order and control, and possibly an inferiority complex prompting him to display his wealth. A man like that would want to feel bigger than his son, so I sat down in the chair across from his desk.

"What is it?" he asked.

"It's business." I leaned back and crossed an ankle over my opposite knee, folding both hands in my lap in a casual gesture. But there was nothing casual about my tone when I said, "I don't want to work for you anymore."

In my experience, messages carried more power when they were short and to the point, so I stayed quiet and left the ball bouncing in Constantine's court. While he processed my words, I maintained eye contact with him, refusing to so much as blink and give him the slightest reason to doubt me. I could almost see the wheels turning behind his eyes, calculating my weaknesses and preparing himself to exploit them. I predicted he would test the boundary I had set, and he proved me right with a dismissive shrug.

"What you want doesn't matter," he said. "You should have learned that by now. Go back to your room and stop being a little *cyka*."

I didn't need to be fluent in Russian to know that Constantine had just called me a little bitch. Maybe it was testosterone overload or just empathy for Blade, but his dad's response really pissed me off. I leaned forward and propped both elbows on my knees.

"Let me clarify," I ground out. "I *won't* do it anymore."

As I bored my gaze into his, I felt my heart thumping hard inside my rib cage, heat spreading through my veins and rising quickly into my face. My fists clenched, followed by the sudden urge to drive one of them through the mahogany desk and straight on until I punched Constantine right in his cold, black heart.

Oh, yeah, definitely too much testosterone, but I didn't care. I wanted nothing more than to put Constantine Romanovitch in the ground, and I could tell that he knew it. He took one look at my flaring nostrils, and the sneer disappeared from his face. He wheeled back an inch or two in his chair, watching me as he sucked his front teeth. We sat there for the longest time, staring at each other. If nothing else, the break gave me a chance to calm down.

"So," he finally said, "I guess Ben Mitchell was right about you."

I had to fight to maintain my poker face. Constantine had caught me off guard. I had no clue what he was talking about.

"Last year was a test," he went on. "When you were arrested on that bullshit charge. Ben used to help me test all my men from time to time. He would pay a dirty cop to make an arrest, and then Ben would turn the screw, apply more pressure to see who would crack and make a deal with him. How do you think you did on that test, my son?"

I didn't have the foggiest idea, so I clenched my jaw and refused to answer.

Constantine wobbled a hand as if to say *so-so*. "Ben told me you wanted out. He said you even asked him to help you start a new life somewhere else. You wanted to abandon your papa." For the briefest of moments, hurt flashed in his eyes, and then it was gone. "But when he asked if you would testify against me, you said no. That was the only part of the test that you passed. I didn't raise a snitch." He exhaled bitterly. "If nothing else, at least I can say one good thing about my son."

I tried to play it cool while my mind reeled with this new information. My instincts about Ben Mitchell had been right all along. He had been more crooked than a crossword puzzle. Now I understood why Blade had hated him so much. Blade had asked Ben to help him go straight, and in return, Ben had stabbed him in the back and sent him to prison.

"No, I'm not a snitch," I agreed. "But I guess your friend Ben was."

"Of course he was. It's what I paid him to do."

"And the new district attorney?" I asked. "Is he in your pocket, too?"

Constantine frowned. "Not yet. But I'm working on it. If he doesn't come around, the next one will. Everyone has a price."

I believed that part. But one thing didn't make sense to me. If Ben Mitchell had been on Constantine's payroll, then why had Ben fought so hard to convict Blade of a bogus charge instead of sweeping it under the rug for his boss?

Constantine must have seen the question on my face, because he unleashed a vile grin and said, "It was me. I was the one who gave the order for Ben to prosecute you."

My eyes flew wide. *"You?* You had me sent to prison? Your own son?"

"My son who wanted to abandon me," he clarified, as if that made it all right. "I hoped prison would change your mind, that it would give you time to think, time to appreciate the life your papa has given you. But it didn't work. You don't care."

Oh, it definitely hadn't worked. Constantine had no idea, but his scheme had blown up in his face. If he hadn't sent Blade to prison, then Blade never would have taken the class that sparked his love of motorcycle engine repair. Blade had learned a brand-new, legitimate trade to support him in life, and he had his father's betrayal to thank for it. The irony of the situation was so delicious that I couldn't bring myself to feel salty about it.

"Thank you, Papa," I said. "You did me a favor."

Constantine blinked in confusion.

"I forgive you," I told him, and then I stood up and peered down at him, unafraid of making Constantine Romanovitch feel every bit as small and as shitty as he was. "I never wanted to abandon you. I still don't. I won't work for you, but I'm willing to be your son. You can take that offer or you can leave it. The choice is yours."

And then I turned on my booted heel, and I walked away.

Chapter Nineteen

THE LAST DREGS OF ADRENALINE LEFT MY SYSTEM by the time I returned to the pool house, so I no longer felt the urge to Hulk-smash the hedges lining the sidewalk. But that sneaky bastard testosterone had another surprise in store for me. As soon as I opened the door and caught a glimpse of Nash resting peacefully on the bed, a rush of emotion welled up inside me, and before I knew what was happening, my body started to react—in a physical way.

Basically, I got ambush-aroused. Turned on against my will. And because of my new equipment, the experience was the absolute worst kind of mind freak. To anyone watching, I probably looked like a drunken fly, buzzing around the living room, uselessly flapping my hands in an effort to make the intrusion in my pants go away. All I had wanted was to finish this job and eat a donut, but now I couldn't stop thinking about how soft Nash's lips were and how good his neck always smelled in that one spot below his left ear.

Damn it, I seriously needed to stop taking male clients.

I whirled away from Nash. Since I couldn't return Blade's body to him in its current condition, I sat at the foot of the bed, closed my eyes, and practiced one of the calming meditative exercises that Val taught me. When that didn't help, I tried a different strategy and calculated some algebra problems in my head. I figured that since math killed all joy, it might work on boners, too.

I was right.

A few minutes later, after my figurative pool noodle had deflated, I stretched out next to Nash on the bed. From there, I was able to lull myself into a trance and meet Blade inside the imaginary room within his mind. I knocked on the closet door to summon him, and when he opened it, he asked me the same question that all of my clients asked at the end of a job.

"How'd it go?"

"It went well," I told him. "But not without complications."

I motioned for him to leave the closet and follow me into the pretend room, where we could talk. For some reason, my clients responded better to tough news when I explained it inside their minds as opposed to waiting until I returned to my own body. (Or in this case, Nash's body.) At least here, Blade would see me represented as my real self, and that might put him a little more at ease.

Since beating around the bush never helped, I got right to the point. I explained the whole encounter with his father, reciting the conversation word for word. Blade chewed on his thumbnail while he listened. When I reached the part of the story involving Ben Mitchell and Constantine's betrayal, Blade covered his mouth and went so still that he might have stopped breathing.

"I know it's a lot to take in," I said, giving his arm a reassuring squeeze. "I was surprised, too. But listen, I made a judgment call, and I hope you're okay with it."

Blade took his hand away from his face. "What did you do?"

"I told your dad that I forgive him."

Blade didn't react. Not a single blink. His poker face was even better than mine.

"Hear me out," I said. "I thought about what you learned in prison, and how you might be able to start your own shop someday because of the class you took." I shrugged. "That doesn't make your dad innocent. He royally screwed you over, and there's no excuse for what he did to you. But the way I see it, fate handed him a giant Uno reverse card when he sent you to prison. He tried to trap you, and instead, you came out of your cage with a free pair of wings that you didn't have before. Now you can fly wherever you want."

Blade cracked a smile. "Tia Dante. That might be the cheesiest thing I've ever heard."

"Okay, I'm cheesy. But am I wrong?"

"No," he admitted. "You're not."

"So are we good? Did I make the right call?"

"Yeah, probably," he said. "I would have done things different. But worse. I would've blown up and broken some stuff and said a bunch of shit that I can't take back. Your way was better. Smarter. But I'll have to stay away from my dad for a while. I can't forgive him like you did. It's not that easy for me."

"Of course it's not," I agreed. "It's only easy for me because he's not my father. I don't care about him one bit. If it was my dad, I would be so crushed right now that I'd eat my feelings until my stomach exploded. Well, technically *your* stomach, but you get the idea."

Blade chuckled.

"Oh, by the way," I added, "if Marta hates you even more than usual, it's because there's a hole in the kitchen wall that you need to fix. It's right behind the door. You can't miss it."

"Good to know."

"Well, I guess this is it," I said. "Now that we're even, I can give my friend his body back, and we can call it a day."

"Wait," Blade told me. "One thing first."

I raised a questioning eyebrow.

"I want to do this while you're still you," he said, and then he took my hand in both of his and bent down to place a gentle kiss on my knuckles. The tender brush of contact set my stomach fluttering, even though the experience was all in my mind. Blade winked and released me. "Your friend is hairy. . . . It would've made this weird. No offense."

"None taken."

"Thank you," he told me. "I won't forget what you did for me."

"Well, I would say *anytime*, but let's not make it a habit."

"Agreed," he said, and he gave me one of his rare genuine smiles— the kind that electrified his blue eyes and made it impossible to look away. "I like you, Tia Dante. Hit me up if you ever want to hang out sometime. You're pretty cool for a snitch."

As I smiled back at him, I caught myself biting my lower lip like some shy little freshman. Not a good sign. I hated to admit it, but I liked Blade, too.

More than I should.

.   .   .

Roughly an hour later, after switching back into Nash's body, I dropped off Blade at the Saint Valliant's parking lot so he could retrieve his motorcycle, and then I continued to the nearest fast-food restaurant for a chocolate shake. I had just pulled into the drive-through lane when Nash's phone buzzed with a text.

I glanced at the screen.

Someone named Kenzie asked, Where r u?

Kenzie? Who the hell was that?

I swerved out of the drive-through lane and pulled into a parking spot so I could investigate further. I tried scrolling up in the text thread, but there were no previous messages between Kenzie and Nash . . . obviously because Nash had deleted them. That must have been what he didn't want me to see.

But why? Was she his girlfriend?

I noticed that Nash hadn't uploaded a photo of Kenzie. Her default icon was a circle containing the initials *MM*. I opened her contact page and tapped the *info* icon to access the pictures and files she and Nash had texted to each other. His cloud brought up the last sixty days' worth of content. I held my breath while I scrolled, afraid of what I might find. Sweat slicked my hands when I imagined coming across photographic evidence of Nash with another girl. I knew it wasn't healthy for me to snoop and that I should stop. What I was doing was the dictionary definition of hurting my own feelings. But putting down his phone was like trying to look away from a car wreck. I couldn't do it.

At first there wasn't much to see, mostly pictures of random buildings and landscapes. I kept searching and eventually found a selfie of the two of them together inside what appeared to be a science lab.

Right away, I recognized the girl's pretty face.

MM stood for Mackenzie McDonald, aka Corporal Diaz, the college girl who had impersonated a soldier to weasel her way into my house so she could try to recruit me for her Scooby Gang of head-hoppers, the Immersionist Liberation Organization.

Did that mean my instincts about her had been right? Was Mackenzie the girl who had replaced me?

I had to find out. My sanity depended on it.

U coming? she had texted.

I replied with a simple ???

The meeting! she said. Srsly bruh! Ur the one who called it!

Instant relief washed over me, and I relaxed the shoulder muscles I had unknowingly been clenching. Nash was supposed to be at an ILO meeting. I still didn't know if he and Mackenzie were a thing, but at least they didn't have a date tonight. I tried not to dwell too hard on why that news made me happy.

Sorry, I told her. Crazy day. Lost track of time.

She replied, so r u coming?

My thumbs were poised and ready to type *no*. But then curiosity forced me to think again. Nash must not have told anyone in the ILO where he would be tonight, otherwise Mackenzie wouldn't have texted him. That meant I could show up to the meeting as Nash, and no one would have any reason to doubt me. This might be my only chance to find out what the ILO and Nash were hiding—the real reason he had kept his ability a secret from me for so long.

The only downside was that Nash would definitely find out. I couldn't impersonate him at the meeting without someone eventually talking about it and tipping him off. There was no point in trying to hide it from him, and no matter which way I spun the truth, he would be furious with me for violating his trust.

I felt a sharp tug in my gut when I imagined his reaction, but then I reminded myself that Nash had violated my trust first when he had kept secrets from me. The way I saw it, if I could forgive him for shutting me out and breaking my heart, it was only fair to expect him to forgive me for taking his place at one teeny ILO meeting.

It was decided.

Plus, there might be snacks.

I texted Mackenzie, On my way, be there in a few.

Chapter Twenty

NASH'S BODY GAVE ME MORE THAN ENOUGH ENERGY to burn, but I felt an eerie sense of déjà vu as I left his car in the parking lot at the bottom of fraternity row and climbed the steep hill toward campus. A blanket of clouds concealed the moon and the stars, leaving a few scattered streetlights to illuminate the road ahead of me. With no sidewalks and a solid line of cars taking up both sides of the street, I had no choice but to walk in the middle of the road again, following the same path as the night I had almost been un-alived by a Tesla.

I glanced over my shoulder every few seconds until I reached the top of the hill, where the narrow road ended at a stop sign. On the other side of the intersection, a newer stretch of pavement indicated where the campus began. A sidewalk appeared in front of me, leading to a network of cross streets and dozens of boxy brick buildings of various sizes and heights. I found myself relaxing as I followed my GPS to the student union building a few streets ahead. The campus was well lit by towering lampposts, and the open thoroughfare allowed me to see all around, with very few places for a murderer to hide and jump out at me.

I reached the student union building and paused for a moment to shake off my nerves before I opened the door. The lobby was silent and deserted, with no signs telling me where to go. I picked up the faint echo of voices and followed the sound to a room at the end of the hall.

There were more people at the meeting than I had expected, about twenty or so sitting in a circle of chairs. I didn't see any snacks, but I spotted Mackenzie sitting next to an empty seat that was probably intended for Nash. Exhaling one last anxious breath, I loosened my joints and loped into the room as my ex-boyfriend.

"Sorry," I muttered with a general wave at the group. "Man, I can't believe I blazed on you guys. I feel like such a dick. I appreciate you waiting for me." I took the empty seat and looked to Mackenzie, who I assumed was in charge. I couldn't recall the title on the business card she had given me, but I remembered thinking she seemed important.

"All right," Mackenzie said with a single clap. "Now that Nash has finally joined us, we can get started." She glanced at me. "Do you want to take it from here?"

"Uh . . ." I stammered. "No, no, you go ahead."

"You called the meeting," she reminded me.

I had forgotten that part. I gripped my temples and faked a wince of pain. "Yeah, I know, but I'm getting a migraine, and I'm *really* off my game tonight. Can you take over? You'd be doing me a huge solid. I wouldn't ask if I didn't feel like total dog shit."

She stared at me for a moment or two. Mentally, I crossed all of my fingers and toes and hoped that Nash had told Mackenzie enough about the meeting for her to run it.

"I mean, we can reschedule if we have to," I added. "I just don't want to waste any more of anyone's time. It's bad enough that you had to wait for me."

"That's fine; I'll do it," she said, and watched me for another charged beat before returning her attention to the group. "Okay," she called out. "At the last meeting, Nash made a motion, which was seconded by Todd, to debate the issue of data security and possibly schedule a vote on whether or not to destroy our research."

A debate? And a vote?

I began to see a critical flaw in my plan. Even though I knew Nash inside and out, he had kept this part of his life a secret from me. I was out of my depth trying to impersonate him around his head-hopping friends. Not only did I have zero clue what Mackenzie meant by data security and research destruction, I didn't know how Nash felt about either issue. This wasn't something I could fake.

"Some of you already know how I feel," Mackenzie went on. "I spent the last year and a half on this research. I worked too hard to delete it." She hooked a thumb at me. "Plus, it helped Nash. Think of all the other people we can help."

I avoided the gazes that turned my way.

"But what about the downside?" a guy asked from across the circle. "You didn't just find a way to turn it on. You found a way to turn it off, too. Think about what would happen if the government got their hands on your research. They already hate us. You know they'll find a way to strip our power . . . except for the chosen few they can control."

My breath locked. The guy had made it sound like Mackenzie

could activate and deactivate the ability to head-hop. But that couldn't be right. Scientists didn't even know how immersion worked.

Or so they claimed. . . .

I thought back to what Nash had told me last week, right before our big fight. He'd said that the way he had discovered his ability was "unusual" and "not an accident." That hadn't made sense to me at the time, but what if Mackenzie had somehow switched on his gift? And if so, did that mean she could turn anyone into an immersionist? Was the entire human population capable of trading bodies with one another?

If so, life on Earth was about to get a lot more confusing.

Mackenzie shook her head. "How could they take away our power? They don't know who has the mutation and who doesn't. And even if they did, they don't have the manpower to hunt down every single one of us and forcibly inject us with the cocktail."

The mutation. That answered one of my questions. Not everyone could head-hop.

"It doesn't matter," the same guy argued. "They could dose us through the water supply, or crop dust every city until they get us all. No one would see it coming. Think about biological warfare, or fertilizer runoff that carries nanoparticles from rivers to oceans and spreads across the world. Or even something as innocent as adding fluoride to the drinking water. There are a hundred ways to disseminate chemicals to the population. It's not like the government hasn't done it before."

"Okay, so we'll keep the research secure," Mackenzie said. "Like it already is. All of the files are saved on a separate disk drive that never connects to the internet, so they can't be hacked. The drive is locked up in a bank vault that no one can access except for me. Then there's the fact that nobody outside this group even knows that the research exists. So unless one of you thinks you can make millions by selling our secret to the government, we don't have a problem. But you know what? Even if we do have a traitor in the group, they would never be able to access my data. Believe me, our secret is safe."

Nash's words echoed in my mind: *The secret wasn't mine to tell.* Now it all made sense. I understood why he had hidden the truth from me, and also why he kept pressuring me to join the ILO. Nash hadn't told me about his ability because Mackenzie had activated it. He had been sworn to secrecy, just like the rest of the group, and if I joined the ILO, then Nash wouldn't have to keep secrets from me anymore. He never stopped trusting me. Nash had honored the promise he'd made to protect the research . . . because Nash was an honorable person.

Me? Not so much.

I felt a throb of guilt. I shouldn't have crashed the meeting.

"Come on, Nash," the guy said, jutting his chin at me. "Back me up, bro."

I supposed that told me how Nash felt about the issue. "Yeah, man, I agree with you," I said, my gaze fixed on the floor. "Even if the risk is small, I don't think we should take it. The stakes are too high. Too much can go wrong if the research gets leaked or stolen." For what it was worth, I believed every word I had said. I added, "Nothing stays a secret forever. Eventually the truth comes out."

The group continued their debate, some of them in favor of destroying Mackenzie's research, others of them opposed. I tried to act sick, slouching over and rubbing my belly, so I could make an early exit. But the longer I sat there ruminating about how selfish I had been, the less I had to pretend. The thought of confessing the truth to Nash had twisted my stomach into a double knot. I didn't even want a donut or a milkshake anymore.

I excused myself and strode out into the hall. Thankfully, no one followed me, so I kept going and returned to the parking lot. I had just started the car when Nash's phone buzzed with a text. The screen displayed *Tia's new number*, along with a heart icon.

He saved me as a heart. Why did that make me feel even worse?

You okay? he asked from my phone. Thought you'd be done by now. Val had to leave.

I typed, Just finished. On my way.

K, he said. Come to the back door. I turned off the alarm.

The back door meant my bedroom window. Sneaking in was probably a good idea. I could avoid raising any questions from my dad about why Nash had come back to the house, and as a bonus, Nash would have to keep his voice low when I told him what I had done.

Chapter Twenty-One

ADMITTING THE TRUTH TO NASH HAD GONE BETTER—
and worse—than I had imagined. We had traded bodies, and then I'd
delivered the news to him in my usual way, quick and to the point,
ripping off the Band-Aid like a waxing strip. My decision to wait to
tell him until *after* the body swap had been deliberate. If I had confessed the truth to him any sooner, he might have insisted on having
a conversation inside one of our minds, and a full discussion on the
topic of my assholery was the last thing I wanted. My strategy worked
a little too well. As soon as I finished telling Nash the truth, he had
turned around, climbed out my window, and I didn't hear a word from
him for two days.

Two terrible, horrible, no good, very bad days. And not just
because of Nash. My trial date was creeping up on me, and so far, my
public defender hadn't come up with any brilliant ideas to get me off
the hook. He'd said there was no legal precedent in my favor, and that
my best option was to make a deal with the district attorney. I didn't
even have the court of public opinion on my side. A new poll showed

that the majority of Americans wanted to see me locked up for criminally negligent manslaughter. To them, it was my body, my crime. (But not my choice.) People on social media didn't support me either. Twitter users were the meanest—no surprise there—but I was getting dragged harder than a suitcase full of quarters on the other apps, too.

The universe didn't seem to love me anymore.

But at least my father did.

"You ready?" he asked, handing me an egg-free, dairy-free, gluten-free, joy-free breakfast bar from the kitchen pantry. "We gotta go. You can eat in the car. It won't look good if you're late."

That was putting it mildly. My lawyer had set up a meeting with the acting district attorney, Shane Douglas, to talk about a plea deal for my case. Mr. Douglas claimed his schedule was so packed that he could only spare a few minutes for us if we arrived at dawn and met him in the courthouse lobby. I didn't know if the DA was actually that busy or if he was just flexing on us, but either way, he had all the leverage. So I dragged myself out to the garage and followed my dad to his car.

"Now remember," my dad said as he pulled out of our driveway, and then he proceeded to remind me of every negotiation pro tip he had taught me in the last seventeen years. We both knew I didn't need the repeat lesson. But because he also taught me that people overtalked when they were nervous, I let him ramble on while I ate my breakfast.

There was plenty of open parking along the street when we reached the courthouse, but my dad had this weird paranoia about the acidity of bird poop ruining his car's paint job, so he paid extra to use the multistory parking garage. We drove in circles until he found a spot near the elevator, about two levels up from the ground floor.

"We're early," I said, checking my phone. The district attorney and my public defender wouldn't be in the lobby for another ten minutes.

"Better than late," my dad muttered.

"Yeah, I know, but maybe we should wait here for a few?" I said. "The enemy of power is desperation. I don't want to look too eager."

My dad grinned and patted me on the leg. "You really do listen to me sometimes."

"Sometimes," I agreed.

We passed a small but strategic amount of time in the car before we made our way to the elevator. I had just pressed the call button when a man wearing a suit and tie strode toward us. I didn't pay much attention to the guy at first. Until he walked near enough for me to recognize him from my pretrial hearing.

"Good morning, Miss Dante," said District Attorney Shane Douglas, my prosecutor and the closest person I had to a mortal enemy. Or the second closest. The number one slot belonged to the head-hopper who had stolen my body and used it for murder.

I gave him a tight smile.

The three of us stood in front of the steel doors, waiting for them to open. When nothing happened, I pushed the call button again.

"That doesn't work, you know," Shane told me. "You have to be patient."

I pushed the button five more times, just because I could. The fixture above the steel doors lit up to indicate that the elevator was on its way up from the floor below us. A few moments later, a soft *ding* announced that our ride had finally arrived. But before the doors parted, a much louder noise echoed from the vacuous space in the parking garage behind us, and all three of us turned around to see what it was.

I heard the revving of a thunderous engine and tires shrieking like a banshee. The smell of burned rubber crossed my nose, and the next thing I knew, a silver pickup truck was speeding past us. It came to a halt with a terrible screech and then flew into reverse. As the truck passed us again, this time going backward, I caught a glimpse of a young male driver peering at us through an open window. A flicker of recognition tickled my brain. I had seen the man before. But I barely had a chance to gasp before he thrust a pistol out the window and fired three shots into Shane Douglas's chest.

After that, several things happened at once: I released a primal scream, Shane collapsed to the ground, and my father tackled me into the open elevator, where we hit the floor and rolled behind the protection of the front panel. Without hesitating, my dad reached up and slapped the elevator buttons. I curled into a ball and covered my head, flinching as two more shots rang out. I stayed like that, frozen in the fetal position, until my body's downward momentum told me we had escaped. From above, I could hear the retreating screech of tires as the truck sped away.

I pushed into a sitting position and patted myself down, checking for damage. My dad sat beside me and did the same.

"You okay?" he asked me.

I nodded. The hard landing had probably left me with some sprains and contusions, but I wouldn't know for sure until the adrenaline wore off and I could feel pain again.

"You?" I asked.

He flapped a beefy hand. "I'm hard to kill."

I turned toward him and wrapped my arms around him in a hug. He squeezed me close, and even though my heart was still racing, I had never felt more secure. "Thank you, Dad. You saved me."

"That's my job, little bee."

"Well, I'm glad you're so good at it."

He chuckled. "Me, too. You have a way of keeping me on my toes."

The elevator doors opened to the ground floor of the courthouse. My dad supported my elbow and walked me to a nearby seating area, and then he jogged to the security station to report the shooting and call an ambulance.

While I waited, I couldn't stop replaying the attack in my mind. Over and over, I envisioned the truck whizzing past me in reverse, and the quick rotation of the driver's face as he fixed his gaze on Shane Douglas. This was no random drive-by. Three bullets to the chest was a textbook hit, and Shane had been the target. The driver would have happily killed me and my dad, too, but only to eliminate the witnesses.

Two district attorneys shot at the same courthouse in the same month.

What the hell was going on in this town?

My brain continued to focus on the driver's face. More than a trauma response, I sensed something niggling at the back of my mind, a tingle of awareness, like I had almost found the missing number to an equation. The harder I tried to coax out the answer, the further it slipped away. It wasn't until my pulse slowed down and I finally recovered from the shock of nearly dying that I realized what my subconscious had been trying to tell me.

I knew who the driver was.

I had seen his face before, first in mug shots, and then on the surveillance video footage I had captured using a borrowed drone. He was Richard Franco: convicted felon, halfway house resident, record-holder for the world's worst grandson, and employee of the Russian mafia. Last week I watched Blade Romanovitch deliver an envelope full of cash to Franco. Now I had a pretty good idea what the mob had paid him to do. I should have put it together after my talk with Constantine Romanovitch. He said that if Shane Douglas refused to do business with the mob, then the next DA would.

Shane must have held his ground. And in return, Constantine repaid him with three bullets to the chest.

* * *

Shane Douglas died at the scene.

The news of his death broke while my dad and I were still giving our statements to the police. Detective Roberts was in charge of the investigation, and he had given me that same disapproving look, as if my presence was the reason for all the chaos in our town. After my father and I were released, a journalist filmed us driving out of the courthouse parking garage, and by the time we got home, a conspiracy theory about my involvement in Shane's murder was already making the rounds on the internet.

"These people can't be for real," I told Val, who had come over for moral support. We were stretched out on my bed, scrolling through our social feeds. I showed her a meme of my face photoshopped onto a Lord of the Rings actor. The text read, ONE DOES NOT SIMPLY . . . APPEAR AT TWO MASSACRES AS A CASUAL OBSERVER. "The garage security cameras caught the whole thing," I went on. "The police already released the video. How does anyone think I managed to shoot the DA while simultaneously dodging the next bullet?"

Val read from her phone screen. "According to this guy named Big Dong Daryl, all head-hoppers can secretly project their minds into multiple bodies at once. He says you split your consciousness in half and took control of the truck driver, forcing him to—and I quote—'do your bidding while you played the victim.'"

I leaned over and glanced at Big Daryl's picture. He wore wrap-around sunglasses and a beard down to his chest. He looked as dumb as he sounded. "You know what's really scary? This guy can vote and we can't."

Val cringed. "That explains a lot about the current state of our nation."

"Facts."

"Don't worry about these people," Val said. "They're the same ones who think the earth is flat and birds aren't real. No one takes them seriously."

"Not believing in birds? That's a thing?"

"It's actually a funny story," she said. "It started out as a conspiracy theory parody of a conspiracy theory, but it took on a life of its own, and now it has real followers."

"Huh. Conspira-ception."

"What about the drone footage?" she asked. "Are you going to turn it over?"

I shook my head. I had told Detective Roberts that I recognized Richard Franco from his online mug shot, but I hadn't mentioned using the drone to follow him. If the police learned about the drone footage, then I would have to surrender it as evidence, and the video would implicate Blade in the hit. I knew that Blade was innocent. Constantine had only used him to make the payoff because Blade had already proven that he wouldn't testify against his father. It was Constantine who hired Franco to kill Shane Douglas. But I couldn't prove any of that, and I refused to watch Blade go back to prison for his father's crimes.

"I deleted it," I told Val. "So if anyone asks . . ."

"It never existed," she said. "You should tell Nash the same thing, just in case someone asks him."

"Maybe you can tell him for me," I said. "He's not picking up my calls, and even if he was, this isn't the sort of thing I want to say over the phone."

Val pulled her lips to the side in disapproval.

"I promise I'm not avoiding him," I told her with a lifted hand. "I tried to apologize a bunch of times. He won't listen."

She held out a palm for my phone. "Prove it."

I didn't want to show her.

"Let me see," she pressed.

Heaving a sigh, I gave her my phone.

"Oh, my god, Tia," she said. "You sent him one *I'm sorry* text."

"And a sad-face emoji," I pointed out. "It's crying a tear."

"That's not apologizing a bunch of times."

"It is for me."

She gave me back my phone. "Maybe the universe has a lot more to teach you than I thought."

"Let's focus on my personality flaws another day," I suggested. "My trial is coming up. Or at least I think it is. I don't even know who's prosecuting me anymore, but I'm pretty sure I'm going to end up in prison if I can't find the person who used my body to kill Ben."

"Well, we can probably rule out the mob," Val said.

I agreed with her. Constantine Romanovitch had no motive to kill Ben Mitchell. Ben had been an asset to the mafia, and his replacement had been a liability. By default, that also eliminated Richard Franco as a suspect, because he worked for the mob.

"Hey, what about the ILO?" Val asked.

I raised an eyebrow. "The head-hopper union?"

"Yeah, think about it. When you strip away everything we've learned about Ben Mitchell, we still only know one thing for sure about his killer."

"That they're an immersionist."

"Maybe we should have started there."

I couldn't deny that Val had a point. As much as I hated the idea of joining the ILO, it would give me access to their membership information. But not every immersionist belonged to the ILO, and even if they did, I wouldn't know what process of elimination to use to narrow down who had a motive to kill Ben.

"I don't know how much that would help," I said. "Nash has already seen the names on Ben's case list. If he recognized anyone from the group, I'm sure he would have said something."

"Unless he's more loyal to the ILO than to you," Val said. We looked at each other for an uncomfortable beat of silence, and then she added, "But I can't see that happening. Can you?"

"No, but now I'm second-guessing myself," I told her. "Thanks for putting that idea in my head."

"Forget that I said anything," she said, waving me off.

"Either way, I need more names to cross-reference if I'm going to join the ILO. Otherwise it's a waste of time." I chewed the inside of my cheek, wishing I had access to Ben's phone. "I don't suppose you're dating anyone who can borrow Ben's cell phone from the police evidence locker and download his contacts for me?"

"Sorry, no," Val said. Then she tilted her head as if something had just occurred to her. "But what about his calendar?"

"What about it?" I asked.

"People like him sync their schedules and contacts with office staffers," she said. "I learned about it from Mrs. K. She can log in to the principal's calendar and see everything that he sees. She adds, deletes, and changes his meetings, she sets auto-reminders, and she updates his contacts when someone's email or phone number changes."

"Ben's assistant would have all of that," I realized.

"Do you know who his assistant was?"

"No, but I can find out. That's the easy part."

"Hacking their calendar, not so much," Val said.

I smiled at her. I had an idea for that, too.

Chapter Twenty-Two

LEARNING THE IDENTITY OF BEN MITCHELL'S ASSIStant had taken less than sixty seconds. I simply called the district attorney's office and claimed that I needed to confirm the cancellation of a fundraising event for one of Ben's charities. After that, the office had given me his assistant's name and contact information, along with her email address, which allowed me to move on to phase two of my plan.

Phishing.

More specifically, *spear* phishing, which meant targeting an individual with an email that was designed especially for them. I had learned the term from my former client Josh Fenske. I didn't know anything about hacking office systems, but Josh did, and he was more than happy to help me clear my name.

"Okay," Josh said, sitting cross-legged on the futon in my shed, a laptop balanced on his knees. "I just sent the email. Now we wait."

"For what?" I asked. "What happens next?"

"She'll click the link in my email, and then we're in."

"Just like that?"

"Just like that," he said. "The link downloads malware directly onto the office network. It only takes a few seconds for the malware to install, and then I'll have access to the whole system for as long as it takes the IT department to figure out they've been hacked. Then they'll shut down the server. We could have fifteen minutes; we could have an hour. It all depends on how good their security is."

"Sweet," I said. Fifteen minutes should give us plenty of time to download Ben's calendar. I could examine it later in detail. "You're the best, Josh."

His cheeks colored as he gazed into his lap. "Well, this whole thing is kind of my fault when you think about it. If you weren't fighting Mark for me that day in the lunchroom, you would have been in your own body, and no one would have stolen it. You would still be in school, and Ben Mitchell would be alive."

"I don't believe that." I nudged Josh's shoulder until he looked at me. "Really, I'm serious. Whoever stole my body knew that I was a head-hopper. That means they were already watching me. They had the whole murder planned out. All they had to do was wait for the right time. If you hadn't come to me that day, they would have just taken my body at my next job. It would have happened sooner or later. Ben was marked for death. It sucks, but that's the truth. The only person to blame is the one who pulled the trigger."

Josh chewed his lower lip. "I guess you're right."

"Besides," I said. "Kicking Mark's ass was the highlight of my year."

Josh grinned at me. "I watched the fight on YouTube. It was awesome. Sorry you got punched in the nuts, though. I can't believe you didn't barf."

"Oh, I did." The reminder made me cringe. I had barely gotten to the bathroom in time. For real, no more male clients. "But it worked, right? Does Mark leave you alone now?"

"Everyone does, just like you said."

"Then it was worth it." I extended a fist to bump. "No regrets."

"No regrets," he agreed, tapping my knuckles with his.

A chime rang out from Josh's laptop. He glanced at the screen. "Showtime."

"That was fast. She clicked the link already?"

"Yeah, I always send my fake emails from human resources," he said. "People open those first because it might be about their paychecks or their vacation requests."

"Time and money," I mused.

"The two most important things in life," he said.

"Damn, Josh, you're diabolical. I knew there was a reason I liked you."

With laser focus, he stared at his computer screen while his fingers flew over the keys. I sat back and let him work his magic, trying not to distract him. He must have known exactly what to look for and where to find it, because a few short minutes later, he held up his hands in victory and announced, "Done!"

"You got it?" I asked.

Josh pulled a thumb drive out of his computer and gave it to me. "Ben's schedule, his emails, his contacts, and the notes he made about his cases. It's all on here."

"No way." That was even more data than I hoped for. I bounced up and down on the futon cushion, smiling and clutching the thumb drive to my chest. "Thank you, Josh! You're a rock star."

He beamed, his cheeks pink. "I hope it helps you find whoever killed him."

"So do I," I said.

My future depended on it, because if this mother lode of information didn't give me the answer to Ben's death, nothing would.

* * *

A few hours later, I was hunting in the kitchen for a snack when my phone rang. The screen showed a blocked number, but I answered the call anyway, just in case it might be Nash.

I hated that my mind went straight to him, but it did.

As it turned out, Detective Roberts greeted me instead.

"Oh, hi," I told him. "Is this about the shooting?" It occurred to me that I should clarify which shooting I meant. "The one in the parking garage?"

"No," he said. "I wanted to let you know that the lab finished testing the samples we took from your shed. I already sent a copy of the forensics report to your lawyer, but I promised I would call you when the results came in."

I propped one hip against the counter. "What does it say?"

As soon as Detective Roberts exhaled hard into his phone, I knew the news wasn't good. "Not a whole lot. The lab singled out a strand of hair that doesn't belong to you or your client, but when they ran the DNA through the system, there was no match."

I took a beat to consider what that meant. DNA was usually catalogued from samples taken from suspects in criminal cases. "Okay, so the killer hasn't been in trouble with the law before. That still helps us, right? We can rule out convicts or anyone who ever gave the police a DNA sample."

"No, we really can't," he said. "You're assuming the hair belongs to the killer. We don't know that. You could have tracked it in on the bottom of your shoe. We still have to consider everyone a suspect."

I disagreed with him, though I didn't argue. I had tracked in plenty of grass clippings and leaves on my shoes, but I couldn't think of a single time I had walked across a random person's hair and brought it inside with me.

"What does the hair look like?" I asked.

"Medium brown color, medium to fine texture, three inches in length. But before you get too excited, that doesn't tell us as much as you think it does."

I wasn't excited at all. It didn't tell us much of anything. "Medium brown hair" described roughly half the population. And three inches could mean the suspect had short hair, or long, layered hair, or bangs, or even brand-new growth sticking up on their head.

Still, I tried to look on the bright side. At least we had a DNA sample to link the killer to my shed . . . assuming I could find them.

And for that, I needed Nash's help.

*   *   *

I didn't share Val's belief that the universe was a sentient being, and even if I did, I wouldn't believe that such a powerful cosmic force would even notice me, let alone take the time to meddle in my life. But I did agree with Val that I was trash when it came to apologies. And because my actual future depended on getting Nash to speak to me again—not to mention that I really did care about him—I had been forced to go online and watch instructional therapy videos until I learned the proper way to apologize to someone I had wronged.

Thinking of it that way, maybe the universe *had* taught me a lesson.

But whatever. The point was I knew what to do now. I packed a shoulder bag with my laptop, a water bottle, a few snacks, and the thumb drive containing all of Ben's information. After waiting for my dad to finish his dinner and leave for his shift at work, I snuck out my bedroom window, crossed through two backyards, and met Val in the discreet spot where she had parked her van.

To be safe, we sat there for a few minutes, scanning the roads and sidewalks for anyone who might have followed me from my house. Once we were certain I had dodged the media, and more important, the person who tried to run me over, Val started the engine and began driving toward Nash's dorm on campus.

Nash still wasn't taking my calls or returning my texts. So the plan was for Val to drop me off at his place and pick me up later, after I had apologized to him and (hopefully) convinced him to help me cross-reference Ben's list of contacts with the members of the ILO. If Nash wasn't at home, or if anything went wrong and I needed a ride sooner, I would text Val and then wait someplace safe and public until she could return for me.

It was a solid plan, all things considered.

Val pulled up to the front of Nash's building and told me, "Good luck."

"You don't believe in luck," I reminded her as I stepped out of the van.

"Yeah, I know," she said. "But you would just roll your eyes if I told you what I was really thinking."

I pressed a hand to my heart and faced my best friend. "Val, I want you to know that I'm sorry for all the times I invalidated your beliefs about the cosmos . . . and the tarot . . . and ancient aliens . . .

and astrological charts. That's not something a good friend would do. From now on, I promise to listen to you with an open mind. Will you forgive me?"

She grinned, pointing at me. "Hey, that wasn't half bad."

"Thank you."

I curtsied and blew her a kiss, and then I shut the van door and backed away before she could ask me if I meant a single word of what I'd said.

Striding though a pair of automatic double doors, I entered the dorm lobby. The space reminded me of a hotel convention center, with polished floor tiles that led to a wide reception desk along the far wall. An abundance of leather couches and chairs were arranged in small clusters that made it seem like a hot spot for students to hang out. Not only was every seat empty, but the flawless condition of the leather cushions told me what any lucid human being would already know. Who would want to hang out in a public fishbowl instead of the privacy of their own room?

Ahead of me at the reception desk, a flat-screen monitor proclaimed *All visitors must check in. No exceptions!* But as I approached the desk, I found no one there to help me. I even stood on tiptoe to peer behind the counter, looking for a bell to ring, or maybe a note telling me where the receptionist had gone and when they would be back. A desktop computer sat lifelessly on a workstation that was too clean to have been used recently.

"Great," I muttered. "Now what?"

A pair of voices echoed from the stairwell. I turned around and waved at two girls to get their attention. "Hey," I called out. "How do I check in?"

The first girl gave me a *bless-your-heart* kind of smile, like I was a kindergartner who had asked where babies came from. "You don't."

"No one cares," said the other girl. "Just make sure you leave before midnight. That's when they do the slut sweeps."

"Slut sweeps?" I repeated.

"Yeah, random spot checks," the second girl explained. "If the RAs catch you in the wrong room, you'll get a ticket, and so will the guy who invited you there."

"Cool," I said. So basically, any rando could walk in off the street and wander the whole dorm, including the bathrooms and the showers, but the students who actually lived there would be punished for a late-night hookup. Solid logic. Glad to know campus security had its priorities straight.

I left the reception desk and then headed for the stairs. Until now, I had never visited Nash in his dorm. He dumped me before I'd had the chance. But his room number was permanently seared onto my brain. I climbed the steps to the third floor, and from there, I followed the numbered wall placards until I found room 315.

I lifted my chin, took a deep breath, and knocked on the door.

A skinny guy with purple dreadlocks answered, bringing with him the skunky smell of a hundred joints. The guy blinked at me, and then his puffy eyes lit up, and he smiled.

"Hey, I know you. You're that head-hopper, Tia Dante."

"The one and only," I said. "Is Nash here?"

The dude's eyebrows rose up his forehead. "You know Nash?"

I wasn't expecting him to ask me that. His question caught me off guard, and I stood there, frozen, until I realized my mouth was hanging open, and I closed it. Nash hadn't mentioned me to his roommate? I didn't know how to feel about that. Actually, I did know how to feel: sick, queasy, like a contestant in a hot-dog-eating contest.

"He's not here," the guy said. He thumbed behind him. "But, hey, you can totally wait for him if you want. I'm super down to chill. I always wanted to meet a real head-hopper. I have so many questions." He gasped in excitement. "Do you want to be on my podcast?"

"Oh, uh . . . maybe another time," I said. "You mind if I leave him a note?"

"Sure, no prob. I'm Stu, by the way."

Stu handed me a notebook and a mechanical pencil, and I scribbled a quick apology to Nash.

Hey, listen, I know you're mad at me, and you should be. You had my back. You trusted me with your life—literally—and instead of honoring your trust, I took advantage of you. I was wrong, and I'm sorry. You deserved better. I hope you can forgive me so that we can be friends again. Even though I can take care of myself, it would be nice to have an extra pair of eyes looking out for your girl. ~T

I folded the note in half and gave it to Stu.

"Hey," I said. "Can I ask you something about Nash?"

"Sure, go for it," Stu said.

"Does he have a girlfriend?"

Stu gave me a sympathetic look. "Listen, I wanna tell you to shoot your shot, but to be honest, the dude doesn't date. He went out with, like, two girls last fall, and then nothing." Stu slashed a hand through the air. "Nada. Either some girl messed him up real bad or he's not into chicks. You're wasting your time on that one."

I hid a smile and then thanked him before walking away.

Now I felt even better about what I had written to Nash. I figured

Stu would read my apology letter as soon as he shut the door. Not that I blamed him. I would have done the same thing. But strangely, I didn't care if he read it. I wasn't ashamed of what I had written because it was true, and for the first time in my life, deep down inside my core, it finally occurred to me that admitting I made a bad choice didn't mean admitting that I was a bad person. If anything, it made me a better person to own up to my mistakes than to pretend they didn't happen.

I beamed as I walked back toward the stairwell. Val would be proud of my new progress. I had made the kind of breakthrough she would call "spiritual growth."

I would brag to her in person. For now, I texted: Nash isn't here.

She replied with a sad-face emoji. I'll come get you.

I made it to the bottom of the stairs and peered out at the vacant lobby, filled with cushy furniture. Actually . . . I added. Can you come in half an hour?

You sure? she asked.

Yeah, I want to hang here for a few, in case Nash comes back. I rested my bag on the sofa farthest from the front entrance. The lobby's kinda nice. I can go through Ben's file while I wait.

Okay, she said. Text if you change your mind. I'm doing an online sound bath for my subscribers, but I can quit early if you need me.

I began to teasingly suggest: Make sure you use extra sound soap on your dirty bits, but I deleted the joke and typed Thank you instead.

Spiritual growth for the win.

Chapter Twenty-Three

IF I HAD EVER HAD ANY INTEREST IN GOING TO LAW school, the idea died as soon as I opened Ben's calendar. I didn't know how much money prosecutors made. I didn't care. There wasn't enough cash in all the bank vaults in all the world to convince me to wake up at four o'clock in the morning to do case reviews, trial prep, document revisions, warrant requests, and police consultations. And that was *before* the start of Ben's official workday at the courthouse, where he had ricocheted like a pinball from one hearing to the next, one meeting to the next, eventually landing in his office and staying there until ten o'clock at night. He even worked weekends.

But what really blew my mind was knowing Ben had taken money from the mob, and there hadn't been a moment in his schedule for him to spend it. What was the point of compromising his integrity and accumulating all that wealth if it meant also having to work a hundred hours a week, the equivalent of two full-time jobs? Ben's dirty cash hadn't followed him when he'd died. According to the will his assistant had filed, he had left everything in a trust for his goddaughter, Molly Kazinski.

I almost felt sorry for Ben. Even in life, he'd had no life.

Scanning through his emails was no easier than reviewing his schedule. Ben's inbox contained more than two hundred unread messages, most of them received the day of his murder. I began to see how naive I had been to think that Nash and I could sit down for a couple of hours and cross-reference Ben's contacts with the names of the ILO members. Ben's contacts weren't compiled into a tidy, alphabetical list. They were spread out over emails, notes, and appointments that would take weeks to process.

Weeks I didn't have.

My phone buzzed with a text from Val.

OMG so sorry! she said.

I was about to ask her why when I checked the time and discovered she was five minutes late to pick me up. I had been so immersed in Ben's file that I had lost track of time.

Engine won't start! she added.

No worries, I typed. I'm fine here. TBH, I didn't even notice.

I'm working on it, she said. If I can't get the engine to turn over, I'll call Drew for a ride.

Who's Drew? I asked.

The Gemini

I grinned to myself. Val had named him. She must have caught major feels for the guy. I practically had to wrestle my own thumbs to resist the urge to type an innuendo about the ride Drew could give her, but I did the mature thing and sent her a smiley face. I could tell she was stressed, and my humor—primo as it was—wouldn't make her feel better.

Again with the spiritual growth. I was on fire today.

I went back to Ben's unread emails. Starting at the top, I opened each message, skimmed the content for any potentially juicy details, and then added the sender's name to a separate document that I had titled *Ben's Homies.*

I made quick work of it, and before long, I had filled my page with fifty names. So far, nothing interesting had stood out in the body of the emails . . . until I opened the next one.

The subject of the message read *final hearing.* I added the sender's name, Christopher Greeson, to my list of Ben's Homies, and then I quickly skimmed the message, not expecting anything useful to stand out. My eyes paused when they landed on the name Michael Kazinski.

Mike Kazinski was Molly's father. And also Mrs. K.'s ex-husband, the same man who had threatened to kill Mrs. K. right after he had sued her for full custody of Molly. I had done some digging into Mike's background on social media. The guy was the dictionary definition of a douche canoe. I had even investigated him to see if he'd had an alibi for Ben's murder.

I read the email again, more carefully.

Ben,

It was good talking with you yesterday. I appreciate the meeting. I spoke with my client last night, and he agreed to all of your terms and conditions, with one minor exception that I'm certain we can resolve over a brief phone call. Let me know when you're available, and I'll have my assistant set it up.

As we discussed, the deadline for disclosure is rapidly approaching. Because I have no doubt that you and my client will reach an agreement, I added you to discovery. A summons will be delivered to you in the coming week, but for your records, the trial date is set for June 15th at 1 p.m. I look forward to seeing you then.

Kindest regards,

Christopher Greeson

Attorney at Law

Re: FC 5867 Michael Kazinski vs. Sharon Kazinski

Having reread the email, I still didn't fully comprehend what it meant. I googled the terms *discovery*, *disclosure deadline*, and *custody hearing*, and then I read the first article that popped up in my search.

By the end of the article, I learned that in every trial, both sides had to tell each other what evidence and witnesses they planned to introduce in court to prove their case. That was the process of discovery, and it had a time limit. If the deadline for discovery passed and either side found additional evidence or witnesses to help their case, then they were out of luck. The court wouldn't let them introduce it at the final hearing.

So . . .

If Mike Kazinski's lawyer had added Ben Mitchell to his discovery, that meant Ben had agreed to testify for Mike at the custody hearing. But that made no sense. Ben and Mrs. K. had been best friends since childhood. Why would Ben testify *against* his closest friend in the world and cause her to lose her only child?

The answer was obvious. I should have seen it at once.

Money. Ben loved money. He had already proven that by taking bribes from the Russian mob. And if Ben had sold himself to the

Russians, it wasn't much of a stretch to assume he had cashed in on the Kazinski trial, too. The email had practically spelled it out: *My client agreed to all of your terms and conditions.* Ben and Mike's lawyer had brokered a deal . . . with Molly as the commodity.

Molly—Ben's own goddaughter.

"Damn, Ben," I breathed. "That's fierce."

I no longer felt sorry for Ben Mitchell. What an absolute, utter piece of shit. He had been rotten all the way to the core. If there was any justice in the universe, his spirit was floating around in the void somewhere, cold and alone.

Mike Kazinski could go to hell, too.

I checked the calendar on my phone. The custody hearing was scheduled for next week, assuming Mike's lawyer hadn't filed for a continuance due to the loss of their hired witness.

Any luck with the engine? I texted Val. I found a lead and want to check it out. I could use a ride to Molly's house . . .

Molly Kazinski? Val asked. And no! Nothing's working! ☹

Maybe Drew can drive us?

I already called him . . . went straight to voicemail.

Ugh

What's this about Molly? she asked.

I gave Val the abbreviated version of events. Ben Mitchell was helping Molly's dad get custody of her.

NO!

YES!

But her dad's such a dick, Val said. He's totally unhinged.

I know, right?

I heard he came to the school, Val added. He tried to kidnap Molly . . . as in literally showed up and dragged her kicking and screaming out of science class. Mrs. K. had to call the cops and get a restraining order.

I hadn't heard anything about that. When did it happen?

I dunno, maybe a week ago. I took a sick day, so I wasn't there.

Val didn't get sick. One of the planets had probably been in retrograde. I wondered if Mike had been arrested and charged that day. If he hadn't, then I had to consider the possibility that Mike had paid off more people than just Ben Mitchell. I remembered shortly after Ben's funeral, when I crossed paths with Mrs. K. at the police station. She had played her ex-husband's threats on speakerphone, and the officer had refused to do anything to help her. For all I knew, there could be a conspiracy that involved the whole legal system in our town.

I needed to talk to Molly and get her story.

I saved and closed my files and then packed up my computer. I could think of one person who wouldn't mind giving me a ride. He hadn't given me his phone number, but I had snagged it from his cell a few days ago when I had worn his body.

Hey, Blade, it's Tia, I typed. Any chance you're free?

Chapter Twenty-Four

I WAITED IN THE LOBBY UNTIL I HEARD THE RUMBLE of a thousand atom bombs, and then I walked outside and met Blade as he pulled up in front of the dorm and slowed his motorcycle to a stop. My text must have caught him in the middle of a party or a formal event, because he wore black leather dress shoes instead of boots, and tailored slacks paired with a sleek button-down shirt instead of jeans and a riding jacket. He rotated his head toward me, his shielded helmet covering his face, his jet-black ponytail dangling between his muscled shoulders. He looked like a younger, hotter version of James Bond.

Annoyingly, my heart quivered at the sight of him.

He handed me a spare helmet and helped me fasten the buckle beneath my chin. Each time his fingers brushed my skin, my insides did that weird quivering thing again, and I was grateful for the mirrored face shield that hid my flushing cheeks. After securing my backpack, I straddled the bike and clumsily searched for the footrests. Blade reached down on either side of my calves and folded out a set of tiny metal pegs.

"First time?" he asked.

I flinched at the sound of his voice inside my helmet.

"Built-in mics," he said, tapping his helmet. "It's the only way to talk while we're riding."

"Fancy," I told him. "I didn't know this tech existed."

"I guess that answers my question."

"Yeah," I said. He was right. I had never ridden on a motorcycle before. My dad had been calling them "death chariots" ever since I could remember. As a bonus, he had also pointed out the messiest deer carcasses on the highway and insinuated that I would end up as a smear on the asphalt if my rear end ever so much as touched the back of a bike. "Let's not die, okay?" I added.

"We're all going to die," Blade said. "We're mortal."

"Not funny."

"Okay, I promise we won't die *today*," he clarified. "Just hold on to me, and don't make any sudden moves. Think you can do that?"

"Sounds easy."

"Ready?"

"Ready."

I wrapped my arms around his waist, propping my chin on his right shoulder as my hands settled on the rock-hard planes of his abs. Touching him there felt wrong, but he tugged my wrists together in a silent command to hug him tighter. I scooted forward and squeezed him, eliminating the last sliver of space between us. His body was warm and firm against mine, and when he accelerated, I was forced to clench my thighs around his hips.

Again with the quivers.

I decided I didn't like motorcycles. They were dangerous in more ways than one.

The road whizzed beneath us, the wind whipping my hair against the back of my neck as we sped away from campus. I stuffed down my fear and focused on navigating to Molly's house. I didn't remember her address, but I vaguely recalled the route my dad had taken the day we had driven her home from school. I directed Blade as best as I could, and after only one or two wrong turns, we eventually made it to Molly's street. From there, we slowed to a crawl, and I peered in the dark for a small but tidy brick Cape Cod with an immaculate lawn and three flowerpots resting on the front stoop.

"There," I said, pointing. "That's the one."

Blade stopped at the curb and turned off his engine. My ears rang faintly in the silence, and I couldn't help but grin at the memory of his wicked tinnitus.

He flipped up his face shield and helped me unbuckle my helmet. I handed it back to him and said, "Thanks."

"Want me to wait for you?" he asked, thumbing at Molly's house.

I was torn. I *would* need a ride home, but not at the expense of Blade getting in trouble with his parole officer for staying out too late. "What about your ankle monitor?"

"I'm not on house arrest," he said. "It's just a tracker."

"Are you sure you don't want to get back to your party?"

"What party?"

I indicated his dress shoes and slacks.

"Oh, right," he said, glancing at his pants as if he'd forgotten about them. "I wasn't at a party. It was a date."

"Must have been a nice date."

He shrugged. "Just a couple of steaks at the Wentworth."

"Oh, is that all?" I asked sarcastically. The Wentworth was the most expensive restaurant in two counties. "Whoever your date was, she's a lucky girl."

He chuckled darkly. "I doubt she sees it that way. I got up and left the table halfway through the appetizer course."

"You left your date?" I asked in shock. "For me?"

"I paid the bill and ordered her an Uber first," he added. "But yeah. She was pretty pissed that I walked out. I think I burned that bridge."

"I'm sorry," I said.

"Don't be," he told me. "I made my choice, and I'm good with it."

I caught myself chewing my lower lip and blushing, so I abruptly shook my head to clear it. "Yeah, if you don't mind waiting, that would be cool."

"We passed a coffee place about a mile back," he said. "I'll go hang there and you can text me when you need me."

"I don't know how long it'll take," I warned him.

"It's cool, Dante." He flashed me one of his lethal grins. "I've got all night for you."

I spun around before my insides could start quivering again. Blade fired up his engine and rumbled away, and I strode up the sidewalk to Molly's house. Judging by the sudden movement of curtains in the front window, Molly or her mom had already seen me. Not surprising, since the noise from Blade's motorcycle could probably be heard from space.

I was poised to knock when the front door inched open.

Half of Molly's face peeked out from behind the door. She pointed in the direction Blade had just driven. "Was that your boyfriend?"

"No," I said with lightning speed. "No, no, no."

"Are you sure?" she asked. "Because it kind of looked that way."

"I'm sure," I insisted. "We're just friends."

"Hmm." Molly seemed disappointed in my answer. She fixed me with a blank stare, the dark circles under her eyes giving her a ghoulish appearance. She resembled more of a fairy changeling than a high school freshman. "So what are you doing here?"

"I was hoping we could talk," I said. "Is this an okay time?"

Still half hidden behind the door, she hesitated, visibly chewing the inside of her cheek. "My mom's not home. She went out for groceries. I'm not supposed to answer the door when she's gone."

"I get it," I told her. Molly had almost been kidnapped. If I were her mom, I wouldn't let her answer the door either. "I heard what happened at school."

Molly groaned. "My dad's such an asshole."

"Yeah, I bet," I said. "That's kind of what I wanted to talk to you about. But I can come back later. No worries."

I had just started to pull out my phone to text Blade to come and get me when Molly waved a dismissive hand and opened the door.

"You know what, it's fine," she said. "My mom will be back soon."

"Are you sure it's okay?" I asked.

"Yeah, she won't mind. She knows you. It's not like you're an axe murderer."

I covered my heart as if swearing an oath. "I would never murder an axe."

Molly laughed in a light, breathy tinkle, almost inaudible. "You're funny. Come in."

I followed her into a miniature foyer that was more of a box-shaped extension of the living room than an actual receiving area for guests. The entrance was more compact than I expected, with barely enough space for me to squeeze past an empty brass coat-tree standing beside the door. On the left was a narrow set of wooden stairs and an adjacent hallway that probably led to the kitchen. The hardwood floors looked historic—wide planks with a dark finish, the surface dented and nicked in a way that seemed classy instead of damaged. To my right, the living room reminded me of an old-timey museum display, with an antique floral sofa and matching armchair, a polished, round coffee table, and a braided floor rug. Not a single item was out of place. Maybe no one used the room, but more likely, Molly's mom was obsessive about keeping it clean. The perfect lawn and immaculate flower beds outside hinted that Mrs. K. cared a lot about appearances.

"We can talk in my room," Molly said, leading me up the stairs.

As I walked behind Molly, I paid attention to what she was wearing: thick fuzzy socks, baggy black sweatpants, and a massive hoodie. She had worn the same basic outfit each time I had seen her, no matter how hot it was outside. I didn't know how she could stand it. Air-conditioning or not, I would be sweating out my soul under all that fleece.

The landing at the top of the stairs led to three bedrooms and a single bathroom. One of the bedroom doors was closed, so I couldn't see inside it. But I peeked into the second room as I passed and found a mahogany bed draped in lacy floral-print linens and covered with about a hundred throw pillows. That room had "Mrs. K." written all over it. Molly's bedroom was at the end of the hall. Much like the rest of the house, her room was small but nicely furnished with an ivory twin-size bed and a matching dresser with mirror. There were no posters or photos on the walls, or any dirty socks or charging cords on the floor. Not even a rogue water bottle. I had never seen a teen's room look so spotless. Maybe Molly had stuffed all her junk in the closet or kicked it under the bed. I had used that "cleaning" strategy before.

Molly plopped down on the bed and sat with her legs crossed. "What do you want to know about my dad?"

"Well," I said, sitting at the opposite end of the mattress, "can we talk about what he did at school? Do you know why he tried to kidnap you?"

"Oh, yeah, that's easy," she said simply. "To take me away from my mom. He hates her. He would do anything to hurt her. Even if it hurts me, too, he doesn't care. He can't stand that I want to live with my mom and not him and Debby."

"Debby?" I asked.

Molly rolled her eyes. "The bitch he cheated with."

"Oh."

"As *if* I would want to wake up to her fat, ugly face every day," Molly said. "Anyway, my dad's been trying to turn me against my mom ever since he left. I found out there's a name for what he's doing. It's called parental alienation. So I told him if he didn't stop complaining about my mom, I wouldn't visit him anymore. He wouldn't shut up about her, so I blocked his number. That was two months ago. I haven't talked to him since."

"Is that when he filed for custody?"

Molly nodded. "I won't live with him, though. Not even part-time or weekends. I don't care what a judge says. They can't make me."

"What about your godfather, Ben Mitchell?" I asked.

"What about him?"

"Did he get along with your dad?"

Molly exhaled into a soft giggle. "Ben didn't really get along with people. He could be prickly a lot of times."

"Did you like him?"

"Yeah, I liked Ben. He was nice to me and my mom. He took care of us."

Did he, though? I wondered.

"He used to come over and check on us and bring us dinner," she went on. "He helped me with my algebra homework, and sometimes at night, when the mall parking lot was empty, he would take me out and teach me how to drive his car. And he gave me money whenever I needed anything, like when I dropped my phone down the stairs and shattered the screen. He bought me a new one. Just like that." She snapped her fingers. "The latest version, too. He didn't care how expensive it was. He was like my own personal genie."

"Lucky you," I said. I phrased my next question carefully, not wanting to traumatize her by announcing that Ben had cut a deal with her dad. "Ben was a lawyer, so he probably had opinions about legal stuff like custody. Did he ever talk to you about that? Or about your relationship with your father?"

"Ugh," Molly said with another eye roll. "That was the one thing I couldn't stand about Ben. He lectured more than he listened. He didn't take me seriously when I told him what was going on with my dad. Ben said I was young, and I didn't know what was best for me, and it wasn't healthy to cut my dad out of my life, blah, blah, blah. So I got pissed off and blocked him, too."

I blinked in surprise. "You did?"

"Just for a couple of days," she said, shrugging. "He came over and apologized and brought me a new computer and promised he wouldn't talk about my dad anymore. So I decided to forgive him."

Something about her story began to feel . . . icky. It was the power dynamic between Ben and Molly. Their whole relationship was super weird, almost as though Ben had been desperate to win Molly's approval. But that didn't match what I knew about Ben's personality. He had been a greedy, stone-cold liar and a cheater who had shaken down criminals for the mob. And Molly had him wrapped in a bow around her pinkie finger. To me, that meant one of two things had to be true: either Ben Mitchell hadn't been as fierce as he had seemed, or Molly was a whole lot tougher than she looked.

An eerie sensation crept up the back of my neck. I looked at Molly with fresh eyes—not as the waifish victim of an abusive dad and a scheming godfather, but as an empowered and perhaps manipulative teenage girl who had just inherited a fortune.

"Did you say that Ben taught you how to drive?" I asked.

"Yeah," she said. "In his brand-new Audi. He was going to give it to me for my sixteenth birthday. I think I'm still going to get it. I'm not sure, though. My mom says it'll have to stay in storage until . . ."

I tuned out her prattle as my suspicions played tug-of-war with my doubts. Was I crazy for thinking Molly could have killed Ben? Or that she could have carjacked a Tesla and tried to run me over with it? She was only a freshman, and a tiny one at that. But then again, I had heard stories on the news about kids younger than Molly who had done far worse things than pull a trigger.

Did Molly even have an alibi for Ben's murder? I didn't know because I had never considered her a suspect. Then there was the fact that Molly was half my size. How had she hijacked my body if she wasn't strong enough to drag me out of my shed and stuff me into the backseat of Ben's car?

Maybe I *was* crazy.

And yet . . .

I couldn't help noticing the short layers blended into Molly's medium brown hair.

Chapter Twenty-Five

SITTING THERE TALKING TO MOLLY, I HAD MORE questions than answers. I didn't know if she was capable of murder, but she was definitely capable of twisting Ben's emotions and milking him like a cash cow. And if she could manipulate a man as cold and calculating as Ben Mitchell, she could pull one over on me, too.

Maybe she already had, starting with the day she had ridden home with me and my dad. Right before we had dropped her off, Molly had asked if I still took clients. She had claimed she wanted to hire me. So *if* Molly was the head-hopper who had stolen my body and killed Ben, what better way to throw me off her trail than to pretend she needed my services? It would be a brilliant strategy, the perfect bluff. I couldn't tell an immersionist apart from a regular person, even while inside their mind. A head-hopper could let me take over their body as easily as any other client. As long as they gave me full control, I would never know the difference.

So how could I find out if Molly was bluffing?

An idea came to mind. I began to see a way to get the evidence I needed, to either eliminate Molly as a suspect or implicate her in Ben's death. Guilty or innocent, I would finally have my answer about her. All I had to do was play my cards right.

"Hey," I said. "Remember when my dad and I drove you home?"

Molly nodded.

"You mentioned wanting to hire me."

"Yeah," she said.

I waggled my brows. "Still interested?"

I studied her face to see how she would react. Her eyes brightened with an excitement that might be genuine, or just good acting. Based on what I had learned about Molly, either one was possible.

"Does that mean you're taking clients again?" she asked.

"Not officially," I told her. I didn't want to tip my hand by coming on too strong. "But I might make an exception for you, depending on the job. Why don't you tell me what you had in mind?"

"Okay," she said. "So here's the thing. There are these girls at school." She rattled off five names that I had never heard before. "You probably know them because they're super popular."

I bit back a smile. "Are they freshmen?"

"Yeah, we're all in the same grade."

"No offense," I told her, "but the only freshman I know is you, and that's because your mom is the school secretary."

Molly's expression fell, but she recovered quickly and went on with her story. "Well, anyway, they're really cool and, like, practically internet famous, and one of the girls, Willow, likes me because we used to hang at youth group. I'm this close"—pinching together her thumb and index finger—"to getting an invite to their big summer pool party, but Willow said her friends don't want me to come because they think I'm emo."

I glanced at Molly's baggy black clothes. "So wear something different."

"It's more than that," she said. "Even in a different outfit, I'm not fun."

Someone more polite than me would have contradicted Molly and told her she was plenty of fun to be around. But I didn't believe in hyping people up with bullshit. Besides, she would see right through me. Molly walked around school like a zombie. She was about as peppy as a funeral, and we both knew it.

"That's why I want to hire you," she said. "To pretend I don't suck."

"Hey, now, that's harsh."

"But true," she said, lifting a shoulder. "The girls will like you better than me."

"I can't be you forever," I pointed out.

"You won't have to. Just long enough to get me an invite to the party."

"So that's the endgame?" I asked. "The pool party? Not . . . joining their friend group or whatever?"

"Pretty much, yeah. The party is instant clout. I can post up and get a thousand likes from all the losers who didn't get invited. If nothing else goes right for me, that'll be worth it."

I seriously doubted that would satisfy her. What Molly craved was acceptance, to be included by the popular girls she admired, not noticed by a thousand "losers" who she didn't respect. But telling her that wouldn't do any good, so I said, "Okay, I can get you in."

"Really?"

"Guaranteed or your money back," I told her. "I never lose."

"So what happens next?" she asked. "Do I pay you first? And how much? And how do we decide when to do the taking-over-my-body thing?"

I told her my fee and explained that she would pay me the day of the job. As for the timing, I would have to study up on all the girls in the group, as well as compare their schedules with mine before I could suggest a good time to impersonate her. That would take days. Right now, I needed an excuse to hop into Molly's head so I could start snooping through her house before her mom came back from the grocery store.

I thought of a quick lie and went for it.

"Tonight we can do the first step," I said. "The brain test."

"The brain test?" she asked. "What's that?"

I pointed from my head to hers. "It's basically a trial run to make sure our minds are compatible. Not everyone can handle immersion. The extra consciousness is too much for some people."

The whites of her eyes grew. "What happens to people who can't handle it?"

I hadn't meant to scare Molly. I didn't want her to back out of the deal because she thought her head would explode. "It's no biggie. Some people's brains are just kind of slippery, like the inside of a Teflon pan, so my consciousness would keep sliding out of their head instead of sticking in there."

"Oh." She lowered her shoulders. "How do we do the test?"

"It's super easy," I said. I explained the process of immersion, including the imaginary room and the walk-in closet inside her mind. "All you have to do is go in the closet and stay in there until I tell you to come out."

"What happens if I come out early?"

I frowned and considered her question. No one had ever asked me that before. I honestly had no idea what would happen if both of us were self-aware at the same time in the same body. Depending on Molly's mental strength, she might push me out. At the very least, I supposed she would catch me snooping through her things. I couldn't have that. So I made up another lie, this one a little more scary, and told her that if she came out of the imaginary closet too soon, she could end up with chronic short-term memory loss, like Drew Barrymore's character in *50 First Dates*. Annoyingly, Molly hadn't seen the movie—because freshman were actual fetuses—so I had to give her a rundown of the plot. Once Molly learned that she might have to start every morning with no memory of the day before, she promised to stay in the closet.

Her twin-size bed was too narrow to fit both of us comfortably, so we tossed some pillows onto the floor and reclined on the hardwood planks, side by side with our shoulders touching. I walked Molly through the stages of deep breathing and relaxation. She did a far better job than I did. Her outer arm pressed against mine, her muscles unwinding; meanwhile I was still trying to slow down my heartbeat because I couldn't stop thinking about when Mrs. K. would come home. I put the ticking clock out of my mind or else I would lose more time. So I used Val's trusty meditation trick to clear my thoughts, and a few moments later, I knocked at the door to the imaginary room inside Molly's mind.

"Cooool!" Molly said, drawing out the word as she answered the door, her eyes wide with awe. If she was secretly a head-hopper, she faked her ignorance like a pro.

I didn't have a minute to waste, so I guided her quickly into the closet. "Remember," I told her, "stay in there until I call for you, no matter how long it takes."

She nodded in agreement, and then she shut the closet door behind her.

Alone in Molly's head, I began the process of connecting with her body, focusing on the hard press of the floor beneath her spine, the weight of her limbs, the feather pillow supporting her neck.

When I was fully rooted in her flesh, I awoke as Molly Kazinski.

Right away, I noticed that something was off. Several things, actually, starting with the sour, sticky taste in my mouth, as if I had eaten a handful of rancid cotton balls. I squinted and blinked against the ceiling light, which seemed brighter than it was before. My stomach ached, my temples ached . . . everything ached, most of all the muscles in my arms and legs. I groaned and curled onto my side. I had only felt this terrible once, in middle school, when I'd had the flu. I remembered how the fever had made everything hurt—my muscles, my bones, my skin, somehow even my hair.

Was Molly sick?

She hadn't seemed like it.

I tried to push myself into a sitting position. The room spun around me, and I slouched over, breathing deeply until the dizzy spell passed. I peered beside me at my vacant body. I knew there was a procedure to follow, a list of things I was supposed to do when I left my body for a job, but I couldn't remember any more than that. My mind was foggy, as though I had just woken up in the middle of a dream, and I was still in that confusing stage between sleep and awareness.

A sudden cramp burned low in my abdomen. When I settled a hand on my belly, I felt nothing except the bunched-up folds of my thick hoodie and my fleece sweatpants. And on the subject of fleece, I wasn't hot. I should have been sweltering beneath Molly's clothes.

None of this made sense.

I had to see what I was dealing with.

Slowly, to avoid another dizzy spell, I rose onto my knees and then gripped the bed for support until I stood all the way up. Inch by inch, I shuffled toward the dresser. Once I had made it there, I propped one hand on the wooden surface and studied my reflection in the mirror. Dark circles under the eyes, waxy skin, dry lips, limp hair. None of that was new to me. Then I lifted up the front of Molly's hooded sweatshirt, and all of the air leaked out of my lungs.

Molly was a living skeleton, her abdomen concave between a pair of sharp, protruding hip bones, her navel barely a slit in the center of her belly. Every one of her ribs was visible beneath her skin. She wore a white bra, but the visible gaps at the top of each molded cup told me there was nothing underneath. I used my free hand to feel along the bony ridges of her upper chest and the deep hollows below her collarbones. How was she even alive?

"Oh, Molly," I whispered in her voice. "What have you done to yourself?"

Even with my thoughts clouded, I knew the answer. Molly was sick, but not with the flu. I supposed she could have been diagnosed with cancer or some other physical illness, but if that were the case, her mother would have kept her at home, away from the viral merry-go-round at school. No, Molly had a different kind of sickness, the kind that couldn't be fixed with medicine. The aches and the dizziness, the weakness and the brain fog: all of it indicated that her body was breaking down. And the fact that Molly had gotten used to the pain—that she had compensated for her symptoms and fooled everyone with her baggy clothes—was even more concerning to me, because it meant she had been hurting herself for a long time.

I refocused and tried to remember what I had learned in

tenth-grade health class. When people starved themselves, their hearts stopped functioning properly . . . something about tissue shrinkage and irregular heartbeats. But there was one thing in particular that the human body needed more than anything else, because without it, the heart would seize.

Electrolytes, I realized. That was what Molly needed.

The search for evidence could wait. Right now, nothing mattered more to me than keeping Molly alive. I used the walls for support and made my way downstairs to the first floor. From there, I followed the dim hallway into the kitchen and turned on the lights. I scanned the kitchen for the most likely places to find a water glass and a pinch of salt and sugar. I opened all the cabinets until I found what I needed. After mixing a basic electrolyte recipe with water from the faucet, I forced it down in three big gulps.

That should buy Molly some time.

Now to eat. And not for fun.

Wiping my mouth on my shirtsleeve, I turned to the refrigerator. I didn't know if Molly had any food allergies because I hadn't bothered to ask. But I had never met another human being who had more allergies than I did, so as long as I followed my own restrictions, Molly should be all right. I opened the fridge and pushed past the containers of Greek yogurt, leftover pasta noodles, hard-boiled eggs, and almond milk. Dairy, wheat, eggs, and nuts were all a no-go. But at the back of the lowest shelf, I spotted a potential winner: a bowl of plain white rice.

"You'll do," I said to the rice as I carried it across the kitchen.

I had just opened the microwave when I heard a key slide into the lock from the other side of the kitchen door. Mrs. K. had come home from the grocery. I froze with one hand on the bowl of rice and the other gripping the microwave door handle. The electrolytes in my system had given me a boost, but my thoughts were still muddy and sluggish. It took me a moment to remember that I had to act like Molly. I slouched over and took some of the spark out of my eyes, staring at the microwave keypad with as little interest as possible.

When the door opened, I deliberately chose not to turn around. It seemed fitting with Molly's character, and besides, I was so exhausted that every movement felt like a marathon. But no sooner had I pressed the QUICK REHEAT button than Sharon Kazinski drew a sharp breath and demanded, "What do you think you're doing, young lady?"

I glanced over my shoulder at her. Dressed in a pair of leggings and a boxy T-shirt, her brunette hair pulled into a messy bun on top of her head, she barely resembled the polished, professional school secretary I had known for so many years. In the crook of one arm, Sharon carried a reusable shopping tote, and in her opposite hand, she gripped the neck of a wine-shaped bottle wrapped in a brown paper bag.

"Just heating up some leftovers," I said.

She splayed her free hand and gave me a look that said *Seriously?* "I told you I was making your favorite dinner tonight."

"I know, Mom, but that'll take forever."

"I bought a precooked rotisserie chicken, so unless forever means ten minutes, I can guarantee it won't take that long." She pointed the wine bottle at the microwave. "Whatever that is, put it back in the fridge before you ruin your dinner."

The steaming scent of rice made my mouth water and my stomach gurgle.

"*Mo-o-om*," I whined.

"I mean it," she said. "I didn't drive all the way to the store to buy your favorite dinner to come home and hear you complain that you're too full to eat it."

That definitely wouldn't be a problem. "I swear to god I'll eat it."

Sharon arched a thin mahogany brow. "What did you say?"

"Sorry," I told her. I should have known that Sharon and Molly were religious. Molly had talked about youth group, and Sharon had mentioned her church at Ben's funeral. I didn't usually make mistakes like that. I blamed Molly's brain fog. If I could put some food in this body, maybe I could think straight. "I'm just so hungry."

"Sweetie, we talked about this." Sharon set her bags on the counter and strode to the sink to wash her hands. "Dinner will be worth the wait. Another ten minutes won't kill you."

"No, Mom, I don't think you get it. I'm literally starving."

"Figuratively," she corrected . . . but incorrectly, because Molly *was* literally starving. "It's okay to feel hungry between meals. Snacking isn't healthy. You know that. It spikes your blood sugar and leads to insulin resistance."

At that point, I was ready to violate Molly's privacy by lifting up her hooded sweatshirt and showing her mother exactly how close she was to dying. But then Mrs. K. said something that stopped me in my tracks.

"With practice, you can get used to hunger," she said, drying her clean hands on a kitchen towel. "And even learn to enjoy it."

Enjoy it?

"You have to think of it like a game," she went on. "To see how far you can push yourself, to show your body that you're in charge. I promise that when you're completely in control of your body and your mind, it's the most powerful feeling in the world."

Oh, shit. Molly wasn't the only one with an eating disorder in this house.

"What do I always say about discipline?" Sharon asked me.

I didn't know. And I didn't want to know, because it hurt my heart to learn that Molly inherited her sickness from her mother, and that Mrs. K. had probably inherited it from *her* mother, and so on, generations of girls infected by the myth that they had to make themselves smaller to fit into the world, instead of planting their feet wide, jutting out their elbows, and taking up all the space they were entitled to.

I massaged my temples. "My head hurts. It's hard to think right now."

"We control our bodies. Our bodies don't control us." Sharon chanted the words like a prayer at Sunday Mass. "You know what happens without discipline. Just look at your father. He's practically a toddler—selfish, throwing tantrums, stuffing his face with whatever he wants, taking out his anger on me while he sticks his dick in anything that moves. He can't control his body because he can't control his thoughts. He's weak. And his weakness is what destroyed our family."

As the electrolytes cleared away more of my mental fog, I could finally see why Molly's father wanted custody of her—and why Ben Mitchell had been willing to help him get it. Mike Kazinski might be a verified, card-carrying asshole, but if he walked into the kitchen right now, he would tell his daughter to eat the rice. But he couldn't do that. He wasn't allowed anywhere near Molly. His daughter hated him, because the parental alienation went both ways.

"So," Sharon said, "who's in control right now? You or your body?"

The pain in my stomach nearly doubled me over. I wanted to

shove a handful of rice in my mouth before Sharon could stop me, but I doubted Molly would do that. I had to play the part or I would out myself as an impostor.

"I'm in control," I told her. "But I won't be if I pass out. I pushed myself too far. Now I'm dizzy."

"What did you eat today?" she asked.

"Nothing, really."

Sharon folded both arms and leaned back against the sink. "What do you mean *nothing really*? Did you log your food in the app, or didn't you?"

"I did. I just forgot my phone upstairs."

"What are your macros?" she asked.

I didn't even know what that meant. I took a stab in the dark and hoped Molly wasn't lactose intolerant. "I had a Greek yogurt at lunch. That's it."

Sharon exhaled through her nose. "You know that's not enough. You have to be careful. Do you want those people coming back to the house? Nosing around and asking questions? Because you know your father won't stop trying to take you away from me."

Mike must have called Child Services. I shook my head.

"Then do better," Sharon said. "You're the only good thing that's ever happened to me, Molly. I love you more than life."

"I love you, too," I murmured.

"I'll make you a protein shake." Sharon pointed at me, her eyes going misty. "Never forget, baby girl. If I lose you, I won't have a reason to live."

Oh, god. Poor Molly. She was going to need so much therapy to heal from this tangled-up mess, and she couldn't heal in the same environment that made her sick. Molly had to get away from her mother, which was the last thing either of them wanted. If Molly was like most victims, she would fight like hell to stay put, even if it killed her.

And it probably would.

Mike Kazinski knew it. His desperation was clear to me now. He had already sued for custody and filed a complaint with CPS, and when that didn't work, he tried to kidnap Molly in broad daylight. Ben Mitchell had probably known the danger Molly was in, too. That would explain why Ben had showered Molly with gifts and apologized to her when she had blocked him—so he could stay in her life and protect her from her mother.

Looking back, I had been wrong about Ben Mitchell. At least partly. He had been a liar and a crook, but he had cared about his goddaughter—enough to take her away from his oldest friend in the world. Ben had agreed to testify against Sharon in the custody hearing because he had loved Molly, not because Mike had paid him.

And Sharon couldn't let them win.

If Sharon hadn't been so sunny and sweet to me all the time, I would have put the pieces together sooner. Mrs. K. was the only person who'd had the motive, the means, and the opportunity to kill Ben. The clues were right there in front of me. Legal discovery would have told Sharon that Ben's name was on her ex-husband's witness list. And then, after she'd learned that Ben had planned to testify against her, she had used her access to his car, his home, his schedule, anything she needed to ambush him. No one would suspect Ben's best friend of hurting him, least of all Ben himself, who hadn't seen the attack coming.

When I thought about it, I even had an idea for how Sharon could have figured out I was an immersionist. Molly told me that rumors swirled for years about a head-hopper at the high school. As the attendance secretary, Sharon had access to the absence reports. She could have used the reports to cross-reference absences on the same day as unusual student behavior, like a shy, skinny geek standing up to a senior twice his size. With enough patience, Sharon could have seen a pattern and pinpointed me as the common denominator.

It all made sense. Sharon had left school, stolen my body from my shed, and killed Ben. And when she had caught me poking around the murder investigation, she had tried to kill me, too. I didn't have evidence, but I was willing to bet that if I searched Sharon's bedroom, I would find a pair of black leather driving gloves and a Hillary Clinton mask.

So what should I do now?

The murderer, who was currently mixing me a protein shake, believed that I was her daughter. If Sharon found out who I really was, or that my body was lying helplessly on Molly's bedroom floor, she could finish me off once and for all.

And as Molly, I didn't have the strength to stop her.

Chapter Twenty-Six

I WAS OUT OF MY DEPTH.

I needed to call for backup, but discreetly, without tipping off Sharon and giving her time to ditch the evidence linking her to Ben's death. Or killing me—I especially didn't want her to have time for that. If I could slip upstairs, I could mute my phone and call Detective Roberts, maybe Blade, too. Most important, I needed to get out of Molly's head and return to my own body. I might have to defend myself against Sharon, and no amount of ass-whooping skills could compensate for Molly's Styrofoam muscles and her matchstick arms. She could break in half with a sneeze.

I would drink my protein shake and then make an excuse to go upstairs.

"Here you go, hon." Sharon handed me a tall glass of chalky liquid with white chunks of powder floating on top. "Down the hatch."

I took the glass and resisted the urge to sniff it. I had never tasted a protein shake before. All of the mixes contained whey or soy or some other ingredient that would send me into anaphylactic shock. From the looks of this drink, I wasn't missing out on anything.

"Down the hatch," I echoed, and then I chugged it all in a few massive gulps. The taste was a delayed reaction that I could only describe as a vanilla war crime. I retched, but caught myself before I puked. Good thing, too, since the flavor wouldn't improve on the way back up.

"Wow," Sharon said. She studied me for a long, silent beat, her gaze moving across my face as if searching for something she'd lost. "I'm impressed. This is the first time you drank it without holding your nose."

Shit.

Did she know I wasn't Molly? At the very least, she suspected.

"I should have," I told her. "I almost got sick. I thought I could show my body who was in charge." I flashed a feeble grin. "But I guess it showed me instead."

She was still watching me, unblinking.

Double shit.

I couldn't afford another mistake.

What would Molly do with the empty glass? Would she hand it back to her mother, or rinse it out and set it in the sink? A glance at the sink found it empty. Sharon kept her house pristine. So I rinsed out the glass and loaded it directly into the dishwasher.

"Thanks for the shake," I said, and thumbed at the reusable shopping bag on the counter. "The chicken smells good."

"Yeah," she agreed, but she made no move toward the bag. She stood in the same spot, a few feet from the pantry, where she had just put away the container of protein powder. "I bought some canned biscuits to go with it, the kind with the butter pieces already mixed in."

She was testing me. And lying. No one in this house ate carbs.

"Why would you do that?" I asked.

"Because it's your favorite dinner."

I huffed a dry laugh. "Chicken and biscuits?"

"Yes."

"Um . . . no. That's not anyone's favorite."

"Oh, really?" she asked, arching that same mahogany eyebrow. "Then what should I have bought instead?"

I didn't have enough clues to answer her. Even guessing was too dangerous. All I could do was dodge the question by putting Sharon on the defensive. I wrinkled my forehead and demanded, "Are you serious right now, Mom? I mean, are you having, like, a stroke or dementia or something? Because you know what my favorite food is. And I'm not someone's old granny in Alabama, so it's not chicken and biscuits."

"'Someone's old granny'?" she repeated. "Not someone's me-maw?"

"Me-maw, granny, nanna," I said. "Same difference."

A slow, devious grin spread across Sharon's mouth. She pinned me with a burning glare and then she said my name. My *real* name. "Tia Dante."

I maintained my poker face. "What are you talking about, Mom?"

"You can drop the con, Tia. I know that's you in Molly's head. And that means you left your body lying around empty again." Sharon made a *tsk, tsk, tsk* sound, glancing left and right as if I had stashed myself right there in the kitchen. "Where's your body, Tia?"

There was no use pretending anymore.

"What's her favorite dinner?" I asked.

"Chicken and biscuits."

"*Seriously?*"

"Yep."

Well, damn. I really blew that one.

"Answer the question, Tia," Sharon ordered. "Where are you?"

"In my shed," I lied. It was a long shot, but with any luck, I might be able to lead her away from the house long enough to get help.

"Your shed?" she asked. "How did Molly get over there? She doesn't drive."

"She called me as soon as you left for the grocery store. I picked her up."

"And who drove you here? Your car's not out front."

"My dad dropped me off. He'll be back for me in a minute."

"That could be true. Or"—Sharon pointed an index finger at the ceiling—"you're upstairs in her bedroom right now."

I swallowed hard and fought the urge to panic. "Go ahead and check. In the time it takes you to get upstairs, I'll already be at your neighbor's house calling the police."

She crept toward me. "If you can run that fast."

Molly couldn't run at all, and we both knew it.

I backed toward the door. "Think carefully," I warned. "If I don't have a body to go back to, I'll have to stay in this one. I'm stronger than Molly in every way. You know I can dominate her. Do you really want me taking over your daughter's life? Because I will, if you make me."

Sharon's eyes narrowed to slits. She advanced another inch. "I can force you out. I know how to do it. I've done it before."

I took a backward step. "But not with me. I never lose a fight."

"All minds can die." She inched closer. "Even yours."

As I retreated another pace, Sharon sprang forward—but not at me. She lunged toward a kitchen drawer and yanked it open, and then retrieved a black handheld device that I recognized at once. It was a stun gun. My dad kept one just like it on his bedside table. I scrambled backward until my shoulders hit the door.

"Molly's heart," I said in a rush. "It's weak. You might kill her if you shock me."

Sharon pointed the stunner at me. "I would never hurt my daughter."

I didn't believe her. I cringed, bracing for an attack, but instead of coming at me, Sharon pivoted on her heel and ran in the opposite direction.

Toward the stairs . . . and my empty body.

I exhaled a shaky breath. I didn't know what to do next. I could follow through on my threat and run to the house next door to call the police. But no matter how fast the cops responded, they wouldn't reach me in time. Even if Sharon was wrong and she couldn't force me out of Molly's head, I didn't want to stay there forever. I had no intention of stealing Molly's life. I wanted my own. And that left me with no other choice but to stay and fight.

I pulled a steak knife from the butcher block and headed for the stairs.

An idea came to me when I reached the foyer. I unlocked the front door and pulled it wide open, then propped the coat-tree in front of it and turned on the foyer light. If a neighbor noticed the open door, they might come to check on Molly and Sharon, and then I could scream for help. Another long shot, but better than nothing.

I tiptoed up the stairs as quietly as I could, holding my breath and listening for Sharon's movement. The only sound I heard was the pulse in my ears. My feeble heart pounded so hard against my rib cage that it hurt, but I tuned out the pain and reached the top of the landing, where I paused to wipe off my sweaty palm and readjust my knife grip. I crept down the hallway toward Molly's bedroom. I assumed I would find Sharon there, and I was right. She knelt on the floor, straddling my vacant body and holding a pillow over my face.

"Stop!" I yelled at her. On instinct, I did the only thing that was sure to get her attention. I stood my ground in the doorway and held the serrated blade to Molly's throat. "If I die, I'll take her with me."

The instant that Sharon flicked a glance at me, her lips parted, and she drew a soft gasp, nearly inaudible, but not quite. "You're bluffing," she said, even as she lifted the pillow away from my face and drew it to her chest.

"Am I?" I asked.

I watched the calculation behind her eyes as she weighed the risk of smothering me to death. Sharon didn't like her odds. I could tell from her white-knuckled grip on the pillow, still clutched to her chest. But more than that, psychology class had taught me about projection. Messed-up people tended to believe that everyone else was messed up, too. Liars assumed that everyone lied. Cheaters assumed that everyone cheated. And murderers? Sharon couldn't rule out the possibility that I would kill an innocent girl to protect myself, because she would do the same thing without flinching.

To make my point, I punctured the skin at my throat and drew blood.

"All right," Sharon cried, extending a palm.

"Are you ready to play nice?"

"Yes. Just don't hurt Molly."

"First, get rid of the pillow," I said.

Sharon threw it onto the mattress.

"All of them," I added, jutting my chin at the other pillows Molly and I had tossed onto the floor earlier.

Sharon obeyed.

"Now step away from me," I ordered. A muffled buzz sounded from my body—my phone blowing up in my pocket. I needed to call for help, but not before I forced Sharon out into the hallway and locked the door behind her. If I let my guard down for a nanosecond, she would attack.

"How are we going to do this?" she asked.

"You're going to walk out of this room—slowly—and keep your hands where I can see them. After that, you can wait for the cops, or you make a run for it. I don't give a shit."

"I'm not leaving Molly with you."

"Molly *is* me," I reminded her. "I'll send her out when I'm in my own body. Until then, you don't have a choice."

"How do I know you won't hurt her?"

Something in Sharon's tone had shifted, the slightest hint of a dare. I sensed her testing me, probing for weakness, so I dug in the blade and drew fresh blood.

"You don't," I spat. "Now get out."

She clenched her jaw and held up both hands as she inched her way toward the door. At the same time, I kept the knife at my throat and stepped through the doorway into the room. The tiny space didn't put enough distance between us for my comfort, but I hid my fear. We circled each other in a slow, torturous dance. Sharon had just taken a backward step out of the room when a male voice called out from downstairs.

One of the neighbors must have noticed the open front door.

"Help!" I yelled as loudly as Molly's voice would let me.

Sharon froze in panic.

"Help!" I repeated. "Call 911!"

The man downstairs was shouting something, but I couldn't understand him over my own raised voice. It wasn't until I paused that I heard him call my name.

"Tia!" he shouted. "Tia, are you in there?"

I drew a hopeful breath. It was Nash.

"Nash!" I called. "I'm up here! I'm in a different . . ."

Clomping footsteps drowned me out as he ran up the stairs. It was then that I realized I had taken my eyes off of Sharon. I glanced at her a second too late. In a blur of motion, she grabbed my wrist and twisted hard until I lost my grip on the knife. It clattered to the floor, and Sharon kicked it across the room. The blade slid underneath the bed at the exact moment Nash came sprinting down the hallway, shouting, "You have to go! I just found out something about Sharon Kaz—"

He didn't finish speaking her name. Sharon met him at the doorway with a stun gun to the ribs. Nash went down instantly, rigid as a brick. Before a scream could even form in my throat, Sharon stunned me, too.

A surge of white-hot pain flooded my body, and the next thing I knew, I was on the floor, paralyzed and panting and quite possibly peeing all over myself. My chest was tight and heavy, each breath a wheeze. The agony in my muscles was so overwhelming I could barely think. With tremendous effort, I rotated my eyes toward the doorway and found that Nash was gone. Sharon, too. I didn't know where she had taken him or when she would return, but this might be my last chance to get out of Molly's head and back into my own.

I clenched my eyes shut and fought like hell to shift my focus away from the searing pain in my nerves and to the imaginary room inside Molly's mind. I lost track of how many tries it took me to reach her inner sanctum, but I pounded on her pretend closet door and yelled, "Come out! Hurry up!"

Molly swung open the closet door, her eyes round. "What's wrong? Did I fail the mind test? Do I have brain damage?"

"Never mind that," I said. "Your mom's trying to kill me."

Molly drew back. "*What?*"

"No time to explain." I had to return to my body before Sharon beat me to it. "Just help me." I jogged to the imaginary exit, pausing to add, "And by the way, I'm *really* sorry for what you're about to wake up to."

I hoped Molly had a high tolerance for pain.

Leaving her mind and reconnecting with my own was such a relief that it was practically orgasmic. The absence of pain, the absence of weakness, the ability to draw a full breath—I had never appreciated my body more than I did in that moment. Until I opened my eyes and Sharon stunned me again.

Every swear word in the English language, along with some Spanish ones, crossed through my head as I clenched my teeth and suffered in silent agony. From beside me on the floor, Molly stirred awake, grimacing and groaning from the pain I had just left behind. Her muscle control had started to return. She curled into the fetal position, and Sharon knelt down next to her, smoothing a hand over Molly's hair.

"Baby, are you okay?" Sharon asked.

Molly answered with a whine. "What happened?"

"Tia Dante happened. How did she get inside your head?"

"I let her." Molly cleared the thickness from her throat. "I feel like I was hit by a car."

"Not quite. You were stunned. Try to sit up." Sharon used an arm to hoist her daughter into a seated position. "Take deep breaths."

"You tasered me?" Molly glanced down at her lap and gasped in horror. "Mom! I wet my pants!"

"Baby, listen to me, I had to do it."

"No, you didn't!"

Sharon pointed at me. "Molly, she *knows*."

I expected Molly to ask what her mother had meant by that. But she didn't. Molly glanced back and forth between me and Sharon, her lips in a perfect O. "Are you sure?"

"Yes, baby. She threatened to call the police. That's why I had to stop her."

"How did she find out?" Molly asked.

To me, the better question was, how long had Molly known her mom was a murderer? Why hadn't she come forward? And had Molly worked with her mother to plan the whole thing? Had she participated in Ben's shooting? Had I just been so stupid as to ask Sharon's coconspirator to help me?

"It doesn't matter how she found out," Sharon said. "She's a threat to us."

Molly peered at me. I couldn't speak yet, but I mouthed the word *Why?*

She chewed the inside of her cheek and averted her gaze with enough shame to tell me she was nothing like her mother. Deep in my gut, I knew Molly hadn't killed her godfather. She had probably protected her mom for the same reason most people would. She wouldn't snitch on her own mother. But there was a big difference between covering up a murder and committing one. If I wanted Molly to help me, I had to make her understand that difference.

"Tia's always been nice to me," Molly said.

Sharon laughed without humor. "So nice that she tried to slit your throat. She almost got away with it, too."

Molly probed her neck and then studied her blood-coated fingers.

"No," I croaked. "I . . . never . . ."

Sharon turned around and stunned me again. I cried out in choking sobs while distantly I heard Molly pleading with her mother to stop hurting me.

"Mom, come on. Maybe she won't tell."

"And maybe she will," Sharon said. "We talked about this. What happens to you if I get caught and go to prison?"

"I have to go live with Dad."

"Is that what you want?"

Molly wrung her pale hands. I wished she would look at me so I could tell her with my eyes that living with her father couldn't possibly be worse than sitting by and watching Sharon murder me—and murder Nash, too, if he wasn't dead already.

"Mom, please." Molly shook her head. "I can't."

Sharon cupped her daughter's cheek. "Sweet girl, you don't have to do anything except walk away. That's all. Just walk away. Go downstairs, put the biscuits in the oven, and eat your dinner. I'll take care of everything, and at the end of the night, it will be like none of this ever happened."

No, I thought. *Don't leave me.*

If Molly would just look at me, I could make her understand. But she didn't look at me. She wiped a tear from her cheek and then she stood up. I couldn't turn my head to watch her as she strode to the dresser to retrieve a clean pair of clothes. Her socked feet only returned to my field of view when she walked out the door and gently pulled it closed behind her.

Chapter Twenty-Seven

SHARON WAS EFFICIENT—I WOULD GIVE HER THAT. She wasted no time in snatching a pillow off the bed and holding it over my face with enough pressure to make my nose bleed. Hot liquid flowed down my throat as a metallic taste filled my mouth. I swallowed the blood and fought the urge to gag. My muscles were clenched and screaming, like having a charley horse in every part of my body at once. The pain overwhelmed my senses so much that I couldn't even feel myself suffocating. There wasn't space inside me for any more agony.

Escape was my only thought.

I had never hidden inside my own mind before. I'd never had a reason to. But right now, I would rather dissociate than breathe, so I closed my eyes and envisioned my own imaginary room, small and sparse, with clean beige carpeting on the floor and a walk-in closet situated at the rear wall. I disconnected from my body, and one heartbeat later, I sat cross-legged in the middle of the room, pain-free, tipping back my head in instant relief.

That was better.

Oh, shit, I realized. No, this wasn't better. Now that I could think again, I knew I would die if I stayed here.

I had to brainstorm, and fast.

I started by reviewing the facts. About a minute had passed since my last breath. Permanent brain damage would happen in the next few minutes, closely followed by permanent death. So the only way to survive was to get the pillow off my face, but I couldn't fight back because Sharon had stunned me. My arms and legs were useless. My entire body was paralyzed.

But what about my mind? I wondered. *That's not paralyzed.*

I could move around in my imaginary room. In fact, I was as strong in here as anywhere, plenty strong enough to kick Sharon's ass into next week. Maybe that was the solution: a mental smackdown in Sharon's head. If I could dominate her mind and take control of her body, I could ditch the pillow and let myself breathe. I had never tried a mental attack before, but I didn't see any other choice. If nothing else, at least I would go down swinging.

Without a moment to lose, I left my pretend room and returned to my body just long enough to push past the pain and isolate the feeling of Sharon's knees pressed against my ribs. Her physical touch allowed me to connect with her. I gave her no warning when I hopped inside her head. As soon as her imaginary door appeared in front of me, I kicked it open and stormed her mind's inner sanctum.

My ambush caught her by surprise. Sharon barely had time to brace herself before I swung hard at her nose and landed a right hook with all my weight behind it. No sooner had her back hit the floor than I heel-stomped her in the stomach. All the air left her chest in a whoosh. While she was struggling for breath, I grabbed her by the hair and dragged her toward the walk-in closet. She wriggled and twisted against me, so I let go of her hair, dropped to my knees, and rained down a fury of punches on her until I couldn't feel my knuckles anymore. She eventually went limp. I finished dragging her across the room, and I shut her inside the closet.

Alone in her mind, I immediately opened my eyes as Sharon Kazinski and lifted the pillow away from my face. The sudden transfer into Sharon made me dizzy, but I ignored the spinning and threw aside the pillow, and then bent down to make sure my real body was breathing. I watched my chest rise and fall, the base of my throat pulsing.

Good. I was alive. Now to stay that way . . .

I patted down Sharon's pockets for the stun gun. When I found it, I stuffed the device far under the mattress, completely out of sight. Sharon wasn't zapping me again—ever.

Next, I reached for my phone, still in my pocket and blowing up with alerts. I unlocked the screen by holding it in front of my unconscious face, and then I ignored eleventy dozen missed calls, voicemails, and texts messages and went straight for the keypad. I had just started to dial 911 when my vision went black. I felt a tugging sensation, a sharp pull toward the floor, and the next thing I knew, I was back in my own body.

I groaned, my muscles as rigid as before. My brain felt like butter being churned. I didn't know what had gone wrong. While I struggled to orient myself, Sharon knelt above me and narrowed her eyes to slits. She reached for the stun gun that was no longer in her back pocket. The look of panic on her face when she couldn't find it was almost worth the agony of being zapped two times.

Not quite, though.

I let out a breathy laugh that seemed to enrage her even more. She wrapped her hands around my throat and squeezed hard while jerking me up and down, my skull pounding against the hardwood floor. Each blow made me see stars. My teeth clacked together, my eyes bulging from the pressure around my neck. But the effort of strangling me must have been too much for Sharon, because she pulled another pillow off the bed and crushed my face with it.

Instinctively, I tried to reach for her. My fingers twitched, and I rotated one wrist. Control had started returning to my muscles, but not fast enough. I couldn't fight her with my body. My mind was all I had left.

And I lost the element of surprise.

Again, I used physical contact as a conduit to Sharon's mind. But this time was different. She was expecting me, and she had rigged the imaginary door so that when I tried to kick it down, I ejected myself and had to start all over. I went back time after time, kicking and shouldering the door, even summoning a pretend axe to try to split it open. Minutes ticked by, and nothing worked. Each failed attempt returned me to my own body, to lungs screaming for air, and I knew I didn't have much longer.

Despite that, I ignored my impulse to rush, and I slowed down. I might only have one chance left, and I refused to waste it. When I stood in front of her imaginary door again, I examined it instead of attacking it. In doing so, I noticed a detail I had missed before. High above the door, so high that I had to stand on tiptoe to reach it, was a security panel. Squinting, I could make out letters populating a tiny LCD screen. I tapped the screen to awake it, and five dashes appeared, prompting me to enter a passcode.

What five-letter word would Sharon choose to unlock her door?

The answer was clear. I stood on tiptoe and entered *M–O–L–L–Y*.

A mechanical *buzz-click* sounded from the door, and it unlatched. Sharon gaped at me as I reentered her sanctuary.

"*What?*" she demanded, shaking her head. "Why won't you die?"

"I told you," I said. "I never lose a fight."

Sharon was ready for me, but her defensive stance didn't save her from the nasty left-jab, right-uppercut combo my dad had taught me. And after Sharon went down and I kicked the shit out of her, I stuffed her back into the closet.

For the second time, I opened my eyes as Sharon Kazinski. I pushed past the dizziness spinning the room and took her hands off the pillow, but before I could remove it from my face, my vision went black again.

"No!" I cried.

Sharon was out of the closet already? I couldn't afford another battle. My body wouldn't survive longer than a few more seconds. Blindly, I swiped at the pillow, hoping to knock it off my face before Sharon ejected me and took over, but the next thing I knew, my arms locked up as a jolt of pure fire shot though me.

I didn't know whose head I was in. I felt myself falling. My vision returned as I hit the floor and landed facing my real body. So I was still inside Sharon's head. She hadn't taken control yet. And the horrible agony exploding along her nerves could only mean that she (and I) had been stunned—for a third damn time!

In Sharon's paralyzed flesh, I couldn't move the pillow to save myself. I hopped out of her head and into my own, hoping like hell that my muscles had come back online. My arms refused to obey me, but I could move my neck just enough to turn my face to the side.

Free from the suffocating fabric, I opened my mouth and drew a great, heaving breath, and then another.

Someone pulled the pillow free. I blinked up and found Molly standing above me, dried blood covering her neck. She held up a stun gun and said, "We have a bunch of these around the house."

I laughed in between gasps. "Of course . . . you do."

"I couldn't let her kill you," she told me. She crouched down beside her mother and secured Sharon's wrists behind her back with a zip tie. "I'm sorry, Mom. Please don't hate me. I couldn't sit in the kitchen and pretend I didn't know what was happening. It's hard enough knowing about Ben and that other guy. I can't keep your secrets. It's not fair for you to ask me to do it."

I wriggled away from Sharon to avoid physical contact with her, just in case she took a page from my playbook and tried to hop into my head. My muscles came back online pretty quickly after that. Molly helped me sit up, and I called the police. It took another few moments for the shock to wear off, and then I remembered something Molly had told her mother.

Ben . . . and that other guy.

What other guy?

"Molly," I said. "Who's the other guy you were talking about?"

Molly dropped her gaze. "I don't know his name."

"Did your mom kill him?"

She nodded. "I think so. He's at the bottom of the stairs."

My heart turned cold.

"Nash," I whispered. The other guy was Nash.

Chapter Twenty-Eight

THE NEXT MORNING, DETECTIVE ROBERTS VISITED me in the hospital.

He strode into my room with a smile on his face and a bouquet of daisies in hand, but he stopped short at the sight of a hundred balloons, an army of stuffed bears, boxed chocolates, baked treats, and floral arrangements filling every flat surface available, including the window ledge.

He held up his daisies. "Guess you don't need these."

"It's the thought that counts," I told him from my bed.

"You must have a lot of friends."

I chuckled. "See that vase of roses?" I asked, pointing. "They're from CNN. They want an interview. And that pineapple explosion over there," I said, gesturing at an arrangement of skewered fruit designed to look like flowers. "That's from an agent who wants to get me a book deal, for a fat cut of the advance, of course. And the cookie bouquet is from the ghostwriter who's working with the agent.

My friends know I can't eat brownies or chocolates." Those gifts were from prospective clients. "Let's just say the balloons aren't the only things in here with strings attached."

"What about this one?" the detective asked, stopping in front of the largest, most lavish floral arrangement in the room, a collection of tropical flowers that looked like they had been hand-plucked from an island paradise and spritzed with morning dew. He sniffed an orchid. "Whoever sent this wasn't playing around."

I didn't say so, but that gift was from Blade. He had included a card, which I'd hidden underneath the breakfast tray on my rolling bedside table. *You're a riot, Tia Dante,* he had written. *Not trying to take credit for your win, but I did promise you wouldn't die today. Lucky I was right, or I might not ever get the chance to put you on the back of my bike again. And wouldn't that be a shame? You know where to find me. ~B*

"It's from a reporter," I lied. "They're relentless."

"Don't I know it?" the detective agreed. "But that's the reason I'm here. I wanted to tell you the news in person, before the press conference this afternoon."

"Good news?" I asked.

"I think so," he said. "Sharon Kazinski agreed to a plea deal. She confessed to everything last night, and first thing this morning, she pleaded guilty on all charges and asked to start serving her sentence right away. So it's over—no trial, no testimony, no drama."

That was fast, but I could kind of see why Sharon had decided not to fight. If she had rolled the dice and gone to trial, she would have forced Molly to testify against her in a scandalous case with the whole world watching. In Sharon's twisted way, she loved her daughter. Now she was finally acting like it. Molly had suffered enough. At that very moment, she was three floors below me in a psychiatric unit, being treated for a whole lot more than just malnourishment.

"How long is Sharon's sentence?" I asked.

"Twenty years."

"So she might get out in . . . what? Fifteen?"

"With good behavior," he said. "It's possible."

Note to self: Watch my back in fifteen years.

"Did she say how she pulled it off?" I asked. "I know how she stole my body, but I can't figure out how she got out of my head and back into hers after she shot Ben. The police were right there. They arrested her—well, *me*—as soon as she fired the gun."

"Ben's car," the detective said, placing his daisies at the foot of my bed. "She parked it on a side street that connects the back of the courthouse to the jail. She knew the officers would take her that way if they arrested her. So after she switched into your body, she hid hers under a blanket in the backseat. She locked the car, snuck into the courthouse through a ground-floor window she unlocked the night before—"

"Oh," I interrupted. "That's how she got the gun past security."

He nodded. "After that, you can probably guess what happened."

"She went to the lobby," I said, "the most public place in the courthouse, and waited for Ben to come back from lunch. She shot him, surrendered to the cops, and then they took her exactly where she wanted them to—right past Ben's car, close enough for her to hop out of my head and into hers."

"That's when you collapsed and went into a coma."

"Smart," I had to admit. Sharon had thought through every

detail. I almost hated to ask, but I had to know. "Was she sorry at all? When she confessed?"

The detective flattened his lips in a tiny cringe that gave me my answer.

"She's not, is she?" I asked.

"I can promise you this," he said. "She's definitely sorry that she got caught."

"That's something, I guess."

"But I have even better news for you," the detective said. He paused, splaying both hands as if to build anticipation. "The new district attorney dropped the charges against you. You can go back to your life."

My lawyer already told me that, but I smiled and acted surprised anyway. "Sweet! Does that mean I'm done? Or do I have to go back to court?"

He made a slashing no-go motion. "Please never come back to the courthouse."

"It's a deal."

"So, now that you're officially free," he said, glancing at the gift shop eruption in my room, "when can you go home?"

I shrugged. The doctor handling my case insisted on testing my blood oxygen level every six hours, never mind that I felt fine. Well, not *fine*. The back of my skull still throbbed like a heartbeat, and my eyes were completely bloodshot, but only time would fix that.

The detective gave me his card and made his way toward the door. Right before he left, he paused and turned to me with a grin. "You know, it just occurred to me that we've come full circle. Isn't this the same room where we met?"

I thought back to that fateful night when I had worn Josh Fenske to the hospital to visit my comatose body. "You might be right."

The detective made a teasing finger-gun at me. "How do I know that's really you inside that head, Miss Dante?"

I still remembered his favorite line from his favorite television show. I told him, "Curse your sudden but inevitable betrayal."

"I never doubted you for a second," he said. "Behave yourself."

"Not a chance. Why be a role model when I can be a cautionary tale?"

"Very funny," he told me, and waved good-bye.

Actually, I wasn't joking. I had no intention of behaving myself.

I had already plotted my escape . . . to the seventeenth floor to see Nash.

The fascists in hospital admin had restricted Nash's visitors to immediate family, which was extra cruel because they wouldn't tell me anything about his condition. To hell with medical privacy laws. Privacy was overrated. I had already sent Val to stake out his room last night. She had used the leftover surveillance brooch from Ben's funeral to learn that Nash had a broken wrist, twenty stitches in his forehead, and a concussion from Sharon pushing his paralyzed body down the stairs. Nash wouldn't be in the hospital if it weren't for me, and I refused to go another minute without seeing him for myself.

I waited for the next shift change, and then I tied the back of my flimsy hospital gown, slipped on my grippy-bottom socks, and wheeled my rolling IV stand down the hall to the elevator. Sneaking out of my room was easier than it should have been. There must have been a staffing shortage, because no one noticed me when I arrived at the seventeenth floor either. I scanned the employee badge I had "borrowed" from one of my nurses and unlocked the double doors leading to Nash's hallway. From there, I simply wheeled my way to his door.

Labor shortage silver lining.

The hardest part of my plan was juggling the open door and my IV stand while trying not to trip over my intravenous line and rip it out of my arm. The window blinds were closed, the room dim, with a single bedside lamp glowing faintly behind a fabric curtain that concealed the bed. If Nash had been asleep, my entrance had probably made enough clattering to correct that. I heard him clear his throat, and then I pulled aside the curtain to peek at him.

My chest warmed at the sight of Nash semi-reclined in bed, tucked beneath a white blanket and wearing the same flimsy gown as me. The nearby lamp cast his face in shadows, exaggerating the lump on his forehead and the swelling along his left cheekbone. But even bruised and battered, he was more beautiful than any boy had a right to be.

He sensed me watching him, and he met my gaze. His eyes were sleepy, but he grinned and said, "I hope you're here to give me my sponge bath."

I bit back a laugh, knowing it would make my head hurt. Nash was still a pervert. That had to be a good sign. "I'm actually here to take your temperature," I said. "*Rectally.*"

He winced and patted the spot beside him. "How about you sit down instead?"

I pushed past the curtain and wheeled my stand next to the machine that monitored his heart rate with a soft, steady series of beeps. He scooted over, and I sat facing him, the outside of my thigh pressed against his. Gently, I reached out a hand to brush back his hair and skim a thumb over the strip of bandage on his forehead.

The beeping noise picked up speed.

Grinning, I nodded at the machine. "You can't hide it. You like me."

Nash settled a hand on my hip. "Who said I was trying to hide it?"

If he could hear my pulse, he would know that his touch made my blood rush, just like it always had. "How are you?" I asked. "Really."

"Heavily medicated," he said. "But I'll be all right. Really."

I covered his hand with mine. "You scared me."

"Same," he told me. "Let's not do that again."

I nodded in agreement. When I had gone through my missed calls and texts, I had put together what happened the night before. Nash had discovered Sharon in the ILO database, but under her maiden name. Apparently, she had been expelled from the group years ago, after an incident that had put another immersionist in a permanent coma. Nash had tried to tell me right away, and when I hadn't responded, he called Val. After learning I had gone to Sharon's house, he had sped there to warn me.

"Thank you," I told him. "For coming to help me."

"Always, T."

"Does that mean you accepted my apology?"

"What apology?"

"The note I left with your roommate," I said, and then I realized that Nash hadn't gone back to his dorm last night. He had never seen my apology. "You didn't get it. And you came for me anyway."

"Of course I did. Do you know me at all?"

"Nash . . ."

He shushed me, and then he cupped my chin and drew my face toward him, closer and closer, until nothing but a mingled breath separated our lips. "I accept your apology," he murmured against my mouth. "Now stop talking."

I eliminated the sliver of space between us and brushed his lips with mine, just a soft sweeping motion, a whisper of contact that electrified every cell in my body. It had been so long since our last kiss, but my heart remembered him like a favorite song—his touch, the smell and the heat of his skin, the throaty noise of pleasure he made when I licked his upper lip. It didn't take long for the kiss to turn hot and urgent. Just when things were getting good, his monitor went berserk and forced me to pull away.

I groaned and gripped his shoulders. "We're going to get busted."

"So what?" he asked, his gaze on my mouth.

"I'm not supposed to be here. Family only, remember."

"We'll say you're my sister."

"Not funny," I told him while stifling a laugh.

"All right, fine, I'll behave. But only because I don't want you to go." In a moment of vulnerability, he dropped his gaze and then looked back up with a question in his eyes. "So, uh," he began, "what happens when we finally get out of here?"

I understood what he was asking. He wanted to know where we stood, whether we could be more than friends. I wanted that, but I didn't know how to define us. I had no idea what my future would look like after graduation. One thing was certain, though. Judging by all the gifts in my hospital room, business would be booming.

"What would you say to a partnership?" I asked. "I have more clients than I can handle. I could toss a few cases your way."

"Interesting. Like 'Dirty Deeds Done Dirt Cheap'?"

I shook my head. "More like a variety of deeds done at fair market value."

"Well, that doesn't have the same ring to it."

"Is that a no?"

"Let's call it a *soft* yes."

"How do we turn that into a *hard* yes?" I asked. When he waggled his eyebrows, I added, "Never mind. Don't answer that."

"All right, you wore me down," he said. "You've got yourself a deal."

"Partners?"

He extended a hand for me to shake. "Two head-hoppers are better than one."

I shook his hand, and then he kept my palm and placed it on his chest, where I could feel his heart beating strong and steady and only for me. The intensity in his warm brown eyes told me what I should have known all along. Nash was on my side. He always had been. And that had made him my partner long before our handshake.

"Besides," he added with a grin, "someone has to look out for my girl."

Acknowledgments

WRITING A BOOK IS NEVER EASY FOR ME, EVEN after a dozen completed manuscripts. It's a group effort to produce a novel, and I'm eternally grateful for my team.

Many thanks to my editor, Kieran Viola, for loving this book as much as I do, and for taking my craft to the next level with thoughtful suggestions that amaze me every time. Additional thanks to Candice Snow for assisting with edits and for keeping the production process rolling smoothly. I appreciate you both, and I'm so glad that the universe brought us together.

Much gratitude to my literary agent, Nicole Resciniti, for finding the perfect home for all of my novels, and for being an amazing advocate and friend. We've accomplished great things during our decade together, and I'm beyond lucky to have found you.

Big hugs to my dear friend and critique partner, Lorie Langdon, who is not only a thoughtful beta reader, but a mega-talented author, too! Thank you for taking the time to read literally every single thing I've ever written. Your feedback has helped me grow, and I appreciate you. Bonus hugs to my author friends Jen Osborn and Carey Corp, who are always willing to lend an ear and support me along this journey.

Much love to my family and friends for their never-ending support, and a huge shout-out to my readers, who warm my heart with every email, tweet, video, and post. Hearing from you is the very best part of my job . . . even better than working from home in my pajamas. :)